Oh Dear Silvia

DAWN FRENCH

MICHAEL JOSEPH
an imprint of
PENGUIN BOOKS

MICHAEL JOSEPH

Published by the Penguin Group
Penguin Books Ltd, 80 Strand, London WC2R 0RL, England
Penguin Group (USA) Inc., 375 Hudson Street, New York, New York 10014, USA
Penguin Group (Canada), 90 Eglinton Avenue East, Suite 700, Toronto, Ontario, Canada M4P 2Y3
(a division of Pearson Penguin Canada Inc.)
Penguin Ireland, 25 St Stephen's Green, Dublin 2, Ireland (a division of Penguin Books Ltd)
Penguin Group (Australia), 707 Collins Street, Melbourne, Victoria 3008, Australia
(a division of Pearson Australia Group Pty Ltd)
Penguin Books India Pvt Ltd, 11 Community Centre, Panchsheel Park, New Delhi – 110 017, India
Penguin Group (NZ), 67 Apollo Drive, Rosedale, Auckland 0632, New Zealand
(a division of Pearson New Zealand Ltd)
Penguin Books (South Africa) (Pty) Ltd, Block D, Rosebank Office Park,
181 Jan Smuts Avenue, Parktown North, Gauteng 2193, South Africa

Penguin Books Ltd, Registered Offices: 80 Strand, London WC2R 0RL, England

www.penguin.com

First published 2012
005

CO16471856

02/20

Set in 10.25/18.5pt Gazette LT Std
Typeset by Jouve (UK), Milton Keynes
Printed in Great Britain by Clays Ltd, St Ives plc

A CIP catalogue record for this book is available from the British Library

HARDBACK ISBN: 978-0-718-15606-0
TRADE PAPERBACK ISBN: 978-0-718-15607-7

www.greenpenguin.co.uk

MIX
Paper from
responsible sources
FSC
www.fsc.org   FSC™ C018179

Penguin Books is committed to a sustainable
future for our business, our readers and our planet.
This book is made from Forest Stewardship
Council™ certified paper.

ALWAYS LEARNING   **PEARSON**

For Biggs,
My anchor, and my true love.

Scribentem morbus cepit, dolor, amor.

I am puzzled as the newborn child,

I am troubled at the tide.

Should I stand amid the breakers?

Should I lie with death my bride?

Hear me sing,

'Swim to me, swim to me, let me enfold you:

Here I am, here I am, waiting to hold you.'

'Song To The Siren', Tim Buckley

ONE

Ed

He sits with a sense of being watched, although he himself is the watcher. Momentarily, the others have stepped outside so he is suddenly, shockingly, alone with her. It's odd for there to be no voices. No sound, save those of two human beings just being alive. He becomes acutely aware that for the first time in a very long time, he feels irrefutably more alive than her. She's always making sure you know she's chock-full o' life. She lives big and loud. Right to her fingertips. Her presently somewhat swollen fingertips. Look at them. Someone, perhaps a nurse, has tried to remove the coral-red varnish, but it is stubborn and has bled into her skin, revealing the nails beneath to be unbeautiful, nicotiney. Blotchy red fingers. Yellow nails.

She wouldn't like him to see such a personal thing, so he tries to stop looking . . . but of course he can't. He is transfixed by the unusual sighting. He feels her watching, and although

1

she isn't and although he so wants to remain defiant, he looks away.

So. Here they both are again. Alone. They haven't been alone in a room for ... well, since they were married. What's that? About ... God ... What <u>is</u> it now? Five years? Something like that.

There she is. Breathing.

Here he is. Breathing.

That's it.

Pretty much like it was at the end of the marriage, really. Two people occupying the same air. Nothing else in common. Just oxygen. He remembers when sharing breath with her was exciting, intimate. He would lie close to her in the night, happily breathing in what she breathed out. The breath of life, their joint breath from their joint life.

This breathing now, though, is very different.

He hears his own. It's quick and halting. It fits with his heartbeat, which is anxiously fast and occasionally missing altogether, when he finds himself holding his breath whilst urgent frightening thoughts distract him.

Her breathing is entirely unfamiliar. It's regimented and deep. Her lungs are rhythmically resonating loudly around the room, chiming in with the bellow-like wheezing of the machine. She's being breathed for, through a huge ugly tube in her throat.

Because Silvia Shute, despite all the supposed life in her, is in a coma.

TWO

Jo

Thursday 2pm

A dervish is whirling around Silvia's bed, gabbling and gesticulating wildly. Her explosion of curly grey hair bobs about busily as she moves. The too many strands of assorted, expensive but meant to look casual beads dance on her bosom, and the clack of her posh but meant to look like working boots resounds off the sparkly-clean-polished-all-the-way-under-the-bed-twice-a-day-check-it-on-the-time-sheet-no-bugs-here-mate floor. This is Jo, Silvia's elder sister. Her mouth has mistaken itself for a machine gun.

'It just bothers me darling, that when you do eventually wake up, I'm not even going to be able to tell you what happened because nobody seems to bloody know! You are probably the only one and will you even remember? God knows. Well obviously <u>God</u> knows, whichsoever God one chooses to align oneself with, of course. I can't remember now

3

if you even believe in God, do you? Oh God, that's awful. No. I don't think you do. I think you're a hundred per cent not quite sure, aren't you? I remember you once saying you thought Jesus wore a blindfold to decide who would get the poorly babies, and how that was terribly unfair, but you were eleven, so you may well have updated your thinking since then.

'I know you like Christmas and weddings and church and stuff, but does that necessarily make you a Christian? It's probably got more to do with fabrics and lights and catering if I know you. Do I know you? That's the big question darling, because I can see all this . . . this hellish situation, there's going to be some major decisions I will probably have to make on your behalf.

'Oh God. Why did this happen?! What the hell were you doing out on your balcony? In the freezing cold? On your own? Have you started smoking again? Oh, darling, look at you . . .'

Jo leans over Silvia's bed, smooths her cheek and runs her fingers through her little sister's hair.

'Desperately need your roots doing, darling. Oh dear. What's happened? Where are you Sissy? Come on, come on. Wake up sweetheart. Wake up and see me. I'm here darling. I'm here for you. Always here for you. Big sister to look after you. Just as it should be. Big one looks after the little one. I promised Mummy I would, and I will.

'Come on now, try to wake up. The doctor says you're a long way away, but you're just asleep, aren't you? Very deeply asleep, that's all. Wake up one day, won't you? Yes. Yes, you will. Might be tonight. Or tomorrow. Or soon, anyway. Banged your head, didn't you, silly girl? Banged it when you fell. Does it hurt? They've cleaned it up pretty well. Shaved you a bit there darling, where it's sore, but not a problem, that'll grow back in no time. You've got lovely thick hair. And straight. Always wanted yours rather than mine. Mine's a mess. Yours is sleek, shiny. How hair is supposed to be. Not like this. Mattress has exploded on my head, you said. Everyone loves yours. Loves the colour.

'Come on now, you're just being a silly girl, pretending to be asleep like this. Snoozing. While we're all awake out here. You lazybones. Idle. Selfish. Selfish shellfish. Idle bridle. Lazy Maisie. That's you, isn't it?'

Jo acknowledges the catch in her voice and for the first time alone in the clean clean room with her still still sister, she submits to the tears that have been brimming since she heard the news two days ago. She doesn't want to cry. She knows that if Silvia is at <u>all</u> aware, she won't appreciate this pathetic show. She'd certainly tell her to 'butch up and get a grip', as she has done many times before.

Jo can't stop it though, it's the shock. This sort of thing doesn't happen to anyone she knows, ever. When she first heard the news, she felt as if she was suddenly a character in an American medical show. 'House' was calling her to say that her sister had fallen three floors and sustained a serious

5

head injury. Thank you, Hugh Laurie . . . for giving me this terrible news in your inimitable forthright, some might say even cruel style. Thank God it's you, because now of course, I know it will all be alright for the simple reason that you will inevitably triumphantly and last-minutedly restore my stone of a sister to full health.

Sissy might even seduce him on waking, with her unique interestingness, and win him over to become Mrs Hugh House . . . hmmm.

That first shock of the phone call was awful. But this shock today, Jo thinks, the shock of actually seeing her lying there so motionless save for the hypnotic effort of the enforced breathing, is much much worse. No two ways about it, Silvia is nearly dead.

Look at her. Her skin never usually looks pallid like this.

She must not die. After all, Jo promised their mother to always have a care for her. Silvia shall not die before Jo. Otherwise Jo is even more of a bloody failure. If that's possible . . .

'Hold on, sweetheart. Come on! Keep living. We all love you . . . Well, I do. You know I do. We've had our moments Sis, but the loving you part has never ever been in question. You always love your little sister, don't you? Yes. You do. You have to. That's what you do. You just love them. Whatever they're like. Whatever they've done. However thoughtless or insensitive they might sometimes have been . . . however much they might have hurt you, sometimes carelessly, admittedly, but

6

often purposely, you just keep right on loving them. Whatever you feel. You try to put their feelings first. They come first. Think of others before yourself. Always. Self comes last. Silvia must be protected.

'So that's what we're going to do. Keep you going sweet-heart, at all costs. I'm not giving up on you. There'll be <u>something</u> that wakes you up. I've just got to find it darling, that's all. I'm going to try anything and everything, you wait and see, and one day I will find it and you'll open those beautiful big grey-blue eyes, and I'll be the first thing you see, and you'll know how much I cared and how much I tried, and you'll be grateful and maybe a tiny bit less unkind . . .

'I might well catch you looking at me often in the future, just knowingly, out of the corner of your eyes and I will know you are thinking, "Yep, there she is, my sister Jo, who saved my life, who didn't give up on me, who kept her promise. Who is, truth be told, a bit extraordinary and to whom I owe . . . well . . . everything, really."'

Jo picks up Silvia's heavy dead weight of a hand, noticing the red smudged fingers, and lifts it to her lips and kisses it very much.

THREE

Winnie

Thursday 4pm

Silvia is too hot. Tiny beads of sweat above her lip are the only sign, but it's enough for Winnie, her key nurse, to bring a cool muslin flannel to dab off the moisture and to then rest it on her forehead.

Winnie checks all the machines, could anything be wrong to cause Silvia to be hot?

The ECG monitor is beeping healthily. The read-out is correct.

The endotracheal tube is clear and the ventilator is functioning.

The venous line is in properly, she's getting all her fluids.

Drip drip. That's right.

The nasogastric tube is in place.

She clips a small grey claw on to Silvia's finger and, simultaneously, she deftly folds the large cuff around her arm so that she can check the blood pressure and the oxygen saturations together. She places the grey plastic gun-like infrared thermometer gently into Silvia's ear, and takes her temperature. It takes a moment . . . Winnie always feels like she is pointing a pistol right into the brain of her patients when she does this. She wouldn't say, because it shouldn't, but it amuses her.

Everything is normal. Good. Tick, tick on the clipboard.

Winnie relaxes and starts to sing. She is currently learning a new song for choir. It isn't really new, in fact it's an old traditional American song, but it's new to them, not in their repertoire, which is about three years old now. It's time Calvary Voices had something new. It's coming up to wedding season and they will be asked to sing all the time, sometimes at four weddings on any given Saturday, and Pentecostal services are long. Rarely are the choir invited to the wedding breakfast, so she can sometimes sing at four weddings with only a cold sandwich from the newsagents to sustain her small frame. And is it really right, she wonders, that choirmaster Claude receives £150 for every wedding, but that the choir only receive £10 each from it, and there's only ten of them?

She tries to banish all unchristian thoughts of what an evil selfish bastard Brother Claude might well be, by remembering that Brother Claude is also the official treasurer for Calvary Voices. So presumably there are overheads? On top of which, Brother Claude actually sings <u>with</u> them as well as being choirmaster. He is one of the ten, so he also gets a tenner each time. So . . . that's not good then.

As she toils away, around Silvia, she sings quietly, tenderly. She executes her work with great love.

'As I went down in the river to pray'

She washes Silvia's face

'Studying about that good ol' way'

She washes Silvia's arms

'And who shall wear the starry crown'

She washes Silvia's breasts and shoulders

'Good Lord show me the way'

She washes Silvia's fanny, careful not to dislodge the catheter

'Oh sinners, let's go down'

She changes the sanitary sheet under Silvia's bum, and washes her there

'Let's go down, c'mon down'

She washes Silvia's legs and feet

'C'mon sinners, let's go down'

She straightens up the sheets and tidies Silvia's nightie

'Down in the river to pray'

She brushes Silvia's hair.

When she's finished, she speaks out loud with a pronounced but gentle Jamaican burr.

'Dere you are, Silvia, nice 'n' fresh, yes? Now, we don't want you to be too hot, but I cyan't open the window due to possible cold or h'infection. BUT, mi cyan pull dis down here.'

She pulls down the blind.

'So dere, now you have no direct sunlight on you whatsoever PLUS, mi fetch you up de h'electric fan to cool you, yes? OK.'

She pats Silvia's foot.

She likes to stay in physical contact with her comatose patients at all times whilst she's in the room. It must be very lonely, she thinks, to be so locked away. She has seen this state time and time again, and although she is inured to the shock of it, she still empathizes anew with each fresh patient. No, <u>she</u> isn't shocked, but <u>they</u> are. They have just had all normal life snatched away in a heartbeat, and somewhere, deep inside the brain of this paralysed body, there is life. There are brainwaves.

Winnie saw them when the ITU intensivists and the consultant conducted the EEG scan the evening Silvia was first brought in. There were enough signs of life for them to hook her up, although she scored very badly when they measured the depth of her coma using the Glasgow Coma Scale which Winnie knows all about. It rates:

a. Whether she can open her eyes. She can't.

b. Her motor response. None.

c. Her verbal response. None.

But Winnie knows that just because Silvia doesn't show a response, it doesn't necessarily mean she is not aware. Sometimes Winnie notices the tiniest rise in heartbeat on the monitor when she comes into the room of one of her patients. Not Silvia. Silvia is pretty much spark out, and Winnie can't locate anything she could usefully feed back to the doctors or the family. That doesn't mean she won't though. You have to have two important attributes in this job: patience and vigilance. Oh, and add to those, hope.

Yes, hope, the most important thing of all.

The patients, the doctors, the families and the d'yam hospital itself will give up hope before Winnie does. Winnie's life is about hope. She brings bargain buckets of it with her to work every day. She knows that it's a certain truth, because she's seen it with her own two eyes, that often, it's only at the very edge of life and death that we truly live. Her privilege is to witness that phenomenon daily.

'Phew! You right Silvia, it too hot in here. Mi a burn up. I'll get dat fan, and some remover fi dem red fingers dere. Be right back darlin.'

The door slams shut. Silvia lies alone in intensive care suite number 5, like a marble sarcophagus.

A still, grey effigy.

Cold. But hot.

FOUR

Ed

Thursday 8pm

Ed is standing just inside the door of suite number 5 with his coat still on. He came in easily ten minutes ago but he hasn't quite been able to advance any further into the room or into his visit yet. Although this is his second time here, he is rooted to the spot by the woeful sight of his ex-wife lying so strangely still. He mirrors her inertia, and hasn't moved a muscle except for his eyes which dart around the room, scanning every tiny detail of the grim scene. His paralysis is fed by a creeping sense – one part guilt to two parts irony – as he is remembering with increasing horror how he has actively wished ill on Silvia many times, over the last few, difficult years.

He didn't intend <u>this</u> level of ill though.

All he really wanted was for her to experience, or at least

acknowledge, even a tiny percentage of his pain, rather than parading her new-found freedom with such seeming indifference. It diminished him, and it injured him very deeply. He couldn't believe that so many years of trying and compromising and forgiving and listening were so easily dismissed.

So, in the depths of his humiliated hurt, he had indeed often wished upon her a grisly illness. Something long and slow and debilitating, at least as intolerable as his intolerable suffering.

Now, he numbly stands stock-still, in abject fear that this whole catastrophe may well be his doing. He is as still as her. He wonders what he can do to put it right? That's the job of the man of the family; to put right whatever might be wrong. He is currently the ex-man, so perhaps the job is redundant? He couldn't fix it when they were married, so why would it be different now?

Actually, he thinks, there is one massive irrefutable difference. Now, here, today, he can talk without Silvia interrupting. That was always a big problem. She wouldn't let him speak for long enough without either getting irritated or changing the subject, proving that she simply wasn't interested in his ideas. He was aware, right from the outset, that he wasn't as fizzy as her, he could never think as fast or be as assured. Which is a shame because in fact Ed is every bit as bright as his ex-wife. Just not as confident. Squeaky wheel, and all that.

Silvia told him in the early days that she found his self-doubt endearing. She apparently loved the dichotomy of his tall, imposing angular good looks and yet his many seeming inadequacies. An assured-looking chap who was in fact nothing of the sort. A diffident man, Ed was for her 'a proper-looking bloke' who represented perfect husband and father material. She listened to him more at the beginning, sometimes he would rap on about his dreams and plans for easily twenty uninterrupted minutes before she became fidgety.

If only he'd known then that he would never again have such a window of opportunity to be heard. He might have risked telling her the really big dream. The one he has since realized, unbeknownst to her. The one that gives him purpose and saved his life. The one that offers him the significance he would never find with her.

He is suddenly aware his back is hurting from standing still for so long, so he gathers his achy bones up and moves stiffly to the seat next to her bed.

'Hello Silvia.'

His voice falters, it's croaky, he hasn't used it much today. He secures it with a steadying cough, and restarts.

'Silv. Hello there. It's me, Ed. I'm not sure whether you can hear me, but the doctors have told us to keep talking . . . um . . . at you . . . for you . . . well no, to you. Yes, talking to you. So righto, that's what I'll do. You probably don't relish the idea of me bletheuring on, but I'm hoping that's preferable to the sound of an empty room at least . . . ha ha . . . Christ, I hope it is, otherwise I am genuinely dull. "Duller than the world's dullest-ever thing, so dull it's not worth the time it takes to imagine it," as you not very succinctly put it once, if I remember it correctly. Which I do . . . unfortunately. Anyway love, I'm here right next to you, and I'd like to tell you some stuff. Even if you only hear bits of it, that's OK. Let me . . . just think . . .'

He stares up at the ceiling, wondering where to start. The ventilator wheezes rhythmically and to his horror, he finds he is tapping his toe in time with it. His foot the metronome for her life. He stops immediately. Then he starts again but this time on the off-beat. Something about Silvia being helpless promotes an irresistible urge in him to misbehave.

Can his footbeat persuade the machine to change its tempo? He feels an overwhelming impulse to drum on the bed. She always said he was a child. She used to laugh when she said it. He took that to mean she found some of his more childlike qualities attractive. She giggled at his bad jokes and appreciated his shyness. Slowly, incrementally, that changed though. She didn't call him childlike any more, she flatly called him childish. Well . . . yes, he is, in many ways, and glad of it. He likes doing his silly voices, mimicking everyone that amuses him. He likes tickling and wrestling with those he loves. He likes making faces with his food on the plate, he pretends to walk with a club foot, and he knows he can get babbly when he's overexcited. But he isn't an actual child.

That was another depth charge that hurt so badly when she exploded it.

How did she always manage to insult him with barbs that contained just enough truth to pierce his skin?

She was astute, no doubt about that. He thought he liked smart women, he thought their impressive brainage was an aphrodisiac. He hadn't quite thought through how it would feel when a smart woman decides to round on you wielding her sharpest cleverest incisors, if you fall out of favour with her.

'OK. Well, righto, best to start at the beginning I suppose, which ironically was also the end. The end of us anyway. Just out of interest, why did you decide to become so hellishly unkind in that last couple of months? I knew things weren't great for you in the marriage but honestly I thought we could work it through. Then suddenly I was right royally dumped after twenty-odd years for reasons that are still not clear to me today, apparently to do with "being stuck in adolescence" and "failing to operate as a functioning recognizably human being". I was already in enough distress, did I really need to feel the full power of your turbo sarcasm?

'You really can be cruel Silv, I didn't deserve a lot of what you said. That kind of spite is corrosive, you know. It ate away at me when I was already full of holes. Gouda. I was a living Gouda man. Sometimes, when you attacked, I thought all the holes would just get bigger and bigger 'til they joined up and made one big empty hole. S'pose I'd then be a doughnut man.

'Anyway, it was after I saw the lawyer that I really lost it. Being told you were selling the house. That was a body blow. I signed it all over to you Silv, so you could stay there with the kids. Somewhere secure for all of you, you said. I didn't realize their family time was up too. Neither did they. I know you and Jo were sent out of home so young, I know that, but it was different for you Silv. Cassie was only sixteen, for God's sake. She had only ever lived in that house, that's all she knew. Jamie put on a brave face but just because he's a fella and a couple of years older didn't mean he coped. It meant he "pretended" to cope.

'What did you want with the money Silv? The money from our home, which you swindled the three of us out of?

'What was more important than your family for God's sake?!

'Why didn't we matter?!'

Ed puts his head in his calloused hands and for a moment he relives the heavy empty feeling he used to regularly have in his gut, all those years ago. The familiar wretchedness, the throbbing ache of helplessness. He can't go back to that. It very nearly did for him. It became huge and impossible to endure. He realizes that here and now it's different though, because now he can rant at last. Now is his chance to speak.

'You've got no idea what you did to us. You broke us, Silv. We splintered off in so many bad ways. It's still bad now. Sometimes.'

He pauses.

She breathes. Regular heavy breathing.

She is as impassive now as she was when he arrived. Even if she <u>can</u> hear, does she care? Is she faking it all and purposely sleeping through his torment? Of course not, stop it, Ed. Come on. Courage. Tell her.

'So, one Friday evening, in the middle of the worst of it, when I was so blue that I felt I'd turned black inside, I decided to pretend to be cheerful and do what cheerful people do on a Friday night. Have fish and chips. A normal thing. That's like having your rudder in the water. It's steadying. It's familiar and comforting and keeps you on kilter, upright. It's what normal people are doing in their normal houses on a Friday night. Fish and chips. Normal. I needed some normal, just to get me through the weekend. I was only just surviving, a drip of ordinary at a time.

'I was glad to see the queue at The Plaice To Be was long. I was grateful to have a purpose, to be in the warm, and to have a valid reason to swap cursory pleasantries with other shadows. In fact, I remember very clearly, letting other people go before me in the queue so that my time in the fishy fugginess would be extended. I didn't want to leave there, to sit alone in my car. A car which, incidentally, had a noose in the boot. Well, not incidentally. Purposely. I had made it weeks before and I'd been carrying it around for when the tipping point came. It was close, constantly nipping at me. Up 'til then I knew I could stave it off by thinking about Cassie and Jamie and how much they needed me to stick around.

'Cassie had only just moved into her first flat on her own, she was very scared, Silv. Neither of us could even manage to get the oven on 'til we worked out that the timer was somehow stopping it. That took a whole morning of stomping and swearing. She was so young to be on her own but by then she'd been staying with me at Ma's for too long, and it was all so obviously wrong. The teen and the old mad lady together. Both of them took to sleeping a lot to avoid seeing each other. There's only the one bed at Ma's as you know, I was sleeping on the couch, so Ma slept in the bed all night and Cassie slept in it all day. Shift-sleeping. I knew Cass would crack if it went on much longer, so we went and applied for the flat.

'You should know all of this Silv, I shouldn't have to be telling you . . . anyway, Jamie had already gone along to the Army Recruiting Office in town and they took him immediately. Course they would. A bright, lost, sad young man, full of potential and full of rage. Just what they're looking for. So he was gone. In a heartbeat. She was gone, he was gone, you were gone and I was living with my mother whose bungalow reeks like a tanner's hut. When Cassie complained of the stench, Ma just blamed the cats. The last cat died eight years ago. Ma claims there's still one remaining rogue cat wandering about the house pissing on everything. Cassie agreed that yes, there might well be, and if there was, it would be called "Granma" . . .'

At this point, Ed groans as he gets up and goes to the window mumbling 'living with my mother again, after forty years' and 'bloody appalling' and 'Why d'you sell it anyway?' and 'unkind, truly unkind'. He stretches and scratches. He remains at the window, fixed on the view into a dismal quad, with tall hospital buildings on all four sides. There is a bench next to a bin, and a small lawn, half of which is brown because it never sees the sun, the buildings are too high. Who would ever want to sit there? It looks grim.

Perhaps, if Silvia is in here long enough and the weather gets warmer, if he can stomach still coming to visit her, he will come to regard that bench as his sanctuary. It will be a pleasure to sit on it because it will be wood against his legs, and a relief from sitting in here with Silvia, breathing her same stuffy air and watching her staunchly make no progress whatsoever.

Or maybe not.

Maybe she will wake up soon.

Yes, she might.

All the more reason to tell her. Tell her now.

He girds himself.

'So, that evening, the fish 'n' chips evening, eventually I was at the head of the queue. There was no one else to let in front, so I had to take my turn and give my order. I couldn't steal any more time. As the girl gave me the packet, she said, "Have a lovely night," and I automatically replied, "Yes thanks, I will." I quickly climbed into my car and once inside, I allowed that little comment to land on me. "Have a lovely night." She said it with conviction, actually she genuinely hoped I would have "a lovely night". I wouldn't of course, I knew that, but that wasn't what struck me. The shocking realization I had, was that she imagined "a lovely night" was a possibility for me. Somehow she had the hope I had completely lost. A stranger could still imagine I had the capacity for happiness.

'She didn't know that I was dead inside, that . . . I had ruled out the chance of joy ever again. For that night and every other night to follow. I had fully settled into my unhappiness and wore it comfortably. So comfortably in fact, that it was barely perceptible to others. It just fitted me so well. My suit of misery hung happily on me. So happily that she assumed I could have "a lovely night" in it. The loveliness she referred to was so extremely far out of reach for me. It was as far as . . . the bloody moon.

'The sadness of it all hit me very hard, very suddenly. It virtually winded me. As I pulled away from the kerb, my mind started to chase me . . . towards . . . the bloody tipping point. I didn't drive home. I drove up to Collicott Fields. I parked in the turning point at the end of the lane, you know it. It was still light enough to see, so I grabbed the fish-and-chips bag and the noose, climbed across the wall on that stile they have there, and headed up the field towards the wood.

'No one was about, save a few sleepy cows who gave me that witheringly dismissive glance they do, and then they just resumed their serious chewing job. Four stomachs, apparently. Amazing. As I trudged across the grass, I could see the grove of ancient beeches at the far end of the field, getting closer and bigger, as if they were coming towards me to swallow me up. That's just what I wanted, to be right inside that wood, away from the woodless everywhere else. Away from openness. As I approached the outer edge with the first trees, I could feel the structure of the ground beneath my feet begin to change. The floor of the forest is scattered with the detritus of the massive gnarly beeches, all their droppings. It became quite crunchy and I had to pick my way through carefully. Remember, it was twilight by now, so it was fairly perilous.

'You know where I was going Silv. I headed straight for the massive queen beech at the centre of the copse. She is the mother of them all, I think, the giant shade giver, the oldest. Maybe even four hundred years, possibly.

'You will remember her, you will have looked up past her great knotted trunk into her magnificent dense top foliage that amazing day Silv, all those years ago, y'know the first time. I couldn't believe how young you looked. Easily fifteen years younger than you were. I suppose you must have been . . . What? . . . thirty-three or something when we first met, but with the filtered sun dancing on your skin, so . . . dappled and . . . sort of creamy, you looked like a teenager. You were smiling up at me, giving me permission to go further. Inside the wood, inside you. So breathless and . . . willing.'

Ed looks at her.

Yes, she's still breathless. Different kind of breathless.

That kind, back then, is such a turn-on, he remembers, when

a woman can't find enough breath to keep up. When she has to snatch air between waves of pleasure. Deep, guttural sexual breaths. God, he loves that sound. He hasn't heard it for so long.

So long.

So . . .

Long.

He sighs and looks at her.

'You were the most beautiful sight I'd ever seen that day, your nakedness in amongst those huge snakey roots. It was all . . . earth, or something. Overwhelming. Completely natural. The best kind of beauty. It was a better moment than any I'd ever had. Maybe even than I ever will have, Silv. It was . . . sort of . . . dunno . . . sacred? I know that sounds grand and I'm sorry to say I'm glad you can't respond to it, because I can just hear your haughty derision now. Maybe deservedly. But Silv, I just want you to know how much it meant.

'It was in that moment I genuinely believed in – you know – love, for the first time. Well, for the only time. I believed we would always be one, I wanted that. I thought you did too. I really thought you did. Did you Silv? I would like to know. Yep. Like to know when that all changed . . . Anyway, it was on that day remember, we carved the Latin initials: "CICA" for "Crescent illae, crescit amores", "As these letters grow, so will our love" into the bark of that immense matriarch.

'So that's where I was heading, Silv. I found her, after a bit of

24

palavering about and tripping up. A beautiful, monumental big fat beech with our memento tattooed on her. I felt guilty when we did it, like it was tree vandalism or something, but you said it was a badge of honour for the tree, that she would be proud to display our epigram along with all the other human markings made long before us. By schoolchildren in breeches and petticoats? By lovers in tight collars and corsets? I had to fumble about in my pocket for my keys so that I could use the pathetic little key-ring torch to search the giant trunk to find it.

'It was, of course, further up than we had carved it, twenty-seven years further up in fact, and further in, which isn't so much on a colossal mama like that. I found it though. Still there, holding fast. Unlike us. I sat back down on the ground beneath it. Exactly where we had made love, and I unwrapped the fish and chips. They were a bit cold by then, but I gorged on them anyway. Delicious. "Have a lovely night." I looked at the noose I had flung on the floor nearby. It definitely wasn't going to be lovely.

'The noose was well made even if I do say so myself. I had been practising making it with various kinds of rope, different thicknesses. This one should be just right, I thought. I bought the rope in a chandlers, it was nylon and strong and manoeuvrable where it needed to be. The slip knot was well executed. That was the most crucial part. It <u>must</u> work first time, and it must take my weight. As I fall, I need the knot to jolt my neck forward and snap it cleanly. No fuss.

'Jump. Snap. Done.

'I tied and retied it sitting next to Ma on the sofa whilst she was watching *Midsomer Murders*. She didn't notice.

'I finished my fish and chips, and tidied away my mess. I didn't want to leave a mess. More mess than there already was. Which was a massive bloody godawful mess. Holding the torch in my mouth, I flung the length of the rope over a strong lower branch and secured it to the trunk of the tree. Nothing would loosen it, it would remain firm, I was sure of that. I positioned the noose just above a massive old log that I could use to step off. It was all ready. I realized that these could be my very last moments in this world.

'What does one do? Or say?

'I wanted to be quick or I knew my courage might fail me, so I rummaged around in my brain for <u>anything</u> of significance to think or feel. In the end, I mumbled something pathetic out loud like "Dear God, if you exist, and I'll know pretty soon, help my children to forgive me for this, and please be the strength in them that I can't find in me. Amen. Oh, and sorry for being such a prime tosser . . ."I climbed up on to the log and tried to balance. It was hard because there was slimy lichen all over it, and because I was brimming with tears. Stinging my eyes, then streaming. Thousands of tears. Mostly self-pity I think, and self-loathing. But Silv, I didn't know how to pity and loathe myself 'til you taught me. What an accomplished coach you are. So well acquainted was I with my shortcomings, that

I could end up on a slippy log prepared to donate my life to them. Feeling like absolute shit, Silv. Absolute shit.

'In that moment, all I wanted was for you to find out that's where I hung myself. On "our" tree. Because of you, you, you. So, I reached for the noose and pulled it towards my head. Just as it was slipping over my ears, I lost my footing on the wretched moss and tumbled unceremoniously, arse over tit, on to the forest floor. My back scraped down the bark of the big old dead log and I was scratched to hell. Then the crying turned into sobbing. Completely involuntary. I just felt like such a useless dickhead, I couldn't even off myself well. Couldn't do decent dying, I felt utterly bereft.

'Then, then something happened. Something amazing. I picked up my torch to look at the log that had attacked my back so badly, and d'you know what I saw? Fresh shoots, Silv. In some big storm, this old rotten tree had fallen. But in its new, horizontal position, it had come back to life. It wasn't finished yet, Silv, it had more living to do, that dead old wood. More to give. Yes. It was so clear to me. However battered by our storm, however uprooted I was, I didn't have to lie down and accept that I was felled. I still had strength, I still had sap, and more importantly Silv, and what you will never understand the joy of, I had my saplings to shelter and raise. Of course I did. Of course. I left the noose hanging there and I walked away from that huge tree where only minutes before I had thought I would finish.

'I ran in the darkness back to my car. As I was climbing over the stile next to the gate, I heard a weird flapping noise. With the help of my trusty torch, I could see it was a public notice announcing the sale of Collicott Fields. I read on. It included the beech wood I'd been in, Foy Wood. I didn't know it even had a name! Surrounded by twenty acres of field. Foy Wood, Silv. That's <u>my</u> wood now. I bought it the following week. The down payment was money I nicked from Ma's secret cupboard. Not so secret after all! He he! She counts it every week, and doesn't even know it's gone!

'Yes, that's my wood and I've taken good care of it Silv. And while you're in here, stuck in that bed and stuck in your head, I'm going to tell you all about it, and that way, I'm going to take you there. You may be a cruel old cunt, but everyone is entitled to beauty. And that's what you shall have. The beauty might just save you.'

FIVE

Tia

Friday 10am

'Hello Mrs Shit! Is me at last – Tia!'

Sutiyah Setyawati bumfles noisily into Suite 5, proudly carting a brace of plastic bags with her. She has brought gifts for her employer Mrs Shute. In one bag, there are three Tupperware clipboxes containing three different dishes that she knows Mrs Shute especially loves. She immediately unpacks them and spreads them on the table which swings across the bottom of the big clinical bed.

'I have your favourite. Three favourite. I make for you in my cooker last night. Every in my family try steal! I say no, that for Mrs Shit only. For make her much well. I tell them to do big piss off, not to eat. They have many other to eat. Keep dirty fingers and toes off Mrs Shit food. This goin to make her alive again. If Mrs Shit smell my gado-gado, you think she stay dead? No thank you! She jump up and suck it off very quickly.'

Without even removing her coat, she unclips all the tiffin boxes and takes the lids off, releasing the ambrosial spicy scents into the room. The juicy vapours permeate Silvia's tired dry air with their delicious moisture. Tia, as she's known to all British people who can't pronounce her full name, picks up one of the boxes piled high with delicious fried rice with chillies and anchovies and whole, shiny garlic bulbs. She positions herself near the top of the bed where Silvia's head is slightly lollopped on one side. She places the tub under her nose.

'Come on Mrs Shit. It smell good, yes? You wanna wake up now? I make plenty more if you do. Deal or no deal, come on. This is my special nasi goreng. For warriors. One big lady is easy for this. Will help you fighting. Come on.'

She checks no nurses are snooping through the window, then she dips her index finger into the luscious juice at the side of the dish, slips it into Silvia's mouth, and rubs it all over her gums and teeth.

'Is good. Is very good. Enjoy the juicy and wet. You won't regret. The taste is gentle, hm? Not enough too spice? Just as the lady likes, I think. Who wants food in the tube? How is getting in properly? A tube with bad soup in, no pepper? No please thank you for Mrs Shit. She like hot, ow ow, nice dance on her tongue. Like a bursting she says. Not boring English soup water. Going in a nose hole. How to enjoy that? Aw look at the dry mouth lips.'

Tia replaces the tub of food on the table, and rummages about in her bag 'til she finds a small bright pink tin.

'Here comes! I get this in Jakarta, nowhere in UK can find this, special grease made from tiger ass. Not the bad part where dirt comes through, other part higher in. On two sides, the holes make a juice come out to help the dirt get out easy. But this grease is from that bum juice very fresh, very clean, very expensive. Makes mouth lips fat and slippy. You ever see dry tiger asshole? Never! So, here. I put there for you.'

She opens the tin and spreads the balm all over Silvia's lips and beyond. As high as her nose and as low as her chin, and ear to all-the-way-on-the-other-side ear. The lower half of Silvia's face is now thoroughly glisteningly greased. She looks strangely mannequin-like. For luck presumably, because there's no other earthly reason, Tia adds more grease to Silvia's eyebrows.

'There. No dry left now. Thank you Tia. You're welcome Mrs Shit, have a nice day. Now, what I got next? Oh, cock tosser –'

She takes off her coat and rummages around in the bags. She flits between them like a colourful busy hummingbird, singing Indonesian ditties under her breath, swearing and laughing at little incidental personal jokes. Tia has been taught to swear by her two sons who were born and grew up in England, and who amuse themselves by cajoling her into using utterly inappropriate language. She's not stupid, she knows they are having a laugh at her expense, but she can't be bothered to deduce exactly why, and frankly, she doesn't care.

She's a busy woman. She has two sons at expensive English

public schools, and an injured English husband at home. When he persuaded her to come and live with him in England fifteen years ago, he promised her father he would always look after her, in the manner to which she was accustomed. She was from a good family, her father was a textile merchant and sold beautiful cloth all around the world. The most prized silks in Jakarta. That's what she wore. She still has some, but many of her more valuable possessions, including beautiful cloth and impressive jewellery, have been sold. When her husband injured his head, racing old bangers, he couldn't return to work ever again. If he'd hurt himself at work, they might at least have earned some compensation but no, he was driving round and round at breakneck speed in highly dangerous cars. Nobody pays out if you do that. He's been at home ever since.

Tia didn't mind to begin with, she was determined to nurse him back to health. She felt sure she could do it by dint of food-love alone. Surely her hearty spicy broths would revive him, nourish him, and make him strong? Very quickly she realized that 'husband' wasn't really 'husband' any more. He looked the same, but he definitely <u>wasn't</u> the same person. He was like a tracing-paper drawing of the original husband. Fainter, wobblier, much more distant. His spirit was gone and many many heavy depressions set in. She watched him retreat into his leather lounger in front of afternoon telly, until he was indistinguishable from the chair. They were one item. He wasn't unkind or ungrateful, he just wasn't really there at all.

She is married to a living ghost.

That's why the onus to earn fell on her so severely. That's why ten years ago Silvia Shute and her family became very important. That's why Silvia <u>must</u> stay alive. Silvia is almost single-handedly putting Tia's boys through school. They are good, clever boys. They both have scholarships. But Tia still has to find the money for expensive uniforms and sports equipment.

Tia has to perform many duties for Mrs Shute that she doesn't want to. She is a house-proud woman, it's not that she is shy of hard work, it's just that some of what Mrs Shute requires her to do is extremely personal. It's hard to respect a person when you clean their toilet and wash their pants and see their sex toys in their bedroom drawers. Are you supposed to wash those? Tia doesn't. One of them buzzed once. It scared her. In Indonesia other people would be doing chores for Tia, but she swallows her pride and gets on with it.

Not only does she push on, she does it with massively good cheer, believing that each new day brings a new chance of happiness, new hope. That's how she gets through.

Every morning she sits at her dressing table and makes sure she looks glamorous. She wears a lot of make-up, using bright colours on her eyelids especially. She doesn't understand why British women look so dour so much of the time. They don't know they're born, why don't they try to bring a bit of cheer into their lives? Why choose to wear black and grey when there is fuchsia and turquoise in the world? These are the vivid colours of living nature. Why choose the colours of decay and death? It doesn't make any sense at all to Tia.

From her bright plastic bags, Tia brings out a clutch of magazines. She bought them at the garage, and although they have many different titles, they all seem to be the same, basically.

'I bring you plenty news. I not sure where you gone, but I bet they got no news there. I'm thinking, if I was doin the dead sleeping, I would sure be thinking hey, what's still goin on out where the world is? Someone, quick tell me! We love news, don't we Mrs Shit? So here is . . .'

Tia settles down in the chair with a lapful of magazines. She is going to be here some time. She hums as she riffles through them, stopping every time she comes across a story she thinks Mrs Shute would be interested in.

'Ah, OK, here first big one. "Jordon buying LA pad for eleven million!" Woo! She's givin Peter Andre something to sock in the eye. But who will have kids? No one is telling us. Why not? They all lazy quim-suckers. Next big one is "I married my 28 stone stalker". He he! Look at him! How he do the stalkin? How he follow anyone? He can't hide in her bush, she see him pokin out there! And why she marry him anyway? Should just go out – have a drink, have a talk, have a movie. Not marry. Wanko.

'Ah, this next one very big news. RichardanJudy. We love

RichardanJudy, don't we Mrs Shit? She say no more TV for them, but now please, they just read books. That nice. Judy sit in her big bra readin the books, and Richard makin the coffee. Aw. She say "Oh Richard, I like this book ... about a man ... who does a thing" and he say "Yes Judy, and I like this other book about a girl who ... does a thing ... another thing then the end for everyone to be happy and learn a thing." They very clever up here in the head Mrs Shit. Very clever, cos I read a book, but no one pay me.

'Now, next story is ... oh, <u>big</u> one Mrs Shit, big one, Cheryl Cole is got a tattoo what look like a spider ... I love Cheryl Cole, she a proper nice bollockhead ...'

SIX

Cat

Friday 2.30pm

'Eh eh, yu haffi check wid de desk before you come in please. It just de rules. Nuttin personal. Syame for everyone.'

Winnie is ever so slightly barring the entrance to Silvia's room. She wouldn't be acting in such a brazenly obstructive manner if this visitor wasn't quite so spiky.

'I am a doctor, you are a nurse. Let me through please,' says the visitor, her Irish brogue doing nothing to soften her tone.

'Of course, soon as you sign de book, no problem.'

'Please listen now, whilst I say it again. I am a doctor.'

'Yes ma'am, mi know dat, but not at dis hospital.'

'Oh, for feck's sake . . .'

The visitor retreats and hurriedly, begrudgingly, signs the book at the nurses' station, then bristles into the room, breathing heavily with frustration.

Catherine Mary Bernadette O'Brien is fighting feelings of

36

massive inadequacy in Suite 5. Why, she wonders, do hospitals always represent such a threat to her? This should be where she is at her keenest, completely en pointe. When she was a medical student, this is exactly what she imagined for herself. The cut and thrust of the hospital front line. The white-coated, hugely respected, stethoscope-round-neck, godlike authority of the hospital doctor. It is a much more special role than hers, she knows this, but it is only during visits to hospitals that she is reminded.

Somewhere along the line, and she now can't remember exactly when, she made the less glamorous choice to be a GP. Perhaps the choice made her. Maybe she didn't have the medical X-factor ingredient to make the hospital doctor mark. She mentally kicks herself for thinking that, and for assuming even for one moment that she is somehow insufficient. She is quite the opposite. She is 'The Mighty Cat', as Silvia often calls her.

Right now, she must be the strongest she can possibly be for Silvia. This is when she is needed most, yet ironically, her professional, doctoring skills are redundant in this very specialized situation. She isn't a coma doctor. Until three days ago, she knew very little about this area of medicine. She has internetted and blogged and googled and called informed colleagues non-stop since Silvia's accident, and now she knows a lot more, but of course her voice is a very tiny one in this hospital.

Inaudible.

Not that 'they' are doing anything overtly wrong, it's just that Cat doesn't want to be spoken to as if she's a mere friend of the patient. That is what she is, essentially. A friend of the patient. The patient's best friend, actually. Best best ever friend. Which, in real terms, makes you the most important person in their life. Chosen by them. Not their bloody family, who they don't really speak to, even, who hardly know Silvia any more. Only Cat knows Silvia, the real Silvia. She wishes she could shoo them all out of this room with their ruddy visitors' rota, all these useless hangers-on like Ed and Jo.

Poor Silvia, having to lie there in their dreadful company, unable to resist. They all think they are exactly what she needs to wake her up! How egotistical. Cat is what Silvia needs. Didn't she and Silvia have a special connection from the very first moment Silvia walked into her consulting room twelve years ago to get help with bouts of serious sadness? Cat is the most connected person to Silvia in the entire world – what place do these other fools think they have?

Cat is Blu-tacking to the wall a large printed photograph of the stunning rugged Connemara landscape. This is where she was born and raised, and where she and Silvia have had several remarkable holidays. Wouldn't it be fantastic if this was the first image Silvia saw on waking? Something so evocative and so reminiscent of utter joy?

'Remember Kylemore Abbey, Silly? Sure, I've never seen

you openly weep like that just because of the sheer beauty of a place. And what beauty. Bloody colossus of a mountain with the perky gothic Abbey nestling in its lap. Got a lovely picture of you at the front door. Hat on. And the nuns. Benedictine bats, you said. They frightened you, Silly, I know, God love you, but you haven't grown up with them. I love a bit of a nun, forever flitting about on the periphery of your life vision, providing the moral measure. Personally, I never did come across an evil one, although I always expected to. You hear so many stories, doncha? But no one could verify them. Evil nuns and ghosts – do they truly exist?'

The picture is up. Cat turns from her task and looks at Silvia.

Why is half of Silvia's face covered in Vaseline? she wonders. She unzips a small cosmetic bag she has brought from Silvia's flat. She has keys, and she knows Silvia would use these products if she could choose. She applies plenty of the Clinique toner to a cotton pad and slowly, tenderly wipes all the grease from Silvia's face, mumbling and comforting her all the while.

'Hey there, darlin' one, just get this mess off you. Off your lovely face. Wipe it all off. What're they thinking? There. Gone. Now, some proper moisturizer . . .'

She squirts Silvia's expensive lotion into her hands, rubs them together and positions herself as close as she can get to her. She places them, creamy palms down, on to Silvia's face and starts to rub it in, carefully avoiding her eyes, mouth and so on. She is especially cautious around Silvia's nose, where the nasogastric tube is taped in. Then she smooths out all the remaining cream. Her fingers follow the contours of Silvia's face. It's a face she knows so well and this very intimate touching gives her an unexpected chance to explore it even more closely. Cat relishes this rare opportunity to let her hands echo and confirm what her eyes see. She can't remember when she last touched Silvia's face. And until you touch, you can't know how it really feels.

Now, and only now, she knows that Silvia's prominent but pleasing nose has very fine skin on it. Skin you wouldn't want to be too rough with, lest it split like wet crêpe paper. A fine, large defiant nose, with such a delicate covering. And Silvia's intrepid forehead which has dared a wrinkle to blemish it. Very few wrinkles have thus far had the courage. Freckles, however, are not so lily-livered, they operate in squadrons and are unafraid to muster in such public open spaces as Silvia's exceptionally wide and high forehead. Alongside her phenomenally red colouring, Silvia has had to accept that freckles will forever be her constant companions. Cat knows that in her capacity as an extreme control freak, Silvia wishes she could properly designate the precise locations of the freckles. For instance, she would prefer a cute spattering of them across her nose, rather than the unsightly enclave that have herded together just above her eyebrows.

Ah. Her eyebrows. Cat strokes them with great tenderness. Or rather, she strokes the place where Silvia's distinctive eyebrows ordinarily are. Only now is it apparent that the unique symmetry and shape of Silvia's notoriously perfect eyebrows is entirely fabricated by Silvia and her handy eyebrow pencil. She has always used a very particular shade of reddish-brown that is completely believable, expertly applying it with tiny hair-like flicks that go to make a very authentic effect. Silvia copied the shape from the glamorous old Hollywood starlets, Marlene Dietrich, Jean Harlow, Bette Davis, Elizabeth Taylor. A small square box above the nose, with an elegant high arch bowing outwards. Silvia is expert at this and somehow a daily glamour is achieved with this simple but effective trick. Not now though. Now she has two blondey-red wisps, two crummy excuses for eyebrows.

Silvia's eyes are closed. That's the most difficult part. How Cat would love it if they would suddenly open, big and grey and blue and blousey like they are. Cat would know so much if only they would open. She could read Silvia then. Lying there, eyes shut, Silvia is closed, and Cat can't bear the consequent rejection she feels, however ludicrous that is. A slumbering torment.

Her fingers are at Silvia's mouth, where the venom is stored, a dangerous place, a wide, expressive powerful mouth. So many have wanted to kiss it, because those full lips would surely be so well equipped to do a proper job of the kissing.

You would be folded into those accomplished lips, they'd surely wrap around your measly mouth, around your resistance and your willpower. You'd be helpless if those lips were kissing you. They are especially impressive when outlined in Silvia's trademark strong coral red and filled in with a gloss version of the same. Silvia ALWAYS wears lipstick. In colours that argue loudly with her hair. Colours that confound your notion of taste, that dare you to be as loud and brashly confident as her. Now, though, her lips are natural, and even more pink than any lipstick.

Cat pushes gently up at each side of her wide mouth.

'Smile, darlin'. Life is still worthwhile. If you just smile . . .'

No, it's too grotesque.

Cat stops and cups Silvia's face in her hands, enjoying the plumpness of her cheeks against her palms. The softness and warmth feels, just for a moment, like health. She reaches down and kisses her on that fine freckled forehead.

'C'mon Silly. You can do it, so you can. Just hold on.'

Silvia's sleek hair falls back and away from her large English face, revealing telltale grey roots all around, giving her a kind of silver halo. She wouldn't like that, but Cat has always thought Silvia shouldn't dye her hair. She suspected, quite rightly it seems, that Silvia has the type of grey hair that is strong and thick. Metallic. Cat often tells her it would look phenomenal and that she should let it grow through, proudly. She thinks it would give Silvia an air of elegance, and she is annoyed that Silvia won't take her advice. But Silvia will have nothing to do with it.

When Cat and Silvia first got to know each other, Silvia told Cat about how, as a young girl, everyone commented on her strawberry-blonde hair. It defined her and it clearly marked her out as her mother's daughter. Jo had 'brooown' hair – that's how Silvia always said it, with an elongated vowel to emphasize its dullitude.

'BROOOWN. Soooo. Boooring. Jooooo Boooring Haaair.'

Jo looked more like Dad whilst Silvia looked like Mummy. Silvia liked it that way. She loved Mummy more, and anyway, Mummy was female and beautiful. Dad was a man and a very archetypal army officer type of man. Yes, let Jo be the butch one, like him. Silvia wanted to be delicate and feminine. That was always going to be tricky to pull off because, much to her annoyance, she was tall and big-boned like her father, but somehow the essentially female pale red hair was her saving grace. It lent her an unambiguous girlishness.

Why on earth, then, would she allow it to turn grey? No, that was never going to happen, she would go to her grave strawberry blonde. So, Cat thought, she had better organize to get those roots rectified at some point in the next few weeks. She didn't even know if it would be possible or allowed in hospital.

So much to find out.

But for now, she lets her fingers wander from Silvia's face outward into her hair and she gently massages her scalp.

'Amazing hair, Silly. Wonderful head. Great shape. C'mere, does that feel good? You like this normally, if you ever let me get near you! I do know a bit about massage you know, when I was backpacking as a student in Southern India, I did stay on an ashram for a fortnight and we all learned head massage. Like everyone else of course, I preferred receiving it. It's glorious if it's done right. Hope this is good, darlin'. Wonder if you can feel it at all? Oh Silly. I do miss you. I miss that you would be batting me away right now, and not letting me do this. You'd better come through this Sil, I'll be furious if you don't. I mean it. Feckin' fuming.'

Cat hears herself say this but doesn't allow herself to dwell on the thought, it's too grim. However, she is glad she's said it out loud. Silvia likes honesty and would certainly be saying it how it is, if the roles were reversed. Maybe she's locked in there, longing for someone to speak truthfully.

Cat wants to be that person. She yearns for the approval of Silvia, and as yet, she doesn't feel she is fully granted it. Silvia has stepped up for Cat, most especially in one particular instance that was truly remarkable, but that's not quite the approbation she seeks. That was more like a show of courage on Silvia's part, not the pure personal endorsement Cat aches for and feels she deserves.

The irony, Silvia says, is that until Cat grants herself the permission to be acceptable, she is singularly unacceptable.

This is maddening for Cat who, at work, is perfectly assured.

It's only in the orbit of the leviathan Silvia that she becomes such a pathetic jelly on occasion. The very thing that repulses Silvia. This is what Cat has battled with. It's her constant torment. How to win Silvia's affection, how to creep closer into that warm place which is only in Silvia's gift. In the gift of an intrinsically ungenerous person. Not a simple aspiration, admittedly, and possibly self-destructive, but Cat can't help herself.

She's drawn to Silvia like a moth to a flame, and, like moths do, she is willing the flame to burn brighter and higher.

SEVEN

Jo

Friday 4pm

Winnie and the other nurses can see into Suite 5 through the long window on one wall, which enables the staff at the nurses' station to keep an eye on whatever's going on. Very often, with seriously ill patients like Silvia, Winnie and the other nurses will ignore a certain amount of strange behaviour by visitors so long as it doesn't interfere with the actual physical care of the patient. The visitors are, after all, in their own shock and sometimes react oddly.

This afternoon, though, Silvia's sister is sorely testing their patience. She has closed the big outside window curtains and lit many overpoweringly sweet-smelling candles, which are drenching the entire ITU in their repulsive musky pong. She has been repeatedly told not to do this as a naked flame can cause serious explosions when coupled with oxygen, which is clearly in huge supply in ITU. But none of the warnings register with stubborn ol' Jo. She is playing loud Enya-beauty-spa-atmosphere music which is leaking out into the corridor. The music is the worst offence. It is annoying and upsetting other patients' visitors and Winnie even noticed that a fellow coma patient has charted some eye movement for the very first time, perhaps as a protest against the audio torture.

Jo is ensconced in Suite 5, conducting what she considers to be a celestial gathering. Amongst the towering insanity of the bizarre scene, only one fact is a surety. Silvia would hate this. Really hate it.

All around Silvia's head is a halo of different-coloured crystals arranged in an arc on her pillow. On Silvia's chest lies a clutch of white feathers tied up with twine and quartz beads, and a dreamcatcher. Jo is dressed in flowing white linen, an outsized long-sleeved blouse and a long white skirt. Her obvious and hastily chosen black underpants are the day's biggest mistake so far.

Or so she thinks. She is wrong.

Many other much worse mistakes are happening, including her choice of opening line.

'Right, let's begin by getting comfortable. Oh sorry Sissy, you can't of course. Ignore that bit, I'll start again. Hang on, let me get comfy . . .'

Jo is gabbling, as per usual. Gabbling furiously whilst trying to invoke peaceful meditation. She sits.

'OK. Here we go Silv. Oh great masters of our universe

and all the abundant goddesses, hear us in our time of need. Please, if you're not too busy, we beseech you in your infinite wisdom, to summon all the angels and archangels hereabouts and convene them here . . . abouts. I call out to all nearby divine celestials to gather here to pool our combined forces and make a diamond-white liquid lovelight so strong that it will heal my sister Silvia and bring her upwards out of sleep and back to the living plane and to well-being. It doesn't matter if not all the major angels are available, so long as a couple of key ones could come? Michael for instance. I have been reliably told that Archangel Michael can simultaneously be with unlimited numbers of people in unlimited numbers of places? Not sure if that's true, but it would be great if it was . . . so, do come unto here, o great Michael. Keep breathing Silv, inhaling the positive thoughts, and exhaling your tensions. Let them go. Give yourself permission to let them go. And breathe. And breathe . . .'

The machine breathes in.

And out.

And in.

'Good. Come! Come! This is so definitely helping you, Silv, whether you are aware of it or not. Try to relax and allow yourself to feel totally safe. Because you are safe Sis. You're with me, and just as I promised Mummy, I will look after you. I will always keep you surrounded by the highest divine light. You just need to welcome in the world Silv. I know you've always resisted this stuff in the past darling, and I'm still smarting from being referred to as an "insane witch" but when the angels arrive, they will help you to purge yourself of all your toxic anger and bitterness which constantly cloud your experience of the light. You will be cleansed and vitalized, just you wait.

'I invoke you, o angels of light, approach! Come, angels all. Come, Gabriel, Raphael, Donatello, Michelangelo ... Sandalwood ... Um ... Shamu ... Israel ... Zak ... and ... Po. Come close and shower this wretched invalid with your healing vibrations, envelop her in your protective love, and let her body glimmer with light and health. Allow us to feel your presence. Please. Come on angels, please ... soon, please, if you don't mind ... because visiting time is almost over ... please?! I'm sorry to have to make you work to an earthly schedule, all you hallowed ones, but I'm afraid we are a tad bound by tempus fugit. Sorry about that, but if you could convene soon, that would be super ...?'

Jo allows a unique minute of silence to happen. She is looking for any sign of a supernatural presence. A feather, perhaps, or a breeze, or, she dares to wish, a vision? What she wouldn't give to witness a heavenly host. It would be double great, she thought, if the slightly disapproving nurses were blinded by the divine light through the window. That'd teach them she wasn't entirely wacko. Admittedly, as a child Jo had had her wacko moments. She once cut off all her hair and attempted to stick it on to a bald doll with a flour-and-water glue. She kept a pebble from a Cornish beach as a pet until she was well into her teens, and she refused to wear anything that wasn't purple until she left primary school, causing endless problems with uniform. Eventually, the Head gave in when little Jo claimed she would go on a hunger strike if she was forced to give up her royal purple – a colour she claimed kept her alive. All of these eccentricities were par for the course inside the tight unit of four that comprised her family. They soaked it up and accepted her as just 'JoJo', the one who's a bit odd and a bit irritating. That's who she happily is.

Here, now, in this room, she listens. She looks. But silence and stillness are no friends of Jo's. She is intensely uncomfortable in their company. She only has five more minutes, so she has to take matters into her own hands.

'Right, well, shame you couldn't make it in time, Michael and all the others, but I think I know what you'd do if you were here, so Silv, I'm just going to invoke the spirits of them through me to do the healing myself. So, here goes . . .'

She stands up impatiently and walks to the head of the bed, gesturing like a rookie polytechnic lecturer in a science seminar about planets.

'So, I quickly say the angel prayer: "Angels help to guide me, with abundance to provide me . . ." Yes, yes, I feel it now, I utilize Archangel Michael's sacred vacuum to suck up your low and broken energies, through your crown chakra, hoovering up all psychic debris. Be receptive, Silv, you might feel a bit of psychic pulling . . . surrender Silvia, give yourself over to the supreme lord, and let go of all that does not serve your highest purpose ... Submit! Submit! Oh, bugger ...'

Winnie is tapping on the window, pointing angrily at the candles and indicating her watch. Jo is out of time. She has to stop. She slams her hand down hard on the bedside table.

'For God's sake! I was just getting warmed up. Damn it to hell!'

She flounces about, blowing out the candles and clearing up feathers, cursing and putting the lights back on.

Silvia just lies there. Exactly the same. No perceptible change whatsoever.

Jo is furious.

'Thanks a lot Archangel Michael, typical man. No bloody show. Prick.'

She bundles out of the room, too embarrassed and irritated to give so much as a backward glance, intent on devising whatever the next method might be to wake up her frozen sister. She will melt that iceberg, come what may. Yes she will.

EIGHT

Winnie

Friday 7pm

Just before she goes off duty, Winnie pops in to do a few last jobs in Silvia's room. She rips open a new packet of elastic stockings and, singing little snippets of Calvary Voices repertoire under her breath all the time, she replaces the old ones with these new, tighter fresher ones. It takes some doing. Silvia's legs are heavy.

'Sorry Silvia, I know dey not de most glamorous tights dem, but hey, wotcha gonna do? Better you don't get trombosis, darlin. You don't want dat. Pyainful. Yes. Mi see dat hyappen in here, bwoy, de lady was screamin, den, in ten minutes, she a dead! She say no to dese tights. Big mistake. Yes, sista. But you gonna wear dem, Silvia. Yes.'

Once the new stockings are on, Winnie glances around the room, checking everything is correct. She notes all the relevant figures from the various machines carefully into the clipboard log at the bottom of the bed. She looks carefully at how Silvia is lying, and she alters the position of her arm and her head which had flopped sideways more than Winnie considers to be comfortable. She wipes the side of Silvia's mouth where, just today, she has begun to dribble, and she puts a fresh cloth beneath her cheek to deal with it. The room is quiet, save for the constant compressed hiss of the ventilator.

Winnie likes this gentler part of the day. The light is fading outside, it's time for her to go home, but it's only at this twilight time of evening that her motionless patients look right in their beds. It's bedtime, after all, even if they were well, they might just be in bed now. Somehow it doesn't feel so massively wrong to be bedbound in the evening. That's why she elected to do mainly day shifts. She feels that more nursing is required during the day, that this is when she's genuinely effective. She also needs to be at home at night for her son. Her momma can look after him for a while after school but Winnie knows that the few hours the two of them have alone together each evening is the bedrock on which she is going to build his future.

It was her mission once to break the cycle of negligent dads she knew so well and saw all around her where she used to live both in Jamaica, where she was born and raised, and in the West Midlands, where she came to live in her teens. They were all around her, the careless fathers. Her own dad wouldn't recognize her if she bumped into him in the street. Luckily that's

53

unlikely to happen since he stayed in 'Birningham' as her mother refers to it, and anyway, she heard a rumour he'd gone back to Jamaica last year, to spend his last ranting days in the sun and in the rum. Good riddance to him. What had he ever given her except a massive load of stress?

He upset her momma, coming into church disgracefully drunk and demanding money from her while the pastor was preaching. Everyone was looking at them, feeling sorry for their troubles and pitying them. All those other women in their poshest hats, their finest Sunday crowns, all looking away for shame and feeling so grateful it's not their turn today. They all sung louder to drown out his boozy ferocious ranting. So he stood in the aisle and roared louder, snarling and snorting and spitting. He frightened her. Her mother held her hand to comfort her, but those images of his rheumy raging eyes still haunt her. This was the man she was supposed to look up to, to admire and respect. The head of the family. The king, the lion. This man? This poor excuse for a man? This staggering bullish hollow creature? This lumbering dolt? How could she respect him?

She resolved to change it right then and there, she was never going to allow this humiliation into her own life. She would find an honourable man who wanted to step up and be a proper father, and she wouldn't settle for anything less. Her child would have a dad to look up to, they would not have to live with the aching gap where that person is supposed to be and they wouldn't live with the constant nagging toxins of doubt inside them that they somehow weren't good enough to deserve their father's love. That's what it equalled for Winnie. A life of self-doubt. Her mother was always encouraging but a kid never wants the approval they already have, they want the one that's so far out of reach. The impossible one.

How, then, did Winnie make such a catastrophic choice?

Easily. That's how.

The self-doubt builds and builds over all the years until it melts into one great bubbling cauldron full of hot misgivings and poisonous self-hatred, enough to fuel her gratitude for the attentions of such a handsome confident young man as Bradley Daniels. She couldn't believe that from such popular lofty heights, he bestowed an interest upon her. He was valuable. Beautiful and prized among his crew. A leader. Powerful. That power was the magnet for her. She wanted an important, strong Jamaican man. That's who she thought he was. And she might have been right, for about four years of his Yardie early twenties, that's what he was.

Well, in their flats anyway.

Well, on the particular floor of their flats.

He was respected there, and during his short blingy reign, he paid the dangerously inferior-feeling Winnie occasional attention. She said she wouldn't sleep with him unless they were married and so then she didn't see him for six months. When he blessed her with a returning interest, she was so thankful, she settled for the promise to marry as her guarantee of his commitments. Of course he promised that. In her single bed, in her bedroom with posters of a topless Prince on the wall, and with a hot Winnie wide-eyed and ready, he would've promised anything.

The moment he knew she was to be his 'baby mudda' he began his cruel regime of completely ignoring her. In fact, he went out of his way, sometimes, to display his other, newer younger conquests to her. 'Til they also fell pregnant, of course. At which point they also would be discarded.

And on and on.

Winnie decided that the shunning of herself and her beautiful new son, Luke, was not to be tolerated, so she left Birningham and came to this smaller town to start again, bringing her mother with her. She hadn't broken the cycle of damaging irresponsible indifference with Luke's father, but she sure as hell was going to raise a boy that would respect women. <u>All</u> women. And she needs to get home to him now, to make sure he doesn't have any holes in <u>his</u> loving.

Before she leaves though, she stops for a moment to hold Silvia's hand.

'I'm very sorry for your sufferation, Sista Silvia, you mus be truly vex at all this. But, darlin, if you can hear me now, lissun up. Disya situhation is difficult, but not h'impossible. Nuttin in life is h'impossible but you haffi want it to change, yes? Life is only wutless if you deem it so. Is your life wutless? You cyan't tink dat. I am wonderin, what is it you would want to hear someone say or do, dat would mek you wan' come out? Mi no know, darlin, but plenty effort goin into finding out. So you haffi do fi you part too, Silvia. You haffi try, OK? Right, mi gaan. See you tomorrow. Good eveling, sleepy head.'

She closes the door quietly behind her.

NINE

Ed

Saturday 10am

It's a new morning, five days since Silvia fell off her balcony. She hasn't opened her eyes since that moment and, although no one is openly saying it, Ed is acutely aware that generally, hope seems to be diminishing.

He and Jo are standing outside Suite 5. Ed always finds Jo hard going. She is certifiably insane in his opinion, an unhinged person with acres of confidence, which is a worrying combination. Ed has witnessed many of Jo's burnouts. Whether they are hopeless work ideas or doomed relationships, Jo is a comet – fast, brightly coloured – and fizzles out very quickly. She has a short temper and a short fuse but she is packed tight with energy and enthusiasm, for whatever glittery thing has taken her eye at any given moment.

For a while the most important distractions were Ed and Silvia's kids when they were little. Jo temporarily had a surge of regret about not having any kids of her own, so she swamped Jamie and Cassie with her suffocating interest, over-kissing them, buying them musical instruments and taking them to too many after-school activities they didn't want to take part in. What seven year old really wants to do a course entitled 'Junior Buddhism for the Here and Now'? She took them to concerts and plays and museums and galleries and events and blah and blah. Lovely crazy Aunty Jo very soon became quick-hide-in-the-cupboard-to-get-away-from-her Aunty Jo.

It was a shame really, she went at it too fast, too heavy, too hard. Like everything. Why is desperation so singularly unattractive? It's a human design fault really, because at the precise moment we desire something above all else, we are simultaneously singularly unappealing, exactly because of that desire. Kids are the first to sniff out a disingenuous person, and Jo's unfortunate attempts were a massive turn-off for them. It was sad to witness the almost brutal shunning of her by them. They didn't bother with niceties, they simply told her they were now fed up with it all. Thanks, but they'd see her 'laters'. Much laters. Like, not at all. Jo was forlorn and felt she had blown her last chance at family.

Silvia took her out for too many blue cocktails, and told her to shut up and buck up. She'd got it a bit wrong, that's all. Kids are basic and straight up. They could only be the kids they were, not the kids she wished they'd be. She couldn't buy her popularity with them. Maddeningly, she would probably have been much more welcome if she'd just observed from the side-lines, but she attempted full-on friendship. Fatal.

Ed wishes that's what Jo would do now, observe from a distance. Silvia's silent begging for release from Jo's ministrations is audible to him, but he knows better than to come between two fiery sisters. He carries actual scars from making that mistake before. He once caught a splinter from a broken plate in his cheek. It missed his eye by a whisker, and even though Silvia is now unstirring, he still doesn't want to risk it.

Unfortunately, he has to let Jo be the most important person in the Silvia constellation. She must be allowed to shine brightly. She would be even more of a loose cannon if she felt quashed in any way. Strangely, he has witnessed her finding a purpose in this tragic situation. She may be misguided in her methods, but there is no doubt that Jo is up on the balls of her feet, quick and ready to respond. He hasn't seen her keen like this for years, her bipolar lows robbing her of energy all too often. There is much to be said in favour of the quieter, sadder Jo, but no, it's best that she is taking part.

Ed knows that Jo's enthusiasm clearly isn't entirely altruistic concern for her sister. These two are connected in a profound and perplexing way, linked by their common history, not often a happy one. Their dad cracked up after their mum died. He didn't know what he was doing, tanked up on whisky against the pain of grief half the time. He retreated to his default position of army major and his two young daughters somehow, in his soaked mind, became a couple of green recruits who had to be taught life's lessons the hard way. It was a sorry shame.

But still now, the sisters push against each other, constantly vying for position. All siblings are rivalrous to varying degrees, Ed knows, but why are these two so combative? You would think that when two young girls lose their mother at an early age, they would pull together to look after one another rather than regularly tearing each other apart. Yet they can't be separate for too long either, without one needing to know all about the other. Where are they? Who are they with? What are they doing?

Ed has always figured he's just not supposed to fully understand the intricate workings of such an unstable sisterhood, but if he understood anything at all, it was a tiny bit of Silvia. A tiny bit. He doesn't get Jo at all.

Yet Jo is the one he is left with.

The doctor has just gone. She was mercifully straightforward, no tilting of the head or pitiful couching of the facts. Jo has asked Ed to be with her – she knows she can't deal with this kind of conversation alone. She still regards him as Silvia's husband and therefore – besides herself – the next of kin. Silvia's kids were also requested to be at this meeting but neither have appeared. Jamie is still in Helmand showing no signs of returning and Cassie can't face her mother, at all, even under these dire circumstances. Ed has dutifully agreed to relay any

61

information back to them, but he and Jo know that between the two of them they should assume ultimate responsibility.

They look through the small window in the door and watch Silvia. Lying there. She just . . . doesn't move.

Jo says, 'It's only her opinion, isn't it?'

Ed says, 'Well, yes, but she is the doctor, Jo, so her opinion does matter.'

Jo says, 'I haven't even begun my big techniques yet. I really think I can wake her up Ed, if only they'd let me be in there longer.'

Ed says, 'Then no one else would have any time with her, Jo.'

Jo says, 'No.'

'And that wouldn't be right, would it . . .? Jo?'

Jo sighs, 'S'pose not, but I really think I'm getting somewhere, and no one else is.'

'You don't know that.'

'Catherine O'Brien isn't getting anywhere. She shouldn't even be allowed in.'

'We have to think about what Silvia would want, Jo.'

'She's an evil hell-bitch. From hell.'

'OK. But still . . . think of Silv.'

There is a silence.

Then Jo says, 'When that doctor said that we need to decide what we want them to do if she had a heart attack, or whether they should "treat aggressively, should infection occur". What do you think she meant?'

'You know what she meant, Jo.'

'A "do not resuscitate order"? What? Just . . . let Sissy . . . go?'

'Yes. But that hasn't happened.'

'Oh Ed, I don't know if I can take on the responsibility of that decision.'

'Well, I will then.'

'No, I will,' snapped Jo.

'OK. I'm going in now. Otherwise, I won't have any time with her.'

Jo touches Ed's arm lightly, then turns and walks away from the door. She needs to think, and to prepare for this afternoon's sortie on Silvia's senses.

Ed moves into Suite 5 with more assurance this time. He hangs up his coat and sits next to Silvia's bed. He doesn't have long, and he has a purpose.

'Hi Silv. Ed again. Oh, actually, damn, I forgot. I've brought you these . . .'

He goes to the pocket of his coat and pulls out a handful of curled parched brown beech leaves, a few small twigs, and some empty spiky-shelled nuts. He lays them in a neat pile on the bed, just below her pillow so that she might inhale some fresh nature.

'Probably not supposed to bring it in, but this is part of Foy Wood, Silv. There it is. That's what unfroze me. No question. Now, let's see if it will work for you. Of course, nothing's going to work if you don't want it to, you should know that I understand that. It's just something about how . . . <u>living</u> it all is . . . it makes you want to be living at the same time, sharing the same O$_2$. Well, that's how I feel. OK. Silv, I'm going to take your hand in mine, alright? Try not to mind too much, love, I don't intend anything inappropriate!'

He alters his position by her bed so that with his right hand he can take her left, almost as if they are walking side by side. He is lanced by a ferocious sudden shard of memory as he entwines her long fingers in his. His hands are rougher and dirtier these days because he uses them to work outside more than he ever did. These are hands that now know how to chop and saw and hammer and rake and drag and pull. They are battered by rain, sun and wind, and this winter's chills have chapped his fingers 'til they have bled and rutted in some places, but he doesn't care.

Her hands feel the same as they always were, satin-smooth and graceful. They aren't small, Silvia is not a petite woman, but they are classically elegant and he always loved to hold them. He is savouring this moment. He doesn't desire Silvia any more, that particular longing has finally abated, mercifully, but it doesn't prevent him from finding pleasure in this rare instance. There is an added sensuality in it, because his hands are rougher, hers feel smoother in comparison.

He looks down at the two hands. Adam and Eve. Yin and Yang. Black and white. They melt together the way mercury would on corrugated iron. The oppositeness makes it a bit erotic and heightens the aesthetic kick. It's a small but unforgettable vignette of how to be male and female. Together. He can't get over how marbled and sculptured her long fingers appear clasped in his.

'Your hands, Silv, they're lovely still. Very . . . Junoesque. No, I won't shut up, it's liberating to be able to say it out loud, and you can't stop me. The way your fingers lay against each other and the perfect ovalness of your utterly unbitten nails is . . . bloody thrilling. I always liked them, but the difference now Silv, is that I've learned to look up close. To notice. Imagine that! So, with that in mind Silvia Shute, pin yer lug 'oles back, take my hand and come with me to Foy Wood. I hope you can remember it a bit, to help you get there.

'It's at the far end of a huge pasture meadow so you see it from some distance. The field is on the flat whereas the wood is on a ridged incline, so it looks like a great army of huge old trees advancing towards you, a bit alarming. What's unusual, and you don't really notice at first, is that the huge warlike tribe is almost exclusively beech. *Fagus sylvatica.* It's very rare to see that. There's usually a few oak or sycamore or ash in there somewhere. The Romans usually planted them all together, to nourish and protect each other, but Silv, I have had some pollen dating conducted on my oldest ladies and it's possible they first came to life in the Iron Age, isn't that bloody amazing? So, this mammoth stand of beeches looms up from the distance, and dares you to approach them. As you get closer, the magnificence of them can start to over-whelm you.

'There's something about trees that's too much bigger and older than all of us. We've all felt it one time or another. We have an instinctive reluctance to feeling so small and insignifi-cant, so pathetically young. We all want to count, don't we?'

Ed is loving this rare freedom to elegize and is on a roll.

'We need to be making our mark and whilst near these old veterans, it's easy to feel pointless. But we mustn't feel that, because it's all about spans and lifetimes, and our relevance to that. A tree may live for hundreds of years but what if the tree, for instance, compared its lifespan to that of a stone? Com-pared to the thousands and millions of years it takes for a stone to erode and change and move, a tree's lifetime is a flash. It's important to just remember that we certainly belong in it somewhere, that's all, and if we constantly belittle ourselves in comparison with the trees, we're missing the point. I spend each day amongst them gradually learning to be happy to live in the same air, at the same time. Parallel lives. That's my satisfaction.

'OK. So there it is, Foy Wood, a hangar of beeches, beckon-ing you in. You are probably a little bit wary, you can see the wood is dense, you think it will be dark in there, and not easy to move about. But just now, seconds before spring, the branches are virtually bare. Some of the younger, shorter trees will be hanging on for dear life to a few last leaves, but mostly the wood will be a crowd of clean, denuded grey trunks and branches, the late winter skeletons. At least there will be light in there. In summer, the huge graceful giants show off their voluminous hairdos, and the thick dense canopy of leaves high up prevents most of the sunlight from reaching the forest floor, so there's very little chance for wild flowers to grow in the shade.

'BUT, SILVIA, now, today, at the onset of spring, walk towards the towering grey battalion and as you get slowly closer, you will be aware of a hazy low-lying mist gathered around the roots and bottoms of the trunks of these grand dames. The mist is a colour. It's bright bluey-purple. Can you see what it is, Silv? Bluebells. A proper dense forest carpet of them. Thousands and thousands. More than you could ever count.

'As you enter the wood, everything changes. The light dims, the mossy smells intensify and the ground alters beneath your feet. You pass through the portal, out of open air and into the umbrage. As soon as you enter, you stop still to drink it in. The smell of the bluebells; do they have a scent? Or are you, in actuality, smelling the colour? There's a faint aroma of honey, is that them? Bluehoney. How fantastic. Old crêpey winter leaves are around your feet in crinkly heaps, with broken twigs and husks of the mast the beeches produced back in the autumn. The deer and squirrels and mice have eaten the nutritious meat of the nuts, but the little containers remain, brittle and spent. All these tree droppings gather on the forest floor and make a shushing noise underfoot as you wade through.

'Look at the trunks of the beautiful big beeches, Silv. The bark is smooth and thin and a delicate pale silvery grey. The boles are tall and elegant. Like you. And like you, they are so ... completely ... female. They command you to look up and along their sleek lines: "Look at my pendulous boughs, notice my distinctive lineaments, I demand that you respect my impressive stature. Look up, up just as you would to admire the highest heights in a hushed cathedral. See my beauty. Worship me, I am a shade giver, and shade bearer, I am moody and shape-shifting and from my soft timber you can make bent-wood chairs and high heels and toys and parquet floors. My bark is well toned and mossy lichen defines my outline from root to top like a furry glove. The bright green lichen is dry to the touch, but soft. Velvety downy hair covering my entire lanky spire of flesh. Irresistible to touch. You want to stroke it and you want to embrace me. Me and all the other queens here, and all our nurse and maiden trees. You especially want to meet our old and scarred grandmother beeches with their phenomenal genetic intelligence, where sometimes their trunks contain tissue from four hundred years or so. All her experiences are engrained in there, her wood is an ever-accumulating memory bank. You want to know her."

'It's true Silvia, when you are amongst these timber Amazons, you start to be curious about how they behave and what they can teach you. You hear them. These trees have . . . sustained me through such difficult stuff. And by staying still, and listening, I have changed. So can you, love, I hope. We can visit this wood many times Silv, and we can understand some of its lessons but for now, let's lie down, among the bluebells, and just look up. The bright *bright* blue *blue*bells, all around you, soft beneath you, supporting your whole tired body, just sink into them – and keep looking up. Just float Silv, let yourself float . . . let the trees take the pain and do the worrying. It's lovely, isn't it?'

Ed and Silvia lie side by side, eyes shut, hand in hand on the forest floor . . .

TEN

Tia

Saturday noon

'There Mrs Shit! Now you got tasty food to <u>look</u> at, even if no eating. You get more goodness in you to look at this photos than all the bum juice you get given in here called food. I don't think so, miss nursy nursy. Get it away from her.'

Tia is Sellotaping a menu to the wall. It is from her friends' Indonesian restaurant and has photographs of the different dishes next to their names.

'They telling me no food in here, but nobody say no pictures of food! Ha ha, fool you, suckers! You got to go to bed early to catch out Tia. That for sure. Look at this one. Asinan Bogor. Sweet and sour vegetables. One mouth of that make you come awake rise and shine. The peppers put firework in the blood and whoosh, you not sleepin then. <u>Then</u> you one awake mingehead, you sittin up, lookin around, here, there. Hello everybody! Eyes doin open lookin and mouth doin open talking. And sayin sorry to Tia for no pay for two weeks so far.

'I been there, at your flat, usual days, two times now. I go in, Tuesday Thursday, normal. Same as twenty years. First in the big house, now in the little flat. Much tidier when Mrs Shit asleep in hospital, no dirty pant everywhere with poppin socks all over. But whole flat covered in dirt from dust and old ugly cooking, so I clean all, top in bottom. When you not there, I can use the Mr Jiffy what poison the world but is best cleaner. Gets a lemon smell in and gets grease out. Even if it killin trees and children, it still good. I got it in a hiding place where you don't know, where I got white sugar and instant coffee kept too! Things from evil, all in shush box in big clothes cupboard. Secret. I make water on all plants and let the new air in window for little time, and make the bed open to have air in. I also do the bad thing I not like and make the taps on, running the water away for no reason like Mrs Shit say to do, five minutes. In my home, no water wasting like this, water very expensive and important, and nobody making taps on for no reason. BUT that what Mrs Shit say, so that what Tia do.

'So, I doing everything you ask for even when you not there to tell me. So, I thinking for yourself like you say. And one of the have an ideas is happening like this, OK? Let's say Tia is not getting pay even though the work is done, then it is stealing really, innit? Mrs Shit is stealin from Tia. Tia is doing the cleaning and jizz, but Mrs Shit not paying. Is OK really cos Tia know Mrs Shit is having a sleeping accident, but still, Tia got two boys, well three really with the sitting down husband in a chair, so is not OK for no money.

'SO Tia is have a brainthunder and thinking of what way to make it so Mrs Shit not stealin work from Tia. Then, Mrs Shit wouldn't have to be a criminal no more. Cos all this bad enough with the head thump and everything, without Mrs Shit get called thief and stealer. SO, what Tia do . . . is Tia take one very small old phone Mrs Shit never using any more for more than two years, and do selling on the eBay . . . that phone just in the drawer making a clutter . . . Mrs Shit hates a clutter, it very 'volga'. No clutter thank you. So Tia take away the clutter, and the phone sell on eBay spit-spot, and Tia have her pay.

'In fact, too <u>much</u> pay, cos that phone get one hundred forty quids and Mrs Shit only stole one hundred quids of work off Tia, so Tia put the forty quids in Mrs Shit special money tin box with the picture on of a girl in Christmas. There is no money for a long time in 'til this, so new startings. OK, Mrs Shit, that all the home news BUT now Tia tells you the big news . . .'

Tia puts her Boots reading glasses on with the flashy rhinestones around the edge, and retrieves an impressive pile of chatty magazines from her bag.

'You not going to believe this, Mrs Shit, after all that hard work and time, "Nicola Roberts from Girls Aloud is struggling

72

to find her look". Well. We was all thinking thankfuck, because "she has embraced her natural pale colouring at last", and now this. So what is it? She like the white skin, ooo look at me, I'm all pinky white make-up with my face on, for sale? OR ooo don't look at me I'm a ghostie face scary kids off? And now she got huge new lips off a fishface as well. What she thinking? What we suppose to thinking? She do like white skin or she don't? Hurry up Nicola, we want answer! Now! And she decided to do the head extensions. Like we need more hair from her. No thank you Nicola. Stop it now with hair and lips and skin.

'And aw, look Mrs Shit, lady send in a photo of dog and cat and rat and ugly baby together in basket with big bow on. Like the world should be. All together lovin, no fightin. Strange, cos babies and rats always fightin ... Want to know your stars Mrs Shit? The gypsy lady here always right, here's yours, the Goat, "Juggling work and home is harder than you thought, and travel is costly for you this week. Be aware of everything you say and do, and wear your best outfit on Friday, you'll be dressing to impress ..." OOO, sounds exciting Mrs Shit ... what's goin to happen on Friday ... ?'

Silvia keeps on breathing.

And nothing else.

So Tia fills the silence with more and more and more 'news'.

'This is good, Mrs Shit, can you see? "A knork, eliminates the need for a knife". I want that, shall I send off for you too, Mrs Shit? Yes ...'

ELEVEN

Jo

Saturday 2pm

Jo is not relaxed. Decidedly unrelaxed, in fact. She is not a
good enough actress to hide her anxiety, so the nurses at the
station are on alert. None of them trust Jo completely. They
know she is on a mission to revive her sister, and that she will
stop at nothing. All the staff have tried to be understanding
and helpful, but most have had a gutful of Jo's New Age ideas.
When Jo told them she was going to burn a wreath of white
sage and rosemary over a brazier, American-Indian style, so
that she might smudge Silvia's body with the ash, the nurses
unanimously rejected the idea. When Jo proceeded to round
on them, accusing them of preventing her from protecting her
sister against malevolent spirits, they withdrew the metaphor-
ical drawbridge of goodwill.

Today, then, they have their eye on her, especially Winnie
who is, after all, Silvia's key nurse and therefore her chief

protector. Unfortunately, Winnie is very busy today and can't keep as much of an eye on Jo as she would wish.

This is one of the reasons Jo is tense. She can't block the view the nurses have into the room through the internal window, so she tries to keep her back to the glass in a vain attempt to hide today's theme for Silvia's awakening.

Jo has read somewhere that animals have inherent powerful healing powers and, especially in America, they are often used to comfort and inspire the afflicted and infirm. Dogs, apparently, are the most widely used creatures. If an ill person can rest their hand on a dog's fur for even fifteen minutes, they can absorb up to forty doggiewatts of canine healing energy, supposedly. Jo isn't <u>entirely</u> sure exactly how much that is, but she feels confident it can only help. She's not heard of anyone being harmed by overdosing on animal energy, so she has made the decision to go ahead today with a session of animal healing therapy.

Jo doesn't own a dog. Jo doesn't really even like dogs very much, but her neighbour Betty, a seventy-year-old bingo freak who owns the only house on the terrace that hasn't changed at all in fifty years, has an ancient chihuahua called Lady who is presently cowering in Jo's handbag. Jo is wishing she had chosen a different handbag. This one is an old but still valuable Biba original, and was the only one she owned big enough to fit the dog in with a bit of breathing space. There is a regrettable wet patch forming on the bottom of the tan leather bag. How can such a spookily small dog contain so much liquid? She walked it about in the car park before bringing it in, to try and empty it out, but it obviously prefers Biba leather to prickly yellow grass. Never mind, Jo thinks, however leaky it is, it's still a dog, with potentially massive healing power, but how is she going to get it on to Silvia's bed without the nurses noticing?

Luckily Jo judges herself to be no fool and has thought ahead. She owns a host of 'cuddly' toys, which live in well-organized, serried ranks, in descending order of size on her bed. One of the larger teddies is a sinister creature with its own full-teddy-sized Easter bunny outfit. When wearing it, only the teddy's face is visible, surrounded by bunny ears and whiskers on a bunny hood. The whole shocking ensemble comes off easily via one long zip down the stomach of the 'bunny'. Jo thought to bring this outfit as disguise for Lady. So now, Jo is furtling about in the smelly sodden handbag, trying to get the old dog into the teddy's bunny outfit.

After a short while of muffled yelpings which Jo coughs loudly to cover, the dog is finally, undeniably, in costume. Jo hauls the tiny old mutt out of the handbag and places her on the bed next to Silvia. The bunny outfit is a bit too big for Lady so she seems to disappear inside it, leaving the head-space horrifically vacant as if some invisible wraith is in attendance. When Lady does manage to poke her head through, her appearance is that of an Easter bunny with the face of an alarmed and wizened old rat.

'Keep still Lady. Sit! Lie! Sit!'

The mixed message notwithstanding, Lady has no option as to how she is positioned since she is utterly immobile inside the roomy bunny husk. She is also completely the wrong shape for the outfit. She is small-dog-shaped and so therefore her legs and . . . legs don't fit where a teddy's would. Jo picks her up and places her on her back, hoping this will make her look more like a stuffed something innocent. She manoeuvres the mutant toy into the crook of Silvia's lifeless arm. Lady blinks up at Jo from the depths of the deep and empty head. She isn't a happy actor. She has no idea what is happening to her or what is required of her, so she chooses to take the line of least resistance, and simply lie still, hoping whatever this all is will be over soon and she might be returned to her nice gentle farty old owner with the smelly feet and dog chocolates in her apron pockets. Instead of this . . . Hell.

'Good girl, now just stay still and let your . . . canine . . . chakras flow out of you and into Sissy. That's right, good. Heal her, heal her. Health, health. Wakefulness and well-being.'

The veteran mutt stares blankly into the face of the rangy greying woman with the frosted, cheerless curls, whose mouth is constantly moving. Jo is speaking but absolutely no one, especially a dog, knows what she is trying to mean. This is very often the case in Jo's life. Lots of hectic action in the lips department, usually with good-hearted intent, but no connection to any quiet, thinking head department.

Jo doesn't want to risk failure with today's therapy. The dog is the prime player, and she hopes that at some deep human-canine level there will be a kind of holy healing fusion, but she doesn't want to leave it all to chance. It could well be that Silvia might resist the dog energy, although that's unlikely because she does actually <u>like</u> dogs, BUT it has occurred to Jo that this very tiny antique dog just might not emit enough power to raise Silvia. Maybe she should have brought two dogs? Or one big one? She simply doesn't know how to work out the amp-age. So, in the highly improbable event that the dog is underpowered, Jo has brought some other creatures along, and must now try to place them near or on Silvia as discreetly as possible.

She checks through the window to monitor the nurses' attention, and seeing no sign of the eagle-eyed Winnie, she dives back into the Biba handbag and brings out a plastic exercise ball containing Betty's granddaughter's hamster, Justin Bieber. Although only two human years old, Justin is in fact about sixty-five in hamster years and can only do a certain amount of time in the exercise ball without expiring. He's been in there today for about two hours now and is more than a little hot and sweaty. The hammy stench that comes out of the escape hatch when Jo unscrews the top of the ball is truly unpleasant, in an overheated rodent way. Jo doesn't want to put her hand into the hole to extract him, so she turns the ball upside down, and along with lots of tiny torpedo poos and cage debris, the shrivelled hamster plops out on to the bed, landing on its back and appearing quite dazed.

'Oh dear, come on, turn over. Lot of mess, just try to . . . clear that up.'

Jo tries to straighten up the hamster by poking at it with her glasses and she attempts to wipe the mess from the bed. She only succeeds in making it all much worse, smearing the sheets with fresh hamster poo and causing the little creature to scuttle for safety somewhere behind Silvia's neck, deep in the crevice of the pillows.

'No, no, come on out of there. You've got to nestle up to her, not hide behind her, that's no good. Come on.'

Suddenly, the door opens. It is Winnie. Jo hides the ball behind her back.

'Everyting OK?' says Winnie, a little bit sternly.

'Yes, yes, fine thanks. Just . . . brought Sissy a new . . . teddy . . . a bunnyteddy . . .'

From where Winnie is, she can only see the outline of the furry toy. She is too busy to stop for long. Her checks with Silvia aren't due just yet. And anyway, it's best to do them when Jo is out of the way.

'Oh. Dats nice. Real nice.'

Winnie goes.

'Right chaps,' says Jo, addressing her zoo of two, 'time for the last hope . . .'

Once again, Jo plunges her hand into the Mary Poppins

bottomless bag and brings out a small Tupperware container with tiny holes drilled in the top. She's not looking forward to this. She prises the lid off. Inside is a big curling leaf of ivy. Jo looks closer. The pet shop assured her they sold her one large Phasmatodea, a giant stick insect. It's not the cuddliest of creatures, admittedly, but Jo thought that at least she might be able to leave this one in the room after she'd gone, clinging to the blind or something. Even if it only emitted one watt of insect healing power, surely that's better than nowt? Jo is furious that she has left the pet shop with what appears to be a stack of leaves.

'Damn!' she hisses.

The sudden breath of her exhalation wakes up the mighty twig creature who turns out to be the entire contents of the box. It is so surprised that it jumps out and directly on to Jo's face, where Alien-like, it clamps on. Jo screams at the top of her voice and tries to wipe it off by flapping her arms around wildly. The giant knobbly creature is reluctant to leave its craggy new escarpment home but does a little clinging-on bouncy dance instead. It is positively showing off, wiggling its gnarly bottom over her nose.

The screaming has summoned a couple of nurses, including Winnie, who, bat-like recognized Jo's undulcet tones from further up the ward and flew down the corridor at a low stealthy efficient speed, to deal with the noisy crisis. What

Winnie witnesses as she enters the room is difficult for her to decipher.

Jo is shrieking and panicking, her arms flailing about dramatically. What seems to Winnie to be a small branch goes flying across the room, coming to rest on the side of Silvia's face, just above her nasal tube. As Winnie approaches to remove it, a small rat-like creature darts out from behind Silvia's neck and chomps down on the twig which appears to have sprawling legs and be <u>moving</u>, dragging it back into its pillow lair. The other nurses join in the screaming when they see this.

The new volley of screeches persuades Lady, in her dotage and in her quiescence, to quit her suspension and emerge to see what's going on. She may be vintage, but she's still a dog, of sorts, and she's naturally curious. As she shuffles around to right herself, there are loud cries of 'That rabbit thing!'

'It's moving!'

'It's alive!'

'The toy is alive!'

'Dear God!'

Then Lady pokes her head through the rabbit face hole and the whole room erupts into a cacophony of horrified yelping and high-pitched ululation. It genuinely is a terrifying sight, the skinny hoary old ratty face with the bunny ears. Anyone would be petrified. It makes no earthly sense, what they see, they can't process it all in any normal, logical way. The only immediate explanation is supernatural devilment. A live branch, a rat and a teddy/bunny aberration from hell. Neither fish, flesh nor fowl.

Two nurses flee the room still yowling. Winnie remains, but is transfixed by the perversions of nature she is confronted with. Now that the stick insect is off her, Jo calms down somewhat, but she is still panting with shock when Lady, invigorated with new urgent energy from the shrill squawking, gets the smell in her nose of nearby rodent activity. A small mammal is munching on something, and Lady would like to be munching on that small mammal. She wriggles about and tries to free herself from the costume, but fails. Heroically, she lunges forward, virtually at Silvia's face, trying to locate the pesky rodent.

She can smell it, smell it, smell it.

She wants to eat it, eat it, eat it.

Somewhere deep inside the generations of inbreeding that Lady is a result of, where virtually all natural instincts have been bred out, there is still the remnant of a dog lurking inside her shivering delicate lappy skin. For a brief instinctual moment, Lady feels the urge to hunt. Her eyes grow dark, her tiny lips peel back, and she starts to slaver. She wants the prey in her jaws. She is growling and snapping and sniffing and straining to get out of the bloody rabbit head.

Winnie starts to make sense of it all gradually, and fastens

82

her furious gaze on Jo, who is watching the carnage with paralysed fear.

'Sorry nurse. I just thought ... animal therapy ... might
help ...'

Winnie wades in and, in one fell swoop, gathers up both the
snapping dog and the murderous hamster with the insect still
in its mouth, throws them all into the bag and shuts it quickly.

'Now tek it, you dyam heediat – and go!'

Jo exits hastily, carrying the gladiatorial arena of a handbag,
which is thrumming with murderous activity. She would have
some difficult news this evening for Betty or her granddaughter.

Or both.

TWELVE

Cat

Saturday 8pm

Cat is concentrating on Silvia's face. She was furious to discover a couple of scratches there when she arrived this evening, and when she heard the farcical story of stupid Jo and her stupid neighbour's stupid dog, she could hardly believe what had been allowed to happen. In a hospital ITU! She had stern words with the nurses, who were adamant that they cannot control visitors' errant behaviour and that despite Cat's pleas they didn't want to bar Jo from coming since she is, after all, Silvia's CLOSEST RELATIVE.

That did not please Cat. Not at all.

She is now painstakingly trying to apply the delicate drawn-on eyebrows exactly as Silvia does them. It's impossible. Silvia has been doing it for years, she is expert. It's a matter of the slightest flick of the wrist and such a light touch. Cat is never never going to get it right for one simple reason. Although she is using the very pencil Silvia uses, it is blunt. Silvia never allows it to go blunt, because then, each hair is too thick. The secret to this trick is subtlety, artifice.

Cat is an heroic keeper of secrets, but full-strength and enduring pretence is not her strong suit. More's the pity. If only she could hide her feelings and her temper better, she might have succeeded in many areas of her life where her pathological need to express herself has landed her in plenty of trouble. Cat can deal with almost anything in life. Except rejection or injustice. When she is confronted with either of those, she is automatically propelled into a response. Cat's bonnet is a virtual hive of bees.

Silvia often says to her, 'Let it go, Cat.'

Despite knowing full well that Silvia is usually right, Cat just cannot 'let it go'. And the one thing Cat is definitely not going to let go presently, is Silvia. Silvia has changed everything. Since Cat has known her, she has become the centre of Cat's world, and Cat is feeling severely untethered with Silvia in this state. She is trying to hold it together, but in reality, Catherine O'Brien is screaming inside.

She is lost without her Silly.

The eyebrows are dreadful, Silvia looks like an unsuccessful cross-dresser. They are too heavy and, frankly, wonky. Cat decides unwisely to attempt a lip line too, and some coral lipstick, but again her unfamiliarity with make-up doesn't help, and the unsatisfactory result looks nothing like it does when

Silvia does it. She's even <u>watched</u> Silvia do it, so why is it so hard to copy?

Some of Cat's happiest moments with Silvia have been sprawled on the bed whilst Silvia sits at her dressing table painting on her dayface and primping her gorgeous red hair. That's when they are both relaxed, when Silly is at her most unguarded and when they yap away and share all their secrets. This is when Cat gets to know the real Silvia, the one with doubts and fears like everyone else, rather than the somewhat fearsome figure her reputation would suggest. True, that is also a side of Silvia, but it's not the whole picture. Cat likes to think she is one of the very few, perhaps the only one who knows Silvia – the full story. Silvia is seen by everyone as an assured person, but Cat knows that by being steadily, relentlessly pushy, she has eroded some of Silvia's confident veneer, and inveigled her way into her very core.

At the centre of Silvia, there is Cat.

One lodges within the other. Feeding.

Cat finishes the lips. Silvia looks like a latter-day Lucille Ball. The outer line is too heavy and Cat has over-emphasized the bow, making the philtrum seem freakishly small and the lips seem oddly tall, rather than full. Completely wrong. Cat has no idea how to correct it, so she leaves it, reassuring herself that Silvia would prefer some, <u>any</u> make-up, to none.

Then Cat moves to the bottom of the bed and, very carefully, she untucks the neat hospital corners and unpeels the bedding back from the bottom, revealing Silvia's feet.

'There, darlin', you hate your feet being trapped in the bottom of the bed, doncha? Too hot, too tight. You hate that. Let your feet breathe. Much better.'

Cat takes the expensive moisturizer out of Silvia's familiar washbag, positions her chair at the bottom of the bed, and squeezes the fresh grapefruit and mint cream into her hands. She lays her cool creamy hands on Silvia's hot feet, and alternately, she kneads away at them, letting the moisture sink in. She puts her fingers through the toes and rubs them back and forth. Cat is starting to relax. She hopes Silvia is too, wherever she is . . .

'Liking this? I think I would. Yes. I surely would. Lovely feet, Silly. Very strong but very delicate. And so . . . white. Feet can be so ugly, but yours really aren't. I remember the first time I saw them. Was when I first brought you to the cottage. I loved watchin' you see Connemara. Really see it. You'd seen nothin' like it ever before. How couldya? There isn't anythin' like it. "Connemara is a state of light," Michael Coady says, and that's exactly right. I'd grown up with it of course, and you're not exactly goin' about marvelling at the light and the scenery when it's all around you. Never noticed it to tell the truth. Noticed Mary Desmond's new David Cassidy pencil case, and what Sinead Hogan had for her lunch, is all. Bugger the mountains and the lakes.

'When I brought you there Silly, I saw it all through your eyes and, well, I was amazed. I'd spent so long in England just getting on with lookin' after my patients and my husband and not really looking <u>at</u> anything. When I went back home with you in tow, I had my eyes opened. I saw what you saw. I saw the stony greys of the hares and the seals and the granite. The rocks, the mackerel, the bracken and the crooked cottages. The oatmeals of the dunes, the sheep and the tufts of fleece left in the barbed wire, the geese, the flapping sheets on the lines, the salty shores and the skidding clouds in the feckin' amazing acres of blue sky. So much phenomenal sky. The greens of the moss, the grasses, the hills. Although as you said, they are often purple. And browns. Five thousand different browns on one mountain peak. And orange! And black black lakes. Frightening craters of water. Murderous, you said. I knew what you meant. Powerful water, very deep. Lots of secrets. I knew that was right. I just hadn't thought it before. And now, when I see'em, never think anything else of course, so thanks for that!

'Do you remember the cottage we rented, Silly? I was afraid you might find it all a bit too rustic. No heating 'cept the open burner ... and brown water. Two rooms and a bathroom. Tiny. Your face was a picture, so it was. God, I was so relieved you loved it. Getting away from everythin'. That's what you needed and for those glorious four days, that's what we did, didn't we? No kids, no husbands, no jobs, we didn't belong to anyone, we were on our own isolated island of us. I loved that Sill, I really did. It was only when we were away from it all there, that I could see the bigger picture of my life in proper focus. With your help. I could see how empty it had all become, how loveless and habitual everything was. Nothing was as beautiful as us, then, there.'

Cat still massages Silvia's feet. She doesn't want to stop. The physical contact helps her to speak. She feels connected to Silvia and, at this particular moment, that private bond is all she longs for. Besides which, the beauty of her feet helps Cat to raise up some memories, slowly and quietly through various complicated stages of the remember sediment where they have been conveniently buried. This kind of dredging can be painful but it can also be delicious, irresistible. Today, Cat wants to recapture it. She desperately needs to.

'I lived in the flow of your life for those few days Silly, yet you were in my old home. The calm was hypnotic, the turf in the grate, the whiskey in the glass, the books and the cosy. Just the winds making big noise outside, whistlin' round the chimney and the door to remind us there's wildness beyond. It's in that sort of stillness that you get to know each other, isn't it?

'Remember Sil, the day we gathered all those mussels? You wore green shorts, your old school PE shorts I think you said. You'd won some running races in them. They still fitted you. Amazin'. I showed you where to look, under the seaweed, where the sunlight glints off glistenin' rubbery strands, where it looks at first like a clump of mud but in fact, it's handfuls of molluscs clingin' on. Mostly blue shells, but some olive ones, some black, some glowy green. The lovely hollow clack of the shells as they are thrown together in the bucket where they look immediately appetizin', and exactly as they will look when they're cooked, except then, they will be open and hot orange, drenched in briney wine and red onion and chilli. I've even cooked them in vodka before but not this time. Oh the taste Sil. With big chunks of buttery bread and clumps of steamin' spinach. Mmmm. I knew our evening was going to be a delicious one. Knew it.'

Cat finishes rubbing Silvia's feet, and sits for a few moments looking at them, turning them carefully in her hands as if they were priceless antiques.

'Not sure if I ever told you Sil, but I think it was these that started it all off, actually. Yes. That's right. Your daps were wet and too slippery they wouldn't give you any traction on the rocks where you were climbin' awkwardly to get to the waterside, so you swore a lot, and in between laughs, ripped them off, and flung them to the shore. Then the argument between you and the rocks could at least be negotiated by the skin of your feet.

'You were suddenly much bouncier, jumpin' securely from rock to rock, fit as a fiddle and burstin' with well-being. You just looked so . . . vital and strong. Fit. Flourishin' fit. And I couldn't take me eyes off these amazin' feet. I can't think why but somehow I'd never seen them before. So white. Long and elegant with hissing coral-red nails painted on. The audacity of it! Amongst all that nature, all the greys and greens, there

90

they were, showin' off with not a care in the world. Darin' Mother Nature's colours to top your cheeky redness. Red hair, red toenails. Long strong pale feet, clinging on to dark wet rocks. Feet that someone should write songs about, in praise of their many perfections. With lines about even toes and graceful high arches and smooth round heels. Defiant, stampin' female feet. The feet of Athene. God, so beautiful.

'The sight of you, wrestlin' those mussels out of the rocks, it stirred me Sil, truly it did. It lit something in me and I couldn't deny it. I didn't mention it. Thought it would sound a bit weird, so I left it . . . 'Til later.'

Cat gently covers Silvia's feet back up, being careful not to tuck in the sheets too tightly. She sits down, by Silvia's side.

'Soused with wine and whiskey and salty mussel broth, weren't we? I was. You were. You fell asleep by the fire on the carpet. I brought the pillow for your head and a quilt to cover you for when you woke cold in the mornin'. I put all the lights off and sat watchin' you sleep. One of your exquisite feet was pokin' out of the quilt. I must have looked at it, at you in the firelight, for an hour at least, breathing steadily and sliding into deep deep sleep. Bit like now Sil. You miles away, me watchin' you. Lovin' you. I like it like this because then, like now, at least the love can flow back and forth. You can't stop me. You didn't stop me then. That night.

Cat leans in, whispering, 'Did you think at first, it was happening in a hazy dream? That you thought you felt a tiny kiss

91

on your toes? The lightest touch. That someone, that a woman, that I was under that quilt next to you, holding you and rockin' you slowly to bring you up, up a tiny bit, out of sleep, so that you could know the pleasure of it? That each small kiss elicited a faint gasp from you, that not for one second did you resist? That you turned over and in towards me and sought out my mouth? That you invited me in, and submitted to me with moans and eyes wide open. Eyes lookin' right into mine in the firelight. The smoothness, the softness and the salt of you. The complete happiness of making you move like that. Of making you shudder. Then watching you fall back into a panting, then breathing, then breathing slowly, sleep. Sleep. When we woke up Sil, my world was different. It was female. It was new. It was you. I was consumed with you. Still am. You know that.'

Cat is silent for a moment.

'Remember what you said in the mornin'? That it was the whiskey? You thought in your cups that I was Ed? It was silly and a huge mistake? That was cruel Sil. Don't call my love a mistake. Please. Ever. You destroyed me that mornin'. Killed a part of me dead. So you did. And for that Sil, I have always wanted you to have this . . .'

Cat stands by the bed, and, raising her hand high, brings it down sharply, and slaps Silvia's face hard, leaving a furious red welt.

She puts on her coat.

And leaves.

THIRTEEN

Winnie

Sunday 10am

Winnie is bustling about in Silvia's room, completing her first checks of the day. She always tries to keep this part of her nursing as quick and efficient as possible. Two years ago when she was in wards with responding patients, she was proud of the feedback she had about exactly this part of her job. She would receive cards and letters and presents with tags proclaiming the like of 'to Winnie the wonderful', and 'thank you for the best nursing we've ever witnessed, a genuine Florence Nightingale' and 'thanks for looking after our Dad with the same loving care you'd give your own'.

Well, huh. That's not quite true. But great that they thought it was.

If Winnie's father was ill, Winnie would at this moment in life make a point of visiting him just to be sure he was suffering enough. She shudders at quite how unchristian that thought is, but Winnie's God is a merciful and loving God who has looked into her heart and knows the tribulation she carries there concerning her father, so she feels entitled to a degree of healthy, guilt-free hatred.

Winnie likes to speak to her patients exactly as if they could respond, and so she gives a running commentary about what she's doing. She pulls back the side sheets of Silvia's bed, so that she can get to the arterial line entering her groin which monitors her blood pressure and is also used to take samples of arterial blood to analyse oxygen levels. She notices with annoyance that the line is slightly twisted, having been caught in the side bars of the bed rather awkwardly.

'Eh, eh! A wa dis?! Chu. Aw. Sorry Silvia dats not right for you. Musta bin pyainful, yes? Sorry. Sorry. I'll mek sure Nurse Helen check it last ting tonight. She should do it every night, every night last checks. See it deh, mi fix it now. Straight, I turn it yahso. Evryting else look good here, your colour better today. Not so grey more pinky. Dat good. Just check de heart monitor pads still stickin. Yes. Good. And tek your pulse. You mus be fed up wid alla dis, Silvia, I h'understand sista, but we got to do it, while you still so mash up and weak. We got to get yu strong.'

Winnie makes up her own ditty to accompany her duties while she washes Silvia. She is amusing herself as she invents it, and she hopes somewhere that her patient is amused too.

Silvia brok 'er head
Silvia brok 'er head
Silvia brok 'er head
But Silvia nah go dead

Winnie wash 'er bum
Winnie wash 'er bum
Winnie wash 'er bum
But . . . er . . . Winnie not her Mum. He! He!

She's pon di road to well
She's pon di road to well
She's pon di road to well
But . . . Sista Jo can go to hell . . . Ha! Ha!

Sista Jo, she mek mi vex
Sista Jo, she mek mi vex
Sista Jo, she mek mi vex
Obeah man, give she hex! . . . He! He!

Winnie is helpless with laughter now snorting and giggling, she has to stop for a moment to recover.

'Sorry Silvia, but dat sister o' yours she pyure crazy, she mean well but she a fool, she a drive mi to mad an' back wid all her blouse an' skirtery. Oh well we see wat she bring next, yes? Maybe dis time it's a h'elephant, eh?!! He! He! Dere. Tink you done now, Silvia. Nice an' clean. Ready to greet a whole new day. We hope it a good one fi you. I hope de Lord deliver you a whole heap of peace, so your poor tired body can mend. Burdens an' hardships there may be but we have hope an' the sun still shines. Oooo look pon di time, mi late now fe Mrs Wilson, but y'know she fas asleep too, like you, so she won't mind too much. Later. Mi gone.'

She bustles out.

Silvia is alone.

FOURTEEN

Cassie

Sunday 11am

Winnie almost crashes into the young redhead as she bundles out of the door of Suite 5. Cassie was trying to peer in through the glass window in the door. She still hasn't fully committed to the idea of going in and doesn't want to be persuaded by anyone else. She's in that tempting place where she could abandon the whole idea and leave without any further need to feel anything. She can just turn and go, and she won't be forced to think differently. She will continue to feel as she does right now. Utterly bereft. But she's used to that incendiary mixture of pain and confusion. It's become her friend in a way, and a method to escape from every tricky situation and every difficult decision.

When your mother turns you out of home at sixteen, a week after you tell her you are pregnant, it's the killer excuse for every mistake you make thereafter. Absolutely nothing is your fault because, how could anyone survive that cruel rejection? And <u>so</u> young! She's survived a lot more since then. That considerable spurning was the fountain from which <u>so</u> much further trouble sprang.

Cassie remembers it all as if it were two moments ago. In fact, it was two million moments ago, but the stinging pain of it is fresh and raw.

'You've made your choices, Cassandra, mostly against my advice, and now you will have to deal with the consequences,' Silvia had said to her that day. 'It's not wise for you to remain here. The house is being sold, we <u>all</u> have to find somewhere . . . better . . . somewhere . . . else to be. I'm sorry it's like this but life is a total bitch sometimes. Now is one of those times.'

While she was speaking, Silvia couldn't look at her daughter. She was packing up crockery from the cupboard, wrapping everything in newspaper and laying it carefully into boxes.

Methodically.

Purposefully.

'Please look at me, Mum. You're talking as if I'm not Cassie any more, not even your daughter. I'm still Cassie, Mum. Just Cassie who's having a baby, that's all. I said I'm sorry, but I'm not getting rid of it, I can't. Why won't you look at me? Mum!! Bloody look at me!'

What was wrong with her? Cassie knew her mum was tough but she'd never come across <u>this</u> Silvia before. She just carried on packing up, ignoring Cassie's pleas, like a heartless robot.

Yes, this must be a massive shock for her, yes she would probably feel embarrassed among her friends and neighbours about it, and of course it wasn't what her mother would wish for her, but out-and-out rejection? Cassie hadn't anticipated that.

Her mum had changed a lot since the divorce with her dad. She was impossible to talk to properly. Not that she'd ever been such a touchy-feely mum. She always said that people in her family were allergic to physical contact. She called it 'soft' and 'daft', but deep down, Cassie knew she wanted it, because whenever she did manage to persuade her mum into a snuggle, especially when she was little, Silvia reciprocated. Sometimes, Silvia would cry quietly at these very close, very personal and physical moments. Cassie would try to comfort her but would feel confused.

It was at these times Silvia would say, 'No, sweetie, it's not your fault, it's silly old Mum. I'm just being soppy. It's lovely to cuddle you, come here, it's just, I'm not used to it, that's all.'

Cassie saw the same reaction from her mother, even to her father when he sometimes attempted a kiss. She'd bat him away or play wrestle with him, anything to avoid open and easy physical contact, which clearly made her supremely uncomfortable. Why? What could be nicer than people wanting to hold you? That's all Cassie longs for. That was all she needed on that awful day when her mother made it clear she wasn't welcome any more. But Silvia withheld her love from Cassie then, and there has been virtually no contact since.

Her dad brought a small white soft, very soft, bendy bear from Silvia to the hospital when Willow was born four and a half years ago. It was Ben's mum, though, who was at the hospital with her, not her own mum. By then, the chasm was too wide to cross. Cassie couldn't help hoping that this might be the turning point for Silvia, that she would come marching in and claim her daughter and granddaughter somewhere in those last few agonizing pushes. Stomp in and really be her mum. Kiss her brow, grasp her hand and say, 'C'mon little mother, you can do it, you're amazing and strong and beautiful. Keep going!'

Cassie had never needed anyone as much as she needed Silvia right then. Not Ben's mum, not Dad, not Ben, not Jamie. Silvia. Her own mother. She kept looking at the door. Willing it to swing open and for Silvia to sweep in. It would all have been over then, all forgiven, all in the past, in one glorious birth moment. The start of Willow and the start of a new, better love with her mum.

That didn't happen, though.

Silvia stayed away. Stayed cold. Remained cruel.

Ironically, the white bendy bear has become Willow's favourite creature. Of course. Cassie tries to lose it. She shoves it to the bottom of the toy box, or hides it on a high shelf. Willow searches it out every time and cries anxiously until they are reunited. So Silvia's gift has become Willow's comfort. Silvia is getting to be close to Willow, a privilege she hasn't earned.

In any way. She has skipped her own daughter and connected with the very one she took so violently against.

No, Cassie thinks, Silvia doesn't deserve to have Willow's peachy little face resting on her bear every night, or for that bear's paw to be brushed rhythmically against Willow's utterly gorgeous suckly kissy top lip in order to lull her to sleep. Sometimes Cassie creeps in to check on her and Silvia's bear is sprawled across Willow's entire face. It looks like suffocation, but Willow wants full contact with it, she wants to sleep under its certain protection. She loves it. She calls the bear 'Namma' because Ben told her that her Grandma gave it to her and she couldn't quite manage 'Grandma'. Namma was the best she could do. So, Namma is a very important thing in Willow's little life, yet she has never met her. And neither will she.

Not now, and it looks like not ever.

Cassie is aware that she is in the way, standing at the door, frozen like this. She can just see her mother lying there, with frightening tubes going into her and weird machines all around. Cassie whispers, and she can see the steam of her words clouding up the glass in the small window of the door. She whispers louder, but not so loud anyone will hear.

'I hate you, Mum.'

Cassie can't go in. So she goes home instead.

To Willow.

And Ben.

And Namma.

FIFTEEN

Tia

Sunday 2pm

'I not believin for one little minute, that "Charlotte Church has ditched the booze", is you? No way hosepipe. She is always drinkin the Asda plonk to forget all the Gavin things she love so much. Why could she not miss him? He got the orange boy to man face and kind of hot orange bod what make a girl crazy. Any girl he like. All of him is a pleasant view for your eyes and ears. What young girl not want a piece of his orange yum yum? I do, that for sure. I will say "me next" when I see him. For sure. Stupid if you don't. See?'

Tia holds up a centrefold picture of Gavin Henson, oiled up and fake tanned to within an inch of his orange life, titled 'Torso of the Week'.

'His milkshake bring all the boys to the yard. Damn right, it's better than theirs. It true. It true. Drink it up Mrs Shit. Have a look. It worth wakin up just for this! No? Hm. OK, what about a lady what fell in love with the Masai Warrior? Oooo, he very high, with plenty beads and red blanket on. Why he got a blanket in Africa? Did she sew it for him, for a present? She love him mighty fine yes, but she need a ladder to reach him for the lips. He will be happy when he come to live in Southampton with her. He be high enough to see over everyone when he watchin the football! He should need his blanket then. Southampton full of rain allatime. All Southampton ships get waved off in the rain. She better buy him umbrella. He so big and high, he can hold the umbrella and all Southampton people could get under. Cos he so big. And high. Isn't it? He he.'

Tia flicks the pages, looking for more inspiration.

'"Britney and bodyguard in sex scandal". No surprising there. The old lady from *One Foot in the Mud* is sellin funerals. She smilin bout it, with a nice top on. Pink. Nice. Oh, Jedward twin boys done a next album for no one to buy. They keep doin all their talkin at the same time. Stop it Jedward, for tits sake, no one is thinkin clever about that. When will they finish? Soon I hope. "Are you Preppy or Boho?" Oh, not sure. Mostly both, I think, Mrs Shit. Charlie Sheen, no thanks. Tom Cruise and his wife Katie Price, no thanks. "Ask the doc", oo yes, a good bit. Let see, a lady have spots where pants go tight: Wear the bigger pants please! A man have no hair: Get the but-plugs put on like Dwayne Rooney, he got the hair all over now really good. See, I can be the doctor easy, better than her! You ask me the problem, I try the answer back at you . . . Yes, start now . . .'

Silence.

Tia waits.

Silvia doesn't move or speak.

'Oh. I geddit. You is a lady with no speakin. OK. Well, first I am tellin you that I say you did a fall on your head and now you havin a sleep so you don't look at all the messy bad life you got, where you shoutin at Mrs Cat allatime and cryin about wrong things you done. She shoutin, you shoutin, nobody talkin quiet or listen nice. Everyone sad and angry.

'And why not? Cos you should, cause you have pretty daughter and you never see little babygrand. Lovely little girl. Look like you. Bossy like you. Big noisy like you. Willow, yes, she cute as a dicktip. And the mother is a good girl, keep her clean and do cookin, all what the babygrand need. But she sad and angry too, wishin allatime for the magic mother. But none comes. So she pretend she hate the mother so it feels not too much bad. But she don't hate her mother. She need her. Why you not go for her? Whassafatcock up with you? What so big in Mrs Shit new life so you can't be her mummy? You missin alla good stuff with the babygrand.

'I see her last week, go there to help Miss Cassie. I sit on Willow for some hours so Miss Cassie get to go to shoppin and yoga, and to meet her friends for cappychin coffee. That job not for Tia. That job for Mrs Shit. This is true though, sometime I glad you freezin shut off lady, or maybe Tia wouldn't be the babysit. And Willow love Tia, always putting arms out and laugh loud with smiling. Willow like mini angel from God. Four-year-old angel. Only laughin and smilin allatime.

'If you see her now she would make you wake up for sure. She should come in here, but Mrs Shit too shut off lemon lips to talk to Miss Cassie, so the little babygrand not welcome. How?! How can a four year old not welcome? Ever? You crazy-head. And that finish your "Ask the doc" bit. Now Mrs Shit know her problem, she can fix. Up to you. So, what else?'

Tia flicks the pages, wetting her finger and thumb.

'"My daughter is also my sister-in-law". No thanks. "I married my stalker". No thanks. Ah, here is good one, "Madonna's got a megabucks cellulite buster" . . .'

SIXTEEN

Ed

Sunday 6pm

'Kidneys, heart, liver, small bowel, eyes, lungs, pancreas, tissue. What's tissue? What exactly is tissue? Ti-sh – oo –'

Ed says it slowly to try and unlock a non-existent medical encyclopedia in his head. He holds a clipboard with a questionnaire on it, and he is reading a small pamphlet that's been left with him by the donor team. They took him quietly into an ominous side room and explained that, although there were no concrete signs that Silvia might not survive, they like to broach the sensitive subject of donations with everyone in the intensive care unit at some point. This is Silvia's some point, and Ed is the most appropriate and closest kin, apart from Jo, who is staunchly refusing to speak to anyone who is anything other than positive.

She doesn't view organ donation as a positive move. She doesn't want to think about it at all, it interrupts her unflinching desire to facilitate Silvia's recovery. Questions it. Doubts it. Eats away her determination. She has told Ed that she will support his decision, but she doesn't want to know any details.

So it's all up to him. Ed feels immensely alone with it, and more than a little queasy.

'S'pose really, it's skin, probably. Don't think I can tick that box, you need that, alive or ... Otherwise. Keeps everything else in, contains it all. No, that wouldn't be right. Let's see, of all the other organs, which do I think you wouldn't mind giving? Um. Why are eyes the hardest to say yes to? I don't think I'd be able to tick "yes" for my own eyes on a form like this. They've seen such a lot, I suppose, and I imagine my memory of all that would go with them. Idiotic, I know, but I think it's something like that that bothers me. Plus the ridiculous notion that supposing all that Sunday school bollocks was true after all, it would be terrible to arrive in heaven and not be able to actually see it. To have no bloody eyes to witness the wonder, that would be just my luck.

'After years of believing that no God could possibly exist, that it was all nonsense, when push came to jump off a log, it was that same impossible, improbable God I spoke to, wasn't it? Actually spoke to him aloud! Same when you gave birth to Jamie and to Cassie – I spoke quietly to God both times, wanting you all to be safe. Spoke to him when Cassie had Willow too. And when Jamie went off to a pointless war in a big green bus. I murmur something every day for him, in the hope that

God notes it. Y'know, the God I don't believe in? That one, who definitely isn't there at all the important frightening moments in my life, but whom I still choose to address. Him?

'The same one I raise a little prayer to each night for you at the moment, Silvia. I give it a go, why not? What harm can it do? Yep, that's the same God who's gonna be in charge of the whole heaven shebang that I wouldn't be able to see if I give away my eyes. Wouldn't see the gates, the clouds, the angels, Elvis, Ayrton Senna, Kurt Cobain, Shergar, nothing. Wouldn't be able to see you. Not that you will necessarily be there before me but, just, whenever you <u>do</u> turn up.'

He falters.

It occurs to Ed that perhaps Silvia won't be checking into that particular celestial department at all. Maybe she is headed elsewhere, possibly somewhere subterranean, considering how very unkind she has often been. He doesn't say that bit out loud. He isn't as unkind.

'Either way, God or no God, heaven or no heaven, I don't think you would choose to give your eyes up. I don't blame you, so no to that. Kidneys? Yes, OK. Liver? I suppose so, although it will be, how shall I put it, "previously enjoyed". Ha. Bowel? They can have that. Lungs, pancreas, yes yes. Heart? . . . Ah . . .'

What heart? thinks Ed. She used to have one, many years ago, but he imagines if they go rummaging around in her chest, there is every chance they will find only a heart-shaped hole where a heart should be.

In order to make sense of what she did to him and to their kids, he has had to demonize her, he knows, otherwise he would have to face the fact that he might be partly to blame, and that is too hard. When a big hurtful difficult thing happens to you, it can shock and shake all logic or reasoned memory out of you. That hinterland of victim thinking often becomes the line of most comfort. Ed is sure that Silvia's sudden and inexplicable malevolence must have its roots in something he doesn't yet know or understand, but whilst he is ignorant of it, his method of coping is to render her irrefutably spiteful. That, in turn, must mean she is heartless, or at the very most have a heart of flint, only useful as a weapon not as a donor organ. Any recipient of her particular heart would therefore have to withstand its sharp assault from within. A genuine heart 'attack'.

'I'm saying no to heart. That's it. Done. Hope you approve, but, y'know, can't help it if you don't.'

Ed gets a kick out of this glimmer of assertion. Then he immediately feels immense guilt. He is finally squaring up to a helpless woman on the edge of her life. It's not exactly heroic. He jolts himself out of his discomfort.

'The doctor says no change Silv. The lovely nurse, Winnie, says we should find hope in that. Your strength and resilience is keeping you steady at the moment, while your body is trying to recover. That's good. You're not giving in, you're holding fast. That's what I've told the kids. I think Cassie will come to see you. She is thinking about it. Y'know. Finds it hard all this.

I don't want to push her. She thinks you might not want her here, but I've said that's nonsense. I hope that's right, Silv. God, I hope that's right. I wrote to Jamie, he knows what's happening . . .'

Ed has indeed written to their son to explain what has happened to his mother. He has Jamie's reply in his pocket, but he doesn't want to read it to Silvia.

Dear Dad.

Thanks for your letter and for letting me know. Yeah, you're right I could get compassionate leave. I'm not going to bother, the only time I will come to see mum is when she's in a wooden box and even that would be to make sure she really is completely dead. Sorry Dad, but you know how I feel. No time to write real letter now, but will defo do it next week. Promise. Good news re David Bentley. Allardyce making right choices. Gives all us Hammers boys out here a bit of hope. By the way, I defo have enough dosh for my season ticket (nothing here to spend it on!) so can you get mine when you get yours? Let me know about any special offers etc, yeah?

Seeya.
Jamie

PS I am smoking again. Soz.

No, Ed didn't think it was the right letter to read aloud to Silvia. What a shame it's come to this. Neither of her kids want to be with her at this desperate time.

Ed allows a selfish thought to flash through his mind. He hopes and indeed knows that it wouldn't be the same if it were him in that bed. He rests assured that his kids would be there for him. He hasn't deserted them. He knows as well as he knows anything, that what you put in is what you get out, and he's put a lot in these last few years. Two parents' worth of concern.

He misses being a parent alongside her. However irascible she may have been, she was always clever and saw situations looming way before he did. She watched the children very closely. Literally stared at them, fascinated and amused by their growth and their every move. He remembers it all very clearly, but when he looks at her lying there, a stationary lump, he can't believe it's the same woman. Who has she become?

'Funny really, thinking about when the kids were born, and praying to God to keep you all safe. Do you remember it all, Silv? I do. So clearly. Especially Jamie. The first one. We had no clue, did we?'

Ed finds himself touching Silvia's arm. It doesn't feel wrong while he's remembering their shared intimacies. If she was conscious, he wouldn't dare. Face it, if she was conscious, he wouldn't be here, full stop.

'You didn't like your belly being so big and round, you

thought it just looked fat. It didn't. I told you again and again it didn't. It looked . . . full. Actually, I couldn't tell you this at the time, but sometimes I would catch you waddling down our path and I thought you looked like you'd had the most enormous lunch. Not fat. Not fat at all, but full, like I say. And because I couldn't quite believe there was a living baby in there, couldn't get my head around it, it was simpler to imagine you were full of all your favourite food. That perfectly, alarmingly round belly stuffed with toast and mackerel and fudge.

'However prepared you were, with your bag packed ready by the door and the nursery equipped and ready for action, neither of us were prepared for the experience of that birth. The look on your face when your waters broke up on Kot Hill! You said to take you up there because you didn't think you'd manage the steep path again 'til the baby was born, you were getting too big and out of breath. That's the problem with Kot Hill though, you have to leave the car in the car park at the bottom and the rest is Shanks's pony.

'We were so nearly at the top, do you remember? You were ahead of me, further up the muddy path. You stopped still in your tracks suddenly, and turned round. I had never seen that expression on your face before, I didn't know how to read it. It was a mixture of wonder and embarrassment. You seemed far off, as if you were solving a problem elsewhere. It was only when you looked down and I followed your gaze that I saw the spreading stain on your trousers. It's funny really – I must have known your waters were due to break, but I immediately jumped to the mistaken conclusion that you'd wet yourself. My brain wasn't working on that windy hill. All I knew was that something natural but . . . a bit surprising was happening. God, yes, I remember now. You had the sun behind you, filtering through your amazing blowy hair, red hair, and you said "this is it Ed, it's bloodybabybloodywater". That's not a word. While I was momentarily baffled, you took my hand and firmly led me, puffing with anxiety back down the hillside to the car.

'We went straight to the hospital, didn't pick up the perfectly packed bag, and the next sixteen hours were unlike anything I had ever known or been part of before. I watched you change from a woman I knew, into a . . . a grunting animal. You really did become something from another species. You were so intensely focused on getting that baby into the world, and your whole body – your face, your voice, everything – was different. Long low waves of pain to start, then gradually you began to bellow. I didn't know you could make noises like that, they sounded like they came directly from your womb, from him, desperately fighting his way here. I wanted to protect you from him then, he was attacking you from inside, hurting you, making the veins on your forehead and neck stand out . . . all . . . livid and purple. God, yes, a blood vessel in your eye burst with the sheer effort and the white went red. Demon red. I was terrified.

'You growled your way through that stage and out the other

side, into a weird kind of beatific trance, where you were breathing deeply and staring into a holy blissful distance. For one awful moment, I thought you were dying. I did, Silv. I thought I was losing you. I suppose I was, in a way. Losing the all-to-myself Silvia, the before-kids Silvia, the not-tired-and-irritable Silvia. That Silvia was forever gone in that exact instant because that's when he came. Little pink, wrinkled blinking Jamie, who was furious about it all. Started out in a rage and has rarely been out of one since.

'He'd like to feel differently, I think, but just as he was crawling out of his anger – what was he, nineteen? – we split up, and he was plunged right back in. I wish he hadn't joined up in that frame of mind, that wasn't right. It's like being permitted to get married when drunk in Vegas. Young men incandescent with rage shouldn't be on the front line in Afghanistan. Mind you, who else would be as effective? Jamie. The firebrand. Tearing through his life with rage as his fuel. Totally opposite to little Miss Cassie Rose.

'Her entrance was very different, wasn't it? Or maybe you were different by then. You knew how it might be, and you were resigned to it, much calmer. I thought you'd lost it when you said it was all going to happen in a pool. I didn't get it, wouldn't the baby drown? I know, I know. Stupid. Maybe it was because Jamie was in the room, but you remained so entirely . . . contained throughout the whole thing, from the minute you stepped into the shallow pool and knelt down. Do you remember repeating "yes, yes, yes" over and over? The noises this time were rhythmic murmurs, in time with the ebb and flow of your pain. Jamie was copying you and you smiled at him, so he felt included. You were sweating profusely. One final low grunt of "Christ" under your breath, and she emerged, immediately cleaned in the water, lifted up and out of it by you. You turned round and scooped her out, holding her close, and she breathed. It was phenomenal.

'You are phenomenal Silv. You did it twice, that miraculous unbelievable thing. You gave life. Twice. From your "tissue". No one would ever be as mighty. Your body made two other bodies. So. No, actually. They can't have any of it. Sorry.'

He flings down the clipboard, stands and cries.

SEVENTEEN

Jo

Monday 10am

'Jump!'

Jo pleads with Silvia. She is leaning over the bed and has Silvia by the shoulders.

'Just jump, please darling. Try it, come on, for me. Look, I know you hate this stuff but honestly Silv, it could save you. Jump.'

Silvia lies as still as she persistently has for six days now.

'God help me Silv, you've got to do some of the work. Right look, listen, look, we'll rest for a few minutes but then we're going to give it another go missy, OK? And you are going to try harder, OK?'

Jo slumps back down on her chair. She knows it's wrong to feel exasperated with Silvia, but most certainly, that is what she is feeling. Bloody bloody Silvia. Why won't she respond and make Jo feel useful for once? She is shocked by the next thought that flickers through her mind . . . Why doesn't Silvia at least wake up briefly, so that everyone can witness their giant and undeniable sororal bond and then, THEN, OK, she could die, and at least it would've been Jo who roused her. Albeit temporarily.

As the thought ebbs away, Jo feels the flow of the guilt that accompanies such a selfish thought. She shudders and shakes it off, because surely, she thinks, Silvia waking up and getting better is more important than Jo being the one who makes it happen? Surely . . .? BUT . . . oh come on, Silvia, this particular method of rousing seems so phenomenally simple. All Silvia has to do is to take a giant leap between two dimensions. Quantum Jumping.

Jo tried it herself once, and admittedly, it didn't really work for her, but maybe she didn't have the powers of concentration? Silvia is good at focusing, and frankly, what else does she have to do at the moment? She might even be residing somewhere, deep inside her head, where the springboard for Quantum Jumping is more accessible. Yes, maybe that's why it didn't entirely work for Jo when she tried. She is too much anchored in this, earthly, first-dimensional plane. She is too distracted she realizes, by day-to-day stuff. A woman who can devote a whole week to mourning a pair of earrings she decided not to buy on holiday in Crete last year, is unlikely to be able to summon the mental acuity to change dimensions.

But Silvia can. Silvia has intellectual muscle. Her brain is as flashingly sharp as a Swiss Army penknife. Or was. Who knows what she is now? And, oh God, what would she be if she woke up? Perhaps this fall has permanently harmed her, and, oh God, who would have responsibility for her if she is awake and brain damaged? And ... oh God ... no, Jo must banish all thoughts of anything negative and think only of getting Silvia better. She isn't good at thinking one step at a time but to do otherwise is officially terrifying. Stay in the now, Jo, come on.

'Right Sis, I'm going to explain it one more time to you, OK? Please listen, and please try. Bert thing from America, who invented it, is hugely famous and rich for this, so to start off, we know it actually works, yeah? Otherwise he'd be in prison or something, wouldn't he, especially in America where they sue the butt, or whatever it is, off you in a heartbeat. Bert was in the army in Korea or something, and met loads of gurus and swamis and great stuff, so he picked up some amazing insights. He says that in order to Quantum Jump, all you need is an open mind and the willingness to learn. Surely you can muster that, darling, can't you, come on? There's guaranteed success if only you can open the frequency. I know it sounds weird, but apparently, Bert says that all leading quantum physicists agree that alternative universes exist, maybe in infinite numbers. Even that very clever dribbly one in the wheelchair says something similar, apparently.

'So all you have to do is harness the power of your mind,

a power previously untapped Silv, and journey to another, parallel dimension. Now when you get there, you have to find your other parallel dimension self who lives there and . . . sort of . . . feed off them. So, say you jump into a dimension where Silvia is, in fact, a ballerina. Well, just learn to dance, how to move your body, from her and then, when you jump back into this dimension, you will bring that skill with you. Honestly, you really will.

'You should see what Bert's brought back. I mean, obviously, he is a skilled jumper and has travelled many times, but he once met his 'painter' self in a far dimension and now he does amazing paintings here on earth. He displays them on his website for God's sake! You can even buy them, I think. This was a skill he didn't have before Sis, so explain that! I haven't bought any of the paintings myself, it's all in dollars and frankly, they're all a bit . . . hm . . . modern for me, but hey, good luck with that, Bert, it's still beyond belief.

'So imagine Sissy, if you could just try to jump, you could decide to meet your well and awake happy self, and maybe even send her back here instead of . . . this you. I'm not entirely sure how it works . . . so that maybe you could leave this broken you there instead? Hm, not sure, but listen darling, Bert has had profound results, he says, and since he has achieved mental and spiritual enlightenment, he can't remember the last time he made a bad decision. Everything he does, works. Who wouldn't want that, darling?

'You've simply got to awaken the voice of your soul, see the other dimension in your mind's eye, and when the slipstream is right you need to jump in and ride it baby, until you get to your turn-off. I haven't got that far yet when I've done it, so I can't exactly advise you <u>how</u> to turn off actually. Probably, there are signs or something? Mystic signs, maybe? And services, maybe? Anyway, I'm sure you will know. A bit like *Blade Runner*? You will make the slipstream stop with your mind and you will disembark from . . . your mind . . . or will you be in a little rocket-type thing or something? Made by your mind to transport you to the other universes?

'I'm not entirely clear on that practical stuff, but they must have it sorted because Bert has done many many of these journeys, and he's always returned safely, and always always been a better person. He calls it the "Inter-Dimensional Quest For A Better You". All these other people you will meet in the other universes are all your doppelgängers. I mean honestly, I remember being taught ridiculous unbelievable Shakespeare with doppelgängers in the stories, and I can remember thinking it was an impossible word and an impossible notion. No one is exactly like someone else, are they? I mean yes, occasionally, some people look a <u>bit</u> like someone else don't they, like, ooo, I don't know, Princess Margaret and Chucky the evil doll, or that hilarious picture on the internet where a cat looks like Hitler. Well, OK, not quite like that, but you know what I mean.

'But, Silv, surely it's worth a big fat try, isn't it? It's a chance to awaken your soul and call to your soulmate who will give you health and wellness. The journey isn't outside you really, is it, Silv, it's a journey into your inner self. You don't even have to pack babe. It's all good. Think of it like this. You know when people have twins and they use bits of one twin to fix a disease in the other one? Use their stems, I think, or something, it's a bit like that darling. You are going to go and find your not-in-a-coma twin and she is going to inject all her consciousness into you and you will suck it dry and come back to us. The more I think about it Silv, the more real it becomes. Please, please try. Come on now, one big go.'

Jo resumes her position at the side of the bed, kisses her inert sister on the forehead, clasps her shoulders tight, and takes a deep breath. The deep breath is an example to Silvia of how to physically prepare herself. Jo holds her breath 'til she can do it no longer, 'til it hurts her lungs, and then she exhales in a powerful whoosh.

'There. Right, ah, don't think it's working yet. Here we go Silv, one more big big try. And, breathe in, and concentrate, see those other dimensions, there's the slipstream of molten thought lava. Jump in Silv! Come on! JUMP!'

Tension, tension, wait wait.

And exhale.

Nothing.

Bloody nothing.

Lazy stubborn cow.

EIGHTEEN

Cat

Monday 11am

'. . . Maybe I should never have told him. Just left him. Let it all get colder and colder until the whole feckin' sham of a marriage was an iceberg and I could slide off it into the freezing water and swim away. Swim to you Sil. You were definitely the warmer waters. Perilous in your own way, but warmer than him. And anyway, I had no feckin' choice by then, if I'm honest. It had to be you. BUT. It would maybe have been wiser . . . not to tell him everything . . .'

Cat leans back in the chair, takes a big deep breath, and stretches her arms high above her head. She scratches and sniffs. She is tired. She is trying to behave as normally as possible in her injured life, which has been stabbed and is currently on its knees.

Cat goes to work at the practice each day and sees her patients for the allotted fifteen minutes each, or longer if they cry or have to get undressed. Some of her patients are so familiar and predictable that Cat often wonders whether she should just drive around and drop their various drugs in through their letter boxes, like a regular milk round. It would save time, and nothing would be different. Far more efficient really, then she would have time for the other, rarer patients who present with more unusual problems or with internal, emotional issues. She prefers that to flu and rashes and contraception. She likes the crunchy mental stuff, because that's where she mainly lives, in her own head with all the noise and shambles that's there. She gets that.

Normally though, she would be able to share difficult thought processes with Silvia. That's the hardest part, being separated from Silvia's calming and rigorous influence. They have shared so much in the last twelve years, and Cat likes how complicated and entwined they both now are. She even likes the ugly parts of it, of which there are many.

Her Connemara childhood of mountains and sea and nature might have seemed idyllic, yes, but the young Cat was over interested in being outdoors back then, because indoors wasn't so lovely.

Cat has grown up with two bullies. Her father primarily and, copying his idol, her unkind elder brother. Unfortunately for Cat, both men saw her as a chance to flex their alpha muscles, and took every opportunity to demean her. Her mammy was a ghost of a woman, little more than a servant to her much older husband. If Cat had any position of strength in the family, it was over her weak mammy, Bern. When Cat was lambasted by the men, all she knew how to do was the same to her mammy. At least that way, she wasn't entirely at the bottom of the ladder. One rung up. Only one, but an important one. She didn't like the knot in her belly when she was shouting at her mammy, but my God, it was infinitely preferable to how she felt when she was on the receiving end.

So Cat had come to understand how to live with a bullying man. That's what she thought a proper man was. Physically big, physically strong and physically terrifying with a hefty slice of mentally intimidating thrown in. So, when the time came for Cat to find a husband, two key elements were a surety. First, it had to be a man. She didn't pause for one homoment to investigate her latent fancy for other girls. And second, he ought to be a proper man. Like her dad. A man who could dominate her and control her. Y'know, a man, who was recognizably a man. That's why, when the very English, dicky-bowed and bull-necked GP, Philip, asked her to marry him, she said yes willingly and immediately.

Cat is considering all of this as she stretches.

'Honestly, when I think about it now, all the clues were there with that twat, right from the beginning. Sure, even the way he asked me out was an order. "You will meet me at six blah blah blah. You will be back in your home by eleven thirty blah blah blah. We will travel in my car. You will enjoy your meal."

Dear Lord he was a barking Nazi robot, why did I not mind that? Felt safe, I s'pose, familiar. Plus, to be honest Silv, being Irish was like having leprosy then. Everyone thought you were carrying a bomb. I kept saying I'm from feckin' Connemara you eejits, the only thing that explodes our way is the poitin! Wasn't the point, it was any Irish accent. Couldn't make any friends, felt utterly achingly lonely in England, and he pops up from nowhere showing me a deal of attention. In a town of thousands, he was the only person who connected.

'It's bloody grim bein' so . . . so grateful. Ha! Yes, that's it, I was grateful for a controlling freak of a husband. So I bought into it really, didn't I? It is definitely my fault. Partly. Such a bad choice. Ugly, bad choice. Jeez. When I think of how compliant I was. No wonder he took charge. Who was I then? Totally different now. It was so . . . insidious, the way it escalated. I'm sure if someone had said to me, "Would you like to be married to a man who will isolate you and then batter you?" I would have found that preposterous. Yet – look at what happened. Exactly that. Jeez.

'It crept up on me Silly, it starts with orders which, perversely, can make you feel safe, cradled in the regularity and routine of it. I was used to that, so nothing wrong there then. Then, of course, it's stealthy, isn't it? Incremental. Few more orders, unreasonable snipes and before you know it, five years on and subordination has tipped into subservience. I questioned nothing, Sil. I simply obeyed. Even that would have been tolerable if the bastard hadn't thrown in the slaps. Do you mind if? – slap. Could you pass me the? – slap. I'm not sure that's altogether correct – slap. Then the slaps get a bit slappier and a bit punchier and then they are punches. I lost count of how many times I ended up on the floor looking up at him. I didn't beg. I refused to. I always stayed calm. Calmly accepting blow after feckin' blow. From Dr Philip Harris. The respected and much trusted sadistic General Practitioner.

'I wondered sometimes if me being quiet made him worse? It might have. His face was black with violence when it kicked off. He literally went from ruddy to cloudy in seconds. I offended him deeply. Just my nearness, he said. Everything about me was something for him to defile. But he still managed to overcome his repugnance to have me every soddin' night. He could copulate his way through his repulsion, couldn't he? He wanted to put his mark on me, so he hammered away at me and honestly Sil, I had to pretend it was like going to work every day to a grim job I had little to no interest in. Nothing was required of me really other than to be present and not resist. So that's what I did.

'Christ, sometimes these days, I make the mistake of lettin' my mind wander back, and I imagine how many times I laid there, being violated like that. It was ... bloody ... loveless. Vile. I would close my eyes and try to not be there. Sometimes ...'

Cat stands up and moves to the end of the bed, where she

turns away from Silvia. Having her back to her somehow helps Cat not to feel so ashamed.

'Sometimes . . . he would order me to move as if I was enjoyin' it. To make sounds . . . y'know, to help him. I wouldn't. Funny really, I could deal with him rapin' me, but I couldn't act for him. Well now, was he rapin' me? I didn't resist. I knew it was futile and would only hurt more. But when I wouldn't do a performance for him, that's when he was the most insultin'. He would call me evil names, punch me. Never where it would show, o' course. Give it to him, he was skilled at that. I really . . . begrudged being attacked in bed, when I was naked. Just why clothes make such a big difference, I don't know, but they really do. There's something . . . childlike about being naked, so it's somehow more of an outrage. More of an offence, to do that. To a naked person. To me. To a grown child. With no clothes on. Feeling feckin' helpless. Awful.'

She walks to the window and although she is looking out at a bleak hospital courtyard garden, that is certainly not what she is seeing. She is entirely in her mind's eye and revisiting those terrifying years. For the first time though, she is seeing herself there, as a spectator. She has managed to remember it all, but from the outside. She can see her own face, frightened and wary. She sees her own eyes darting about and looking closely at his face, trying to predict his next move, readying herself for another lash out. Constantly reading him and trying to anticipate his sudden astonishing changes in mood and temper. She is on a bed, naked and curled up, looking up at him, the tormentor. She sees the pleading in her own eyes and finds it pathetic, unbearable.

She snaps back into the now. She turns to Silvia. Her darling Silvia, who would never hurt her. Not physically anyway. Where is she? Why hasn't she helped with all this? Being nearly dead isn't how Cat wants her. Cat needs constant reassurance, and this isn't it. She approaches the bed and looks closely at Silvia. She wishes she could feel more sympathy for her. Cat would only truly derive pleasure from the curing of her. That's the doctor in her, she's a solution-driven person.

The first and only time in her adult life she has ever stopped working, and allowed herself to feel something, was when she took Silvia to Connemara and fell in love with her. She tipped into that giant love very quickly and with massive brute force. It was like being at a bacchanalian feast when you have been starving in the desert. The small amount of love that Silvia could show Cat was the most she'd ever had. She was immediately hooked and wanted never to be parted from it. Silvia promised they never would be parted and now look.

So Silvia is a big fat liar.

'Honestly Sil, I'm not really coping with all of this. Without you keeping the reins on me, I'm spinning again. Not sure which way is up at the moment. All these old bad thoughts keep floodin' in, like a tsunami. I don't seem to have the filter

I need. You are the filter, aren't you, for God's sake. I keep trying to tell myself all the things you say. I say, "Calm down Cat, let yourself off the hook. Be gentle with yourself. Breathe. Breathe." Stuff like that, but somehow, when it doesn't come from your lips, it doesn't work. I don't believe myself.

'And actually, sorry to say it, but I am bloody furious with you. Life was already complicated enough without all this. I have been through a lot for you. I mean ... y'know ... the feckin' marriage may have been a sham yes, but it <u>was</u> a marriage and at least there was all the ... the ... respectability ... that went with it, and in a small town like this, that goes a long way when you're a GP, believe me. If he had gone ahead and ... told people ... about <u>us</u>, just as he threatened to, honestly Silly, I don't think I would still be working. Well, not at this practice anyway.

'It's bloody 2012 for feck's sake, who you love shouldn't matter. But it obviously does. Everyone knows everyone and it's all so bloody insidious. Why? Why would lovin' you make me any different or worse a doctor? I don't want to leave my practice. I've spent years building up relationships there, and anyway, why should I? I had as much right to work there as him. Yes, he was the senior partner, but frankly, so feckin' what?!'

Cat raises her hands in a huge resigned shrug, which renders her stationary for a moment, while she recalls the disturbing memories of the dreadful day.

'So ... but ... maybe ... yes, telling him like that, finally letting him know what a prick I thought he was, standing up to
him, maybe I said some things ... yes. I did. His eyes went
really black, I'd never seen that in him before. He always had
a look of ... sort of ... smug entitlement. Assured. Confident.
This was the opposite of that. D'you know, Silv, if I had seen
even a flicker of sadness or regret or something, anything to
show he felt some ... love ... or something ... it might have
been different. Instead he travelled from shock to humiliation
to boiling rage so fast that I felt like ... I would burn like him
if I stood too close. He was red and spittin'. His eyes. Christ
Silv, his eyes. The hatred. Not hurt, just hatred.

'It wasn't about the marriage being over. I think he already
knew that. It was that there was you. You, Silvia. You, a woman.
That a woman could possibly, in the sleepy hours of the dark-
est night-time, make another woman utter those sounds he so
desperately wanted to hear from me. His power diminished in
the instant he realized that. In a second. So, he's yellin'. "Don't
think you will walk away from all this, you boggy runt, you
won't! I will make one call, one pleading call to the right
people, and you, you dirty bitch, you will be sectioned. Fact.
Immediately. Sectioned. Locked up. And I will visit you, with
my kindest face on, and everyone will pity me because my
wife went mad. I might even weep. Watch me! Watch me bury
you where no one will ever find you. In insanity. Of my making. And watch you be grateful for my visits, and watch you

beg me to get you out of it. And watch me give you more tran-
quillizers to put you back in the confused fog of hell where
you belong you perverted bitch . . ."

'On and on like that Silv, 'til it wasn't possible to listen any
more. 'Til y'know, it wasn't possible to let him live . . .'

NINETEEN

Winnie

Monday noon

A s Winnie whooshes into the room, she is wiping her mouth. 'Wha gwaan sistren! Sorry Silvia, mi no like fi nyam in front o' you, but honestly, dis morning so busy, mi no haffi time fe food. No breakfass, no tea, no biscuits. Mi famish! Well, not really famish, like dem poor souls 'pon TV in Ethiopia an' Somalia wid huge sad eye. I feel shame for alla us when mi see dat. How we come to dis? Why we nuh share alla de food for everybody de same? I see dem whole heap o' huge bins at back of Morrisons on a Sunday marnin, heavin wid de out-o'-dates tings, still good to nyam. Jus fe you n'mi to know, mi haffi tek from dem bins sometime, when mi cheque run out. A true dis. Yu haffi dweet, if yu have a h'empty pickney. Evr'yone dweet. No shame in dat, but plenty o' shame lookin at di eyes of dem mawga babies an' dey big bellies dem. Proper shame in dat.

'Some have so much, some have so lickle. We need fe get

dose unfairness sort out, truss mi. If mi a queen o' de world, mi would say the skinniest get most and the fattest get least. Surely dat got to be right. Lord a God. Bless dem, and keep dem safe in hope. But h'anyway, sorry Silvia, fe stuffin mi face. It all gone now. Wasn't even tasty, a muffin from dat h'ugly man at de coffee shop. One poun' forty pence fe dat wortless cake! I only paid it fe hunger. Cyan't believe it. I fill up mi belly so fass, I feel sick now. Cha.'

All the time Winnie is speaking, she is going about her work, monitoring Silvia's current status. Her usual efficiency is tinged with a hint of edginess today. Her work isn't compromised in any way, but she definitely has the air of someone distracted and irked. She starts to hum, which she always does when she's concentrating, but the hum is the clue to her agitated state of mind. The hum is too loud and too vigorous. She doesn't hum anything specific. It is a generic hymn, incorporating the random sounds of many hymns she knows. Winnie can't possibly relax today because she is still stinging from the humiliation of last week.

On Saturday, there were three weddings at Winnie's church, the Word of God Church, near St Stephen's Park. It used to be St Stephen's Church but when it was about to close down due to low attendance, Winnie's pastor suggested her church took over and with growing support and constantly rising attendance figures, the church has flourished.

The only problem Pastor Saul faces is the dilapidated state of the poorly old building. He has received an estimate of nearly two hundred thousand pounds just to secure the integrity of the exterior. This figure is beyond the belief of anybody in the congregation, but they must believe it, because it is true. Pastor Saul tells the truth, and the builder who has given him the estimate is one of his flock, so he is also telling the truth. Two hundred thousand pounds to raise. Astonishing. Shocking. That's before they refurbish anything inside the church. To do that, there would have to be a second push on fund-raising. Pastor Saul has asked everyone to think of ways of raising the money. He himself is going to pray. A lot. And possibly arrange a car boot sale.

Despite their worries for their church building, the choir keep their spirits up by rehearsing for the weddings. Winnie finds the commitment to the rehearsals quite wearing, and she feels guilty about having more time away from Luke, but this is church work, so not up for debate. Plus, honestly, Winnie finds great solace in the singing. She is one of the stronger voices, she knows that. Brother Claude often encourages her to take a solo, and she seizes that opportunity with relish. Her voice is her gift from her God, and she wishes to return her thanks to him when she lifts it up in his name. It's with that intention that she strives to be the best singer she can be, and she attempts more and more difficult arrangements.

When she is singing, Winnie is truly Winnie. She is free from all other restraints. She is no one's daughter, mother, nurse or anything else. She is the channel through which God's word is sung. She closes her eyes, breathes deep into her soul and lets the spirit flow out of her in reverent and supreme worship. It flows like rivers of love and Winnie communes with that love and feels it 'til it fills her up. Sometimes the sheer exquisite pleasure of it causes Winnie to weep with joy.

Yes, she knows how to speak to her God through song, and it matters very much to her, which is why it was so upsetting when Brother Claude ruined it all last week, at the final rehearsal for the weddings. When she thinks of it now, she hums louder to mask the embarrassment.

The rehearsal was going well, although the church was cold and Winnie could see her breath in front of her face. She was wearing the fingerless gloves Luke gave her for Christmas. He had saved his pocket money for weeks and bought them on the market for her. Her favourite colours too, pink and purple together. The only problem with fingerless gloves is that they are fingerless, and it's your fingers that get cold, so what is the point of them? Luke bought them because he thought Winnie could wear them at work and still operate intricate machinery and so on, but sadly, nurses aren't allowed to wear germ-gathering gloves on the ward. Winnie didn't tell him that of course. She kissed his dear head on Christmas morning and thanked him profusely for his kindness, telling him how proud she was that he is such a beautifully generous boy. In her head, Winnie had put the phrase (unlike your father) in brackets, but she didn't say that out loud either, because she too is kind.

The choir had been working hard and it was time to stop for

a quick tea break. Claude had said five minutes, but since most of the choir are Jamaicans, they operate on Jamaican Time, which is different to Greenwich Mean Time, which is truly MEAN. Five minutes accepts thirty minutes in Jamaican time and 'come for ya dinna at one o'clock' accepts turning up at 6pm and it's all perfectly alright. This all leads to an interesting domino effect of later and later weddings on a Saturday. It's advisable to be the first wedding of the day, then at least you can set your own agenda for the tardiness and not be at the mercy of others!

So somewhere in the twentieth minute of the five-minute break, Claude sidles up to Winnie, who was checking messages on her phone. There were none, actually, but no one knew that and checking the phone makes you feel efficient, Winnie always feels. It makes you appear to be connected to a rich tapestry of a world. Winnie was actually connected to a Sudoku app she had downloaded. She turned the phone away as Claude approached.

'You OK deh, Sista Winnie?'

'Oh yes tank you Brother Claude. Very good tank you.'

'You soundin very good tonight. Very strong, very pyure.'

Winnie felt flattered and happy that Brother Claude should be so pleased with her. He knew his choirmaster stuff, and Winnie was a relatively new recruit to the choir, since it had taken a while for her to muster the courage to ask to move from her place in the pews with the rest of the congregation to a seat in the choir, in the revered front row of the choir, no less. Winnie still felt a little in awe of Claude and Claude's wife, Odine, who was his deputy in effect and a formidable woman you wouldn't want to argue with. Odine is always in charge of the refreshments at the tea break. She bakes ginger cake and then overcharges the choir for each slice, and for each cup of tea. Winnie finds this unfair, and expensive, and so has started to bring her own flask and her own munchies from home but that has not escaped Odine's eagle eye which is massively disapproving.

Winnie feared that perhaps this is what Claude had come to talk to her about. Apparently not.

'Seemin very clear to mi, Sista Winnie, dat you have de chops to be a bit of a solo star, yes?'

'Really? Me? Sorry, Brother Claude, how you mean exactly?'

'Well now missy, I'm tinking you know h'exactly what I mean.'

Winnie started to feel strangely uncomfortable and looked to see where the rest of the choir were. They were all gathered by the huge warm tea urn right at the back of the church, nowhere near enough for Winnie's liking at this particularly awkward moment.

'I . . . h'enjoy dis music you've chosen Brother Claude, very much . . . and I tank you for letting mi sing a solo sometimes . . .'

'It hasn't h'escaped mi notice, Sista Winnie, dat you operatin solo mos' o' de time, yes?'

'Well, yes. Dat is true. Sorry, y'mean the singin? . . . Or what, sorry?'

'Mi jus' tinkin you might be needin some company from time to time ... das all ... a man remin' you how fine you look, how h'attractive. Y'know, you definitely the mos' pretty in dis ya choir.'

Winnie's good heart fell into the pit of her stomach. How disappointing. 'Til this moment, she had looked upon Brother Claude as an upstanding man. An honourable, God-fearing man, and yet here he was, yards from his wife, making Winnie feel nervous – as he flirted with her. What a cheek. Winnie had to be sure she wasn't misreading these signals, she didn't want to jump to any wrong conclusions and she didn't want it to be true that it was happening at all. She knew she would have to be bold to be sure.

'Is you sayin, Brother Claude, dat you could be my time-to-time company? Is you sayin dat, I'm wonderin?'

Claude leaned in towards her, as close as he could get without alerting the others. Close enough for Winnie to smell his wife's ginger cake on his breath.

'Perhaps. You could get special one-on-one attention for yuh solos. If you lucky gyal.'

Something about the arrogance of him made Winnie want to gag, she found it so offensive. How dare he assume she would be lucky to have his adulterous attentions? She's felt lucky and grateful before for this kind of paltry offering, and look where that got her. It might have behoven Winnie to have held her tongue a few seconds more until she had thought through the consequence of what she next said. But she didn't.

She leaned in close to him and hissed, 'Wha di blouse an' skirt you tink you doin? Wid ya wifey a stan' over deso? Wha fuckery dis? You tink I dat cheap? You tink I a dyam fool? Go an suck ya mudda before I box ya face. Move yuh bumbaclaat backside! Cha!'

With that, she pushed heftily past him, and nearly knocked him into the next pew. Winnie rushed to the toilet where she sat quietly for the next few minutes, composing herself and taming her racing heartbeat. She couldn't believe she had unleashed her potty mouth so impetuously, but she couldn't entirely regret it either. She wished very much that none of it had happened, and especially in the House of the Lord. She felt shame about that.

Eventually, when she heard the music start, she knew it was time to return to the rehearsals. It was a long walk for her to return to her place and she took comfort from the fact that none of the other eight singers took the slightest bit of notice, so she deduced that no suspicions had been raised, thank goodness.

Her torture began when she realized that Claude was hell-bent on ignoring her. He made absolutely no eye contact with her and even turned his back when her solo came, and started a conversation with the pianist, Nat. He was singularly rude and Winnie felt that he may well be stupid enough to draw attention to something that hadn't even happened, if he persisted, but she carried on as normal, hoping everything would settle down when Claude had had enough time to consider the error of his ways and lick his wounds.

Not Claude. He is too boorish to bow out with grace. As the rehearsal came to an end, Claude asked for attention to discuss the weddings on Saturday.

'Right, now lissen up people. Saturday a big day for Calvary Voices. Three services. So that will be thirty pound each by the h'end of de day. It not sound much, but is God's work and we send praise and thanks. AMEN. Ev'rybody to be here by nine o'clock please and if mi could ask nicely, please all wear correct dress for church. Mi no wan' to point de finger at a particular, but Lord a mercy, Sista Winnie, de folk at de weddin don't wanna be lookin at your chests, thank you, inna di trampy low-cut top like dat . . .'

He pointed at Winnie's blouse, which, as far as she knew, was perfectly respectable. It was a blouse she often wore to and from work, and for one awful, culpable, red-faced moment of hot embarrassment, she felt she may have been horribly unprofessional. She looked down. The blouse definitely covered her breasts, the top button being well above her cleavage if a bit tight. The blouse was not an affront to anyone, it couldn't possibly be.

She eyeballed Claude, in the certain knowledge that this was an attack. An attack she must suffer in silence, as he concluded.

'Not suitable for a place of worship. H'after all, we not visitin de red-light distric, are we? No, we are raisin our voices to God the Father. Who, praise him, would like the women in his house to look smart an' wholesome, in cris clothes. Like Odine always do. No one person should be drawin the eye to jus them, becaa we a team, yes?'

'AMEN,' replied the choir, through their chortles and tuts. There's nothing like the dressing down of a newby to unite a team in their combined Schadenfreude.

That's Winnie told. Good.

Winnie gathered her music up and purposely walked slowly out of the church when the rehearsal was over. She wasn't going to scurry away, she would show she had backbone and dignity, in bucketfuls. She could feel Claude's eyes burrowing into her to check if his lashing had landed somewhere sore but she refused to return his glare. She wouldn't give him the pleasure. She held her head high and she sashayed out of the church, like a queen.

Once outside and out of sight, she ran and ran, gasping for breath 'til she arrived home on her doorstep, panting. She had skipped a whole bus journey home, so vexed was she. Her only comfort was that she knew she had made the right choices, and for that reason she slept easy, until Saturday the day of the wedding triathlon.

Winnie was at the Word of God Church by eight forty-five in the morning, sporting a demure dark blouse and a neat pleated skirt. She knew she looked smart and no one could possibly accuse her of being racy. She had already opened her throat in the steam of her morning shower, and she knew she was in good voice. When the time came for Winnie's solo, she closed her eyes, thought about her redeemer and sung out for the new love of this first fresh-faced bride and groom.

'Let him always walk beside me'

And she tried not to hate Claude standing there in front of her, conducting her even though her eyes are clamped shut

'Let him take my hand and guide me'

Yes, let him guide her away from Claude and his cheating nastiness

'Let me live in the light of his love'

That's God's love Claude, not yours, you idiot

''Til I reach that great tomorrow'

Ah, tomorrow, Winnie can lie in, with a plate of bun and cheese and a cuppa, pure bliss

'Where there'll be no pain and sorrow'

Yes Claude, the kind of pain and sorrow you could so easily bring

'Let me live in the light of his love'

Yes, let Winnie live in the light of God's love and let her always be strong and hopeful, and let this young couple always love each other and be nothing but kind.

Yes Lord.

All of the weddings went well and Pastor Saul didn't miss the opportunity of three different, new congregations to point out the problems with the church building when the collection plate was about to make its rounds.

'Now, I know dese are tuff times for all us. We all havin to

142

tighten the belt, the purse strings and the grip on di coffers but brothers and sistas, dere is no greater glory than to praise your Saviour, the Almighty the Holy of Holies, and where bes' to praise 'im but in his very own house. Dis house. The Word of God Church. Which is your church, people.

'But how you gonna do dat when de house, it fall dung about yi head? Look 'pon the cracks in di styain-glass. Look fe decay in di mullions and filials, whatever dey may be. Look 'pon de rot in de roof wood from parasite death-watch beetle, and look 'pon decay in di sandstone, from the sufferation of pollution and acid rain. The Lord God askin us to save it, so we mus' save it. Unless we no fear de wrath of Hell. I will lead you h'anywhere, people, H'ANYWHERE. But I will not lead you into Hell. No sir, I will not have dat on mi conscience. Ya hear me now? I will allays keep my compass dial set to Heaven, and mi no deviate for no man.

'So, h'unless you want to feel the licks of the fires of Satan, you mus' dig into your pockets and purses to help with dis almighty task God has set us. Don't you worry, Jesus, we are up to it. Can I get a h'aymen?'

'Amen,' came the solid but solemn reply from the congregated gatherings of mostly non-churchgoers, realizing this was the moment they would pay the costs of not attending the church for ages. They knew it would get them eventually. This was that eventually.

Winnie felt compelled to dig into her own purse and put ten

pounds on the plate the first two times it came past that day. Twice. Twenty pounds. Her wages for the day, other than the ten pounds for the last wedding. She didn't mind. She thought it was the right and only thing to do.

In the short break between the second and third wedding, there was a minor but supremely opportune crisis when Odine felt a little bit faint. The delays between the weddings meant that no one could get out to grab a bite to eat, and ironically Odine, the queen of refreshments, had counted on a break between the last two, when she had planned to pop into her mother's house nearby and share a quick plate of ackee and saltfish, her favourite treat. Odine's personal protest was to go a bit dramatically wobbly at the knees when she realized there would be no break. Odine could never be accused of underplaying any moment, and she certainly garnered plenty of attention at this one.

Winnie was trying not to believe that Odine was also suffering from a bad case of 'there are three brides in a row getting more attention than me-itis', but Winnie was failing to dissuade herself of the unkind notion. Odine is the sort of team player who flourishes when all focus is pulled to her.

As she started to waver, Brother Claude had to help her towards a bench outside. For the first time in the day, he reluctantly looked directly at Winnie when he had to ask her to take care of Odine's handbag whilst he supported her. Winnie obliged and sat quietly at the back of the church, guarding the bag whilst the rest of the choir were clucking around Odine.

Winnie had been sitting with Odine's bag for about ten minutes when she realized this was her only chance to nip to the loo before the next, final, and no doubt lengthy ceremony was about to start. She had no option but to take Odine's bag with her and so it sat on the floor of the cubicle while Winnie went about her toilet business. As she sat there, Winnie's eye was drawn to an open and bulging envelope on the top of Odine's bag. Winnie could see that it was stuffed with banknotes, which arrested her attention immediately. Claude and Odine didn't seem like the kind of couple who would flash their money around like this, and goodness, it looked like an awful lot. Despite her best attempt at willpower, Winnie couldn't help but take a closer look at the envelope.

That's when it all made sense.

On the front of the crammed packet were the words 'Brother Claude. SATURDAY. 3 WEDDINGS x £300 = £900'.

Winnie sat completely still, on the toilet, with her M&S pants around her ankles, and stared at those words and that money, to try and process what she'd seen. SO. HANG ON. Claude was charging £300 per wedding for the choir's services. He told them it was half that. He told them everyone, including himself and Odine, received £10 each per wedding, and that, after the ten choir members were paid, there was £50 over to put into a fund for overheads. Winnie had always wondered what those overheads might be but had never felt it was her place to question. She had always been desperate to believe Brother Claude was honourable. But now, sitting here, with all this money in her hand, and the incontrovertible evidence of Brother Claude's lack of moral judgement during the week, Winnie wasn't desperate to believe any more. She simply felt compelled to put it right.

Without another thought, Winnie counted out half of that money, and put £450 in her pocket. She had a plan for that. The envelope now contained the amount it was SUPPOSED to, and Winnie slipped it back into the top of Odine's bag, pulled her big, demure, wholesome, God-respecting pants up and went back into the church, where the guests for the last wedding were dribbling in. Odine thanked Winnie for looking after her bag and Winnie graciously accepted those thanks, with a broad fake grin.

After Winnie had sung her heart out during her solo, fuelled by the fact this could very well be her last time, she sat down to listen to Pastor Saul's impassioned pleas for help with the refurbishment of the church. Winnie smiled a very broad, very real grin when the collection plate passed in front of her and she proudly placed £450 on there, eyeballing Brother Claude throughout, and joining in loudly with a chorus of 'Mi glory glory, mi hallelujah, as I lay my burden down'.

He was baffled, as were the rest of the choir, by her remarkable generosity, but it went unspoken.

Winnie kept her eye on Brother Claude for the remainder of the service, and she watched as the cogs in his head whirred and whirred. As the third happy couple were repeating their vows, Winnie could tell that Claude was finally working out what must have happened. Winnie saw him looking at Odine, and Odine also working hard in the head to come to the only conclusion that was right. They all knew what had happened, and they all knew that they would not speak of it. Claude and Odine wouldn't because they would risk revealing themselves as frauds, and Winnie wouldn't because she is a decent, honourable woman who took the proper steps to put things right.

At the end of the third wedding, Brother Claude thanked the choir, and everyone received their £30 each. He even added an extra tenner for everyone.

'Just becaa ya work so hard, an' sound so sweet.'

'Yeah,' thought Winnie, 'and becaa ya feel so guilty.'

Winnie went home that night, exhausted and amazed at everything the day had revealed to her. She hugged up her beautiful boy and told him all about personal honour and how it matters so much.

She slept well, and woke up on Sunday to find a handwritten note on her front doormat from Brother Claude, explaining that her services in the choir were no longer required. She knew it was as unjust as it was inevitable, and she felt unbearably sad.

TWENTY

Ed

Monday 2pm

Ed sits on the chair next to Silvia's bed. He has been sitting there with his coat on for fifteen minutes now, saying nothing. He is lost in thought and looking at his dirty boots, with the fresh clods of earth still clinging to the soles. He forgot to bring a different pair of shoes for visiting Silvia, so he has been forced to wear these. He twists round to check the floor where he has walked in, and all the way from the door to the chair there are, indeed, big soddy footprints.

He looks at his hands, stained from digging and chopping. There is earth under his fingernails and rough calloused skin where new skin has formed over old wounds. The bottoms of his old trousers are also crusted in brown dirt. Ed reaches down to the fabric by his soggy ankles, squeezes the hem of his work jeans and brings his hands straight to his nose. He can smell the ground in his wood and, faintly, he can even sense the essence of forest foliage. The bark, the sap, the leaves, even the musk of mammal droppings is contained in the scent. He loves it, and he is glad to get a whiff of it in this stale clinical fug of a room.

Each time he visits, he finds it more stifling. For him, it's not just the room, it's how stifled the dynamic of the whole situation has become. Even though it is barely a week since Silvia came off that balcony, the family and various friends already seem as locked into their roles as Silvia is locked into her body. He feels that unless there is a change soon, stagnation will set in and everyone, including Silvia, will start to reek. Ordinary life is carrying on and ordinary change is happening everywhere else, except in Suite 5.

Ed has had to force big change upon himself in the years since the split with Silvia. He feels as if he is a totally different man now, he even feels a little bit like he wishes Silvia had known this man he has become. Perhaps she wouldn't have found him so easily dismissible.

He looks at Silvia closely, searching her face and her body for clues to any change in her condition. He would love to spot something, to hear a difference in her breathing, or see a change in colour in her skin, or a flicker in her closed eyes. He realizes that he probably didn't ever scrutinize her this closely when she was conscious.

He struggles with his tortured imaginings sometimes, and thinks that perhaps when they were together as a couple, they weren't entirely real. In other words the real Ed he knows himself to be, and the real Silvia which only she truly knows herself to be somehow came together to make a third thing, a new entity called 'EdandSilvia' which neither of them knew themselves to be. A new thing, which they became familiar with, but which never felt wholly right. He certainly felt trapped inside EdandSilvia a lot of the time, so she must have too. What a shame, he thinks, that they couldn't rectify it, couldn't speak of it. Why not? Maybe because it would force them to unravel and analyse in a way both of them feared? Yes, maybe.

One thing Ed knows is that he will not put himself in such a vulnerable position ever again. He can't afford to. He would break if he was felled in such a brutal way again. The sure route to protect himself from such pain is never to love again. Not another woman anyway. He does love. He loves his mum after a fashion, he loves Jamie for sure and he loves Cassie hugely. And now, now, he has an astounding new love in his life, one who has stolen his heart in its battered and bruised entirety. Willow is the new commander of Ed's love, and Ed is bursting to tell Silvia all about it.

He has resisted talking to her too much about Willow because he knows it was such a sensitive issue before this accident. Silvia refused to have anything to do with her, from the moment she was born, and didn't like to hear or know anything about her. But now, looking at Silvia lying there so still and devoid of fight, he wants her to hear some Willow stuff.

'Hope you don't mind the woody smell too much Silv, but 'fraid I can't help it. Today was an important day up there, because today was the day Willow planted her first tree. NOT a willow, I hasten to add, can't be doing with them, the Marilyn Monroes of the tree world, exquisitely delicate yes, but shameless show-offs, and high maintenance. Not right for Foy Wood. No, she planted a copper beech, *Fagus sylvatica purpurea*. We spent quite a lot of last week poring through the nursery brochures to find the right tree. I hoped she would choose a beech, but I told her it was absolutely up to her. She did hover around the bonsai selection at the back for a few unnerving minutes, but thank God, something drew her back to the beech section in the end.

'I have her three days a week, Silv, to give Cassie a chance to work. Tia and I split the babysitting between us as much as we can. Blimey, I'm still calling it "babysitting". She's hardly a baby any more. She's . . . four . . . yes four. Wow. Where has that time gone?'

Ed rummages in his pocket and fishes out his phone. He fiddles about until he finds the photos and puts it into 'slideshow' mode. Every picture is either of a tree or of Willow, or of Willow and a tree, the final photo being taken this morning, of Willow hugging the sapling she has just planted.

'There she is. Know you can't really see these, but maybe,

who knows, somehow through your eyelids . . . you might . . . osmosis . . . dunno . . . anyway, thing is, she is standing there in her red duffel coat with the hood, but she doesn't like the hood, she prefers this hat with the monkey head on it, and she wears green wellies with frogs' faces on the toes, and gloves with lions on them and a knapsack with a raccoon's head on it. She is a walking menagerie, honestly!

'What's so funny is she genuinely believes that all the animals would kill each other if they're too close, so she keeps everything very separate. The gloves can't be near the boots, the knapsack can't meet the hat. She's hugely vigilant about it. She's the zookeeper. Each animal is spoken to separately, and calmed in order to keep the peace. She strokes them and murmurs in their ears, it's a full-time job, animal wrangler. I had to wait a full fifteen minutes this morning whilst she separated and negotiated with them before she got out of the truck.

'The sapling was in the back of the truck, so we had to hoick it up to the edge of the wood on a wheelbarrow. Willow sat in the wheelbarrow cradling her tree and keeping it upright all the way. It's a lovely specimen, a two-foot whip, about two years old I think, pot-grown and still with the remnants of last year's leaves hanging on for dear life. Ideally, I'd rather she planted it in the autumn, but she was impatient and I want to plug into her enthusiasm while she has it in bucketloads. I might only have this tiny window of opportunity to lasso her interest in the wood, and who knows Silv, she might be the one to take it on, if she's still interested when she grows up, and when she watches that tree grow up alongside her. I think I know who'll be the tallest!'

Ed stands up and takes his coat off, still chuckling to himself about Willow and the constant animal wars she has to arbitrate. She must be exhausted from it all. He walks to the window and his eye is drawn to any sign of nature in the sparse quad beneath. He looks at the wooden bench next to the bin. This has been his saving grace on many of these visits and he is going to revisit it again any minute now, when he has finished telling Silvia about Willow.

He wants to run away right now, and dodge telling Silvia anything, his life would be much simpler and much more bearable without these interminable visits, but he is compelled to stay and continue. He knows in his deepest place it's the right thing to do. He doesn't owe Silvia anything, but he owes it to himself to remain generous. He was kind-hearted before he met her, and, despite the damage her coldness has caused him, he is determined to remain kind-hearted.

He never wants to be like her. He looks back at her. A motionless mound. No, he will never be like her, as long as he has breath in his body and as long as he has a grandchild like Willow to continue living for and through. Perhaps, just perhaps, if somewhere in her faraway locked-in place, Silvia can want a little piece of the future that Willow stands for, she might push herself upwards, outwards, away from the quicksand of this deep sleep, even if it is simply to assuage her jealousy or her curiosity or, even, her torment.

'Y'know what I think? I think she chose a beech because that's what she sees when she comes there with me. She doesn't really know the difference between all the different trees that are there yet, although I try to tell her in kid-size bites. There's a hoary old poem my gran used to tell me about all the different woods and how they burn, but I can't remember it all, must look it up, something like, "Logs to burn! Logs to burn! Logs to save the coal a turn!" . . . um . . . "Beechwood first burn bright and clear, Hornbeam blazes too, if the logs are kept a year, and seasoned through and through" . . . it goes on like that, um . . . "Oak logs will warm you well, if they're old and dry" dum de dum de dum "pinewood" something "sparks will fly".

'Anyway, it's something like that, and so me 'n' Willow chanted that first bit about the beechwood over and over again on the way to find the spot to plant her tree. It was good. The rhyme fitted nicely with the chug of the barrow's wheel. Better than "Wheels On The Bus". Dear God, save me from any more verses of that monster song. I have taken to making my own lyrics up now to make it vaguely tolerable when she repeatedly requests it. I particularly like "The bankers on the bus go grab, grab, grab" and "The grannies on the bus go get away, get away, get away". Yes, that one is particularly good . . . very . . . um . . . caring . . .'

Ed realizes how supremely cheeky this is in relation to Silvia, and the measure of his own sheer front causes him to laugh. He quickly loses control on the volume of his laughter as it explodes from him and so he is forced to leave the room as quickly as possible. He bursts into the corridor outside, and has to let his laughter rip.

Winnie is sitting at the nurses' station and sees him.

'You OK deh, Mr Shute?'

Ed can hardly speak. He doubles over, and grabs his knees.

'Yes, yes thanks, um . . . sorry?'

'Winnie. Mi name Winnie. Or nurse. Or pssst.'

'Yes. Right. Yes. Thanks Winnie. Just had a weird moment there. Found something funny . . . y'know . . . that I shouldn't?'

'Mi know, yes. It strange, dis ward can mek you do dat. You gotta laff innit, cos if not, it's all tension an' waterwork. Das no good. Not fi you, and certainly not fi dem. I don't tink Silvia mind you laffin. Not at all, Mr Shute.'

'Ed, please.'

'H'Edward.'

'I think she would mind Winnie. That's why I've stepped out, but, goodness. Phew. I feel better for it, I can tell you.'

'Good. Release. Yes, good. You wan' cuppa tea?'

'Yes, that would be good, thanks.'

'Yu mos' welcome. Mi bring it to you in dere.'

'Right. Cheers. Yes. Thanks.'

Ed coughs and shares a smile with Winnie as he briefly

155

bathes in the warmth of her colossal understanding and her undeniable goodness. For a simple moment, they both stand there, each finding a rare comfort for a couple of seconds. It passes quickly enough. But it was definitely lovely.

Buoyed up, Ed returns to his seat in Silvia's room, squelching his muddy boots all the way.

'Sorry about that, love. Just had a ... um ... moment. Where was I? Oh yes, little mite is in the wheelbarrow cradling her copper beech baby. Although it's a different variant to any of the other trees in the wood, it will totally totally fit, and yet it will also stand out. Somehow, in all her tiny four-year-oldness, she knows that. She has learned what a beech is, what the smooth silver-grey bark looks and feels like and how elastic it is, what standing under that huge dome does to your senses, and with the copper beech, when it is mature, and the leaves are fully reddy-purple, she will feel like she is standing in a grand speckled rose-tinted cathedral.

'It's going to be magnificent, but right now, today, it needed her full-on nurturing. She had to be the mum, and honestly Silv, you should have seen the care she took. Her little jaw was set, as soon as we arrived at the spot, just on the edge of the wood, where it would start its new life. She was so attentive to everything I said.

'It's a responsibility isn't it, this age? They look up to you, literally, and believe everything you say, and they want you to know stuff and be right. Christ. I felt so ... what? ... important. Yes. That's it, I am very important to her. Don't get me wrong, I'm not arrogant enough to think I am genuinely important in the greater scheme of things, or even to believe that I am important to anyone else. But. I know that in Willow's little life, I am very important, and so I try my hardest to live up to that. I tell you, I have to up my game, I really do. So. Anyway.

'We stopped at the outer edge of the wood, where there is more space but still enough shelter. The spot was about two metres from a middle-aged Scots pine, one of only three in there, who will act as a nurse for this little beech. I told Willow that transplanting is like minor surgery, and that this young beech could suffer a huge shock and not survive if we drop her or harm her or her roots in any way. She handled that sapling as if it were a Ming vase, and would hardly let me near.

'For one tiny, lovely moment, I asked her to stand still and listen to the wood. Of course she heard the wind in the trees, and birds and rustling and whistling, but I asked her to listen for the music of it. I don't even really know what I mean, except that I listen out for it all the time, it's a kind of vibration and I know she hears it too because she always reacts if something in amongst it is out of place or time. She hummed a long low base hum to me and told me that was the music she heard. Like this . . .'

Ed hums a low steady note, which reverberates around the room.

If Silvia were awake, she would feel it in the pit of her stomach and in her sternum and in the tiny pools of water in her ears.

'And y'know what? That's exactly what I hear. Wonderful. Willow boldly told me that, "Trees need air and water and hugs Granpop, like me." She is right, of course, but I had to make sure the soil is well drained there, beeches won't grow if it's too damp. Compromises the roots. Makes them weak. Well, none of us do well with soggy undercarriage, do we Silv?!

'I had already prepared the site, checked it wasn't clay-heavy, dug it over, killed any enemy weeds, removed stones and mixed in some well-rotted compost. Home-made of course. I gave Willow the spade and she thrust it into the ground directly straight down. She's seen me do it many times. She made the notch in the ground and together we waggled it back and forth to make a larger slit. We placed the baby tree into the notch, taking loads of care to make sure the roots were all pointing downwards, and the collar of the tree, you know the part I mean? Where the trunk meets the roots yeah, well, making sure that was below ground level. Then we pulled the tree upwards so the root collar was level with the ground, removed the spade and firmed in the soil with our feet, trampling it in very carefully.

'Willow didn't want us to kill any worms. So we didn't. She told me not to scrape the bark with my boot. So I didn't. She told me not to stamp too much as that would "hurt the tree's ears". So I didn't. She poured a bucketful of water on to the patch so the new baby could drink. Then I poured some water into her little mouth so she could drink too. She was constantly checking out the tree all the time she was glugging away, making sure they both were drinking.

'I needed to put a loose plastic guard around the tree to protect it from deer and rabbits. Willow decided that she would ward them off by shouting loudly at them "Go away deer! Go away rabbit! Don't eat my tree!" ... which I think may well work. Then I put a stake in the ground and strapped the tree to it. It will only need that for a year or so, 'til the roots establish themselves. Willow insisted I strap her to the spade in the same way.

'She kissed her tree, and we stood side by side, one big, one small person gaffer-taped to a spade, next to our infant offshoot, feeling very proud and very excited about the future of everyone and everything present.

'To be honest Silv, I feel like I planted Willow today, as well as that tree. Yep. I'm confident about how well she can grow. She's going to be fine. She's going to be ... just ... fine. I will make sure of that. I can't ensure the future of that new tree but one thing I know about Willow's future is that it will have me in it. Because being alive means having a future. It does Silv. For the first time in ages, I can see a future. For us anyway. Now you have to decide if you've got one ...'

Winnie opens the door and brings Ed a cup of tea.

'Deh, h'Edward. Someting to warm you ...'

TWENTY-ONE

Cassie

Monday 4pm

C assie is inside the room.

She has just spent forty minutes drinking watery coffee in the café downstairs, trying to pluck up the courage and the willing to come inside Silvia's room and sit down. In the end, she decided to go for it purely because she is frustrated at having made the trip so many times, and only once having been able to get further than the café.

The bus fare and the coffee together have meant that it's all become very expensive. Cassie manages on very little. Ben works hard, but he is an apprentice and every penny counts. Ed sometimes gives his daughter whatever money he can spare but, essentially, Cassie gets by on nearly nothing, and these trips to the hospital have stretched that nothing to the limit. For that reason alone (or so Cassie convinces herself), she has made it, up in the lift, along the corridor to the ITU past the nurses' station and through the door of her mum's room.

Once the door closed behind her, Cassie felt that she was undeniably IN, committed to the decision, and that an about-turn would be out of the question; so she sat down tentatively, in the visitor's chair. That was five minutes ago, and only now is she starting to regulate her breath. She can hear her breathing as if she is a diver underwater, from a long way inside her head.

She becomes aware, in the deafening quiet of the room, just how much she speaks to herself internally and how very desperately she seeks the comfort of that. She is able to both listen and speak to her own soothing voice simultaneously. How? It must come from somewhere other than her immediate thoughts.

From her soul perhaps? Whatever, she hears it . . .

'Shhh, little heart, stop beating so fast. It'll be alright. It's just a woman lying there. Can't hurt you. Breathe deep. In. Out. In. Out. Same as her. In. Out. There, there, there. Shhh.'

Gradually, Cassie calms herself and drinks it all in. The room, the smell, the light, her mother's body, her hair, her hands, her feet which are uncovered at the bottom of the bed. Strange. Why aren't they under the sheets? Cassie wishes she could fold the sheets and thin blanket down to cover Silvia's feet, but she knows this is impossible for her right now. She can't bring herself to touch Silvia. Just looking at her like this, when she is so unanimated, feels too intimate, never mind touching her. Cassie feels the heaviness of guilt – she is invading her mother's vulnerable sick space. By simply sitting here, she is breaking boundaries that have formed like fur on a kettle element, slowly and poisonously. Cassie couldn't bring herself to believe she wouldn't see her mum again back then. She waited and waited so hopefully for a phone call. Prayed for it. She knew it had to come from Silvia. The forgiveness was in her gift. It was surely Cassie who had done the most wrong, wasn't it? Cassie desperately hoped they would mend. But as each unforgiven day went by, it all stayed undone and grew worse.

The mess was very heavy and impossible to shift.

Like any erosion that is subtle and stealthy, it is enormously potent. Especially since Cassie can't work out what she did so wrong.

What would warrant being so totally rejected? Yes, she got pregnant very young and she knew immediately it happened that this would annoy her mother. Her feminist mother. But what is a feminist, then? Isn't a feminist someone who will fight for the rights of women? And didn't Cassie have the right to have her baby? And wasn't the baby also Silvia's grandchild? And wasn't the baby also a girl? Who had a right to be born? And then be loved? By her 'feminist' grandmother? Well, this is how Cassie interprets it anyway.

Why wouldn't she? None of Cassie's questions have been

answered because Silvia has inexplicably thrown her out and pulled up the drawbridge of her love, for Cassie seemingly never to experience it again. And why would anyone suddenly stop loving their daughter? Cassie fleetingly experiments with the thought of ceasing to love Willow. She can't even entertain the idea because it is unthinkable. What happened? Did Silvia suddenly run out of love? Have 'love-fatigue' or something? Or . . . or . . .

Cassie's most profound and dreadful thoughts start to emerge again, dangerously close to the surface now, so Cassie speaks internally, to steady herself.

'Silly woman, doesn't know what she's missing, she's a bloody twat. That's all. Just an ordinary everyday twat from Twatsville. In the county of Twatfordshire. In the United Twat-dom. In Great Twattain. It's her fault. Not mine. Not Willow's. Hers. She's the one who can't do the loving. Not us. Dad can love me. So I'm not <u>that</u> bad. It is possible. I'm not <u>so</u> bloody hideous. I've got mates for God's sake. They love me. So does Ben. And Willow. And Jamie. And lots of people. So it def is possible. I know that . . . For sure . . .'

With those thoughts, Cassie circumnavigates around her biggest fear, a fear she has lived with for four years now, a fear that has pussed up to become a fully infected surety that she is too afraid to acknowledge. For Cassie, the awful undeniably obvious truth is that she is not good enough to love. That's the fact. Her mother's distance is just proof, that's all. After the divorce, Mum couldn't pretend any more to love any of them. Not Dad or Jamie, or her. Especially her. Who had the most need of a mum, because she was about to be one.

Cassie often wonders when it was that her mother fell out of love with her. To know might be truly devastatingly painful, but frankly it would be better than this howling bottomless pit of not knowing. She wonders if it was when she was much smaller. Maybe she did something very naughty? Maybe she was unkind to another child and Silvia witnessed it and found it sickening. Maybe she was selfish and didn't share nicely. Maybe she wasn't very clever and Silvia knew that and found it unattractive. Maybe she was clumsy and broke stuff? Or lazy? Or a show-off? Or ugly? Or, most likely, all of the above.

What Cassie knows for sure, is that it is her fault. No one can disabuse her of that knowledge, not any of the others, not even her tiny cradling inner voice, which tries very hard. Cassie is just not lovable. FACT. Yes, she wishes that stagnant lump in the bed would love her, and more than that, she wishes she didn't wish for that, because the gnawing pain of its continued and constant absence is virtually unbearable. In fact, at this very moment, it's just that, unbearable.

So Cassie gets up, and after an agonizing ten minutes in that awful room, she leaves, having uttered not one word out loud.

TWENTY-TWO

Cat

Tuesday 10am

'So there y'are, strapped to the top of the plane, on one of those standing-up bracket things, it's one of those old-fashioned planes with the double wings, and I'm in the pilot's seat, hilarious, and we are swoopin' over snowy mountains and huge sandy orange canyons, and then oceans and then forests. You are completely safe because I am the best pilot in the world, but it feels edgy, y'know, because we're takin' this huge risk. I can see you, so I can, and you are screamin' and whoopin' with delight. The wind is in your hair and you are so utterly alive and ... having every last jot of that experience ... you are loving it ... you're free and happy and ... well ... awake. God. Yeah. It was amazing.

'I haven't dreamed like that since I was a kid. In proper full colour like that, and a moment that feels so wild and real and goes on for ages. I was devastated when I woke up Silly, truly

165

I was. Jeesuz help me, I plunged badly. Thank God I was comin'
here, otherwise I swear I would have pulled the covers back
over my head and spent the day in bed, tryin' to recapture it.
And failing no doubt.'

Cat finds it hard to sit still, she is restless and jangled. She
needs Silvia to calm her, but this is all she gets from Silvia
now, a considerable amount of nothing at all. Silvia is a colossal torpid heap, and it isn't fair. Cat has been through a lot to
ring-fence this relationship, and look at her lying there. What
was the point?

'Hmm, Jung, I think, wasn't it, who said, "We all dream, just
as we all breathe." Was it Jung? Someone, anyway. Yes. We all
dream, just as we all breathe. So, we all dream then, all the
time. I just don't remember mine I'm guessin'. Not usually.
Just the vivid ones like that. Wonder if it means somethin'?
Maybe just me wishin' it could be different. Wishin' you
were ... back. Christ, Silly. This is torture. Please God, wake
up. There's so much to sort out. I've got to change ... stuff. I
can't do that without you. So. Y'know ... Come on. Bloody
hell ...'

Cat strides to the bottom of the bed where Silvia's feet are
exposed. The feet she was mesmerized by all that time ago.
The same feet that skipped across the rocks. The elegant,
strong, pearly feet Cat loved. They appear entirely different
now. Cat catches her breath as she realizes that the feet are no
longer thrilling or exquisite, they are the leaden, lifeless feet

166

of a dead person. They aren't fascinatingly alabaster, they are deathly drained.

Faded feet. Of a pallid person. A sickly weak person.

Cat is, for the first time, repulsed by them. By her. By chronically ill Silvia. Surely, the point of Silvia is to feed Cat, in every way, to nourish and support her? A useless human fossil like this cannot do that.

Cat's voice is low and hissing when she speaks. She doesn't usually display this part of herself in public. This is the hidden Cat that few have witnessed. But now Cat feels private enough in this room to open her personal curtain a tiny smidge, revealing a glimpse of the darker Cat she hosts, but rarely acknowledges. This Cat is altogether more serious and chillingly selfish and was born all those years ago in Connemara.

She learned there that she could absent her empathetic, feeling self, so that what remained was cold and numb, impervious to pain. Perhaps not entirely impervious though, since some droplets of pain have leaked through the cracks in Cat's façade, and diluted her resolve, to form a deep pool of shame and anger. A toxic mixture.

'For feck's sake, Silly. It will all fall apart if you . . . stay like this. Everyone is askin' questions all the time. Suddenly now, questions about Philip again. After all this bloody time. I thought we were out of that. The story was so good. It fitted so well. Fitted exactly. He always said he'd go one day. His own mother had heard him say it many times, so she totally believed it. She was even suggestin' places he might be. Calling her son "a medical hero, the answer to the needs of the many unseen and unheard". Blah Blah. Hero?!! The man was a feckin' monster. Brutish bastard . . . good thing he never did get as far as the feckin' jungles of Peru or wherever. It wouldn't be disease the bloody Mascho-Piro tribe would be havin' to fend off. He'd've had a ball with some as-yet-uncontacted-by-civilization people. Cos he was the bloody same. Savage.

'She was comfortin' me, for Christ's sake. "How could he? He's so single-minded, I'm sorry it's turned out like this Cat, he always was a selfish boy." I hardly had to say a word. There was only her to convince, and she was doing a good job of convincing me! Once they searched the house, that was it. No further questions. Missing person. GP. Presumed abroad, or abducted, or both. Interpol alerted. Pity the abandoned missus.

'Thank God there are plenty of misguided do-gooders out there wandering into dense foliage, intent on good-doing. Keeps the figures vague. Suits me. Suits us, eh, darlin'?'

Or did, Cat thinks.

Since Silvia came off that balcony, there have been some uncomfortable questions. Two unexplained incidents surrounding one woman. It doesn't help that bloody Jo and Ed are pushing to know exactly what happened. She has avoided both of them thankfully. She hates them, they hate her. It was a deliciously equal stand-off until this happened. The great thing about long-held grievances is that they petrify nicely, until no move is required on either side. That's the stage Cat was at with Silvia's family. No contact whatsoever.

Occasionally there might be a pinprick of communication to puncture the bubble. Like the very irritating letter from Ed early on, where he'd bleated about Silvia cutting herself off from everyone that loved her, and how none of them could understand it. He had said that no one in the family begrudged Silvia's 'friendship' with Cat.

Friendship! Ha! How quaint.

Then again, other than to Philip on that awful day, neither Silvia nor Cat have ever defined their relationship outwardly, openly, to anyone. They have both thought it best not to, for different reasons. Silvia has always found it hard to commit to it out loud, and also neither of them have wanted the gossip which might promote further interest by the police. They have chosen instead to maintain separate flats, at Silvia's behest, but of course, Cat doesn't spend much time apart from Silvia. She refuses to.

Ed wrote in his letter about how, from an enforced distance, it appeared that 'Cat seems to be the ivy growing around you, Silv. Looks like healthy foliage from a distance, but on closer inspection, might well be choking you to death? Please talk to us.'

How dare he? Ed was Silvia's history. Cat is her present. Cat is all Silvia needs. They share important, private secrets that bond them inextricably. They both know what happened to Philip. Cat told Silvia all about it.

That's the glue that binds them.

Cat was furious at Silvia's response to Ed's 'ivy' jibe. Instead of springing to Cat's defence as she should surely have done, Silvia sat on the floor with her head in her hands, sobbing like a baby. Like a bloody useless vulnerable pathetic baby. After everything Cat had sacrificed for her. Cat had committed an act of such heinous magnitude for the sake of this relationship with Silvia. She had sunk lower than she ever imagined and gone to such a black, bleak place. It still haunts her in the form of jagged, fractured slices of gruesome memory in the many sleepless moments of the night. She often wakes to it. To the persistent thudding truth of it banging away in the pit of her stomach. A red mist descends around the appalling imagery that's branded on her mind, and she packs it away somewhere very deep indeed. Usually. But when Silvia collapsed into a blubbering heap like that, Cat found it offensive. Found it spineless. Found it to be a betrayal. Cat couldn't cope with Silvia being such a snivelling boohoo.

So, she hit her. HARD. A thudding blow to her skull. To shock her out of it, and to show her the price of her betrayal, and to teach her a lesson, and to assert some power. All of these, but mainly the power thing. That was the first of many such times.

Thump. Thump.

And now, in this room, alone with her, and looking at her colourless huge ugly feet, Cat feels an overwhelming urge to hurt her again. To break her toe or punch her hard in the stomach. That would be satisfying. But she can't. The nurses would see.

She stands still.

Low, under her breath, but loud enough for Silvia to hear if she is listening, Cat says, 'Get back here to me, now. Do you hear me, you bitch? NOW! I want to love you. I need to love you. Please. Come on. Come back.'

TWENTY-THREE

Cassie

Tuesday noon

Brave, tenacious, ever-hopeful Cassie is giving it another try. Round three.

When she got home last night and fed Willow, who immediately fell asleep on her lap mid-story, she realized that, however difficult it might be to come into this dreadful room, and sit looking at her mother, Silvia is truly out for the count and won't suddenly sit up and snap at her. It seems that was what she feared the most – a swift, sharp shock with devastating recriminations. Cassie just isn't strong enough to withstand that presently, and any remaining courage she does have needs to be channelled into Willow. After yesterday's visit though, Cassie is reassured that there is no immediate danger around her mother.

How ironic. Silvia is in mortal peril, clinging on to the edge of her life by her fingernails, but Cassie senses no immediate danger.

Cassie stands up and moves closer to the bed so as to look at Silvia's face. Everyone's face looks a bit unfamiliar when they are lying down, she knows that, but Silvia seems to have changed a lot. She is thinner, yes, a little bit. Her skin has the sallowness of sickness about it, as if it has absorbed the shock and is still reeling. The colour of her is all wrong, just as the stillness is. Whatever else Silvia has been in her life, Cassie always remembers her mother as colourful and active. She is a force to be reckoned with. Loud and vital. Not lifeless like this pallid wodge of a person.

Is she even a person any more? Are you a person if you have no visible signs of a personality or a spirit? Perhaps, thinks Cassie. Perhaps you are simply only that, a 'sick person'. Defined by illness. That would be a shame. Her mother has hardly ever been sick, in Cassie's memory. In fact she has spurned sickness at every opportunity. She has always been rigorous about health, barely surrendering a day to feeling ill.

Silvia was as tough with herself as she was with the kids. Told them not to be 'sickly'. Told them it was no good to give in to a 'poorly tummy' or 'poorly head'. Perhaps she will emerge from this a changed person, Cassie thinks. Perhaps that is the purpose of this awful situation. Or maybe Silvia was supposed to be rendered motionless, completely still, so that, for once, she might listen. How ironic then that Cassie cannot bring herself to speak. This is her perfect opportunity, and she doesn't feel able to take it. Not yet anyway.

Cassie looks at her mother's features, reminded that she has often been told they look very alike. In the past, when she was much younger, she took it as a compliment. Firstly, her mother is quite a striking woman, albeit in a big, lumbering way. Secondly, and much more importantly for Cassie since she's had Willow, she loves the fact that she belongs genetically to someone. Undeniably connected. That's the part she marvels at. The actual, physical stuff.

Look at Silvia's hands. Beautiful hands, everyone always says, and also Cassie's hands. Same-shaped fingers, same nails, same ivory skin, freckled and pale. Now, though, there is bruising on Silvia's skin, where needles have been for blood tests and so on, but Cassie can still see the traces of the hands she knows so well. She has held those hands in hers. She has put her small hand in her mother's identical but much bigger hand, to cross a road, or to grasp when getting her BCG injection. Those hands have smoothed her hair when her brother hid her favourite blankie, and she sobbed for three hours.

Cassie even relishes that those hands have whipped her pants down and slapped her bare bottom on a park bench in front of everyone when she was particularly obnoxious. A resounding, cupped smack which left a red welt for a day. Those hands did that. They were instrumental in Cassie learning right from wrong.

They are also the hands that waved her away dismissively four years ago, just when she wanted to hold them so badly, but Cassie tries to reject that memory. She looks at those hands lying so still by her side on the bed. They appear to be sculpted, so elegant and shapely are they. Cassie can see the dent where her mother's wedding ring used to be. A dent that may never disappear. Silvia cannot ever deny her family totally whilst she is marked thus. The groove in her skin is the evidence and the history. Maybe Silvia feels exactly that, dented, by having a family.

Cassie wonders if that was the problem? Did having a husband and two kids slow her up or cramp her freestyle somehow? Did she feel that she had consigned her youth to an ugly, slow death? Or did she feel that her exuberance was being extinguished? Or something like that?

Cassie's head hurts from mulling over the many machinations of her mother's possible thinking. She is exhausted from years of investigating what <u>might</u> be going on. Just one solid reason, however upsetting or personal, would help to end the tortuous conjecture. She has even, in massively insecure moments, imagined that her mother's rejection is due to the colour of Cassie's hair.

Yes, really.

Red, like Mum. Maybe Mum doesn't like the red, despite her endless claims that it makes her 'individual' and 'exotic'. Maybe all that is a sham and Silvia caved in, somewhere along the line, under all the teasing and criticism and shamelessly cruel jibes she must have experienced along the way. Cassie is sure

Silvia would have had all that, because <u>she</u> certainly has, and she is much younger and her generation should surely know better. They don't. They think it's OK to make hair a reason to dislike someone. How is that acceptable in any way? Cassie has found a way to fake joining in or even to initiate the scourge herself so as to seem at home with all the taunting. She is a modern-day Cyrano de Bergerac when it comes to insults about red hair. She knows them all. She has even made up some herself to add to her painful repertoire, a favourite being 'I'm as red as a sore fanny'. That seems to shut folk up.

Willow is red too. She is a small bristling burning bush with bright flamey hair. She is more like Silvia than even Cassie is. All of them are connected but Willow is denied the belonging, just as Cassie is now. Looking at Silvia so lumpen in the bed, Cassie realizes that, unless she can find a way through her hurt quickly, Willow may never meet her grandmother. Cassie knows that this is an acknowledgement to herself of just how critical the situation is.

Silvia might just die. This could be it.

Is she, the spurned daughter, strong enough to build a bridge, on her own, at this very moment? It could be a bridge that doesn't go anywhere. Is it still a bridge if you start building one end but the other end doesn't join on to anything? How unstable would that be? Cassie isn't sure she is strong enough to withstand the familiar toppling effect of no reciprocation, but at least this time it would be for a concrete, tangible reason. Silvia is wholly incapable of participating. It's not, for once, that she won't. It's that she can't.

Cassie leans in close to her mother's face. She can see the open pores of the pasty skin on her nose and forehead. Cassie is thinking so loudly, she feels sure her mother can hear.

She thinks, 'Are you, in effect, dead? And if you were, would I miss you? Not really, I don't think. You don't love me, do you? No. Haven't for years. I've learned how to unlove you back. First of all, you feel the cold then you actually get cold, then you freeze, that's how it works. So there, you dead . . . woman.'

Cassie's mobile strikes up the *Mission: Impossible* ringtone. This means Ben's phone is calling hers. Which means it is probably Willow, who loves to pretend to be grown-up by using her dad's phone to call her mum.

'Hello? Oh, hello darling. Yes, of course it's Mummy. Why? Oh, it's just because I haven't been talking much today, so my voice is probably a bit growly, that's all . . . what, sorry? Oh, well, I'm . . . in a room with a silly old lady who's just being . . . silly. Yes, I'm coming home now sweetheart. I'll be there in time for lunch, yes. Cupcakes for lunch? Oh, OK. Yes. We'll make them as soon as I get there. Banana ones. With noses. In about five hundred and thirty-two counts, OK? Start now. One Mr Octopus, two Mr Octopus, three Mr Octopus . . .'

And Cassie, who loves her daughter, and wants to be with her more than being anywhere else, leaves the room without a backward glance.

TWENTY-FOUR

Tia

Tuesday 2pm

'... and then the big fat sisters come on and she says hi, my name is this name, and her name is that name, and we got bad nylon hoodie tops, and now we singin the big Robin Williams song about the angel with all high bits and low bits so wrong, that Simon Cowhead put his hand up beggin for stop. Why not? It his show. He can stop anytime it hurtin his earlobes. Then he says please go home and do another different job for hell's sake please. Then the big yellow hair one punches the other no teeth one in the face, givin her all blame for it bein soundin bad. Just bang like that, right in her nose face to make all blood come out like a river. My two boys laughin and laughin 'til they nearly do a wee, fall on the carpet, then stand up and one acts like the yellow hair, and one acts like the no teeth, and they do it all again! Then, I am laughing all the time till tiny wee comes out. But husband man, he not laughin now at nothing. Nothin. He just stare at telly, and eat curry.

'Two weeks ago he is laughin sometimes usually at wrong stuff, but least he is laughin a small bit. Now he gone all quiet, no speakin, no lookin in your eyes, just telly watchin and has a face what seen a sad ghost on it. My boys stayin out a lot. They don't like him to see like that. Not like their dad. Like dad who they knew him before, long days ago, but now gone, like they dreamed him. And they stop the friends comin back home now. They stop that. Don't like for friends to see the daddy all sad and staring.

'The doctor come over for see husband again last week. His name spell J-E-S-S but my boys says it say "JIZZ". Dr Jizz. He very kind good man, and he say husband need talking medicine where a head doctor talk at him and tell him how to get happy. He say two ways to do it. First is get it at hospital, wait for six months, or get it at private, do it now. I take do it now, cos husband too sad to wait. And Tia too sad to watch him. But, Mrs Shit, listen up this. It costing Tia eighty pound for each go. Tia laughin when head doctor tellin this money. What?! For talking?! Tia can do that, won't cost even ten pound each time, but this head doctor got an exam at uni so she gets to be a lotta money.'

Tia shuffles in her seat. She has something to say. It's not easy.

'That a lotta money. Eighty pound for one hour of talkin. But the talkin gonna maybe fix husband's head where he sad. Human health is biological and mental, Dr Jizz says. So it worth it. But Mrs Shit, eighty pound. So. OK. Here the deal, OK? Mrs Shit is still owin Tia for this mornin workin at your house. About thirty-six pounds is stolen by you from Tia. So. With that money comin from this week, should make nearly eighty pound. So. Tia look around Mrs Shit house to see what can sell on eBay about eighty pound.

'That a good way to do it because Mrs Shit get rid of "clutter" as well. Clutter evil and get dust on, so good if it goes. So. Tia find a little box under Miss Cat side of bed. Just a little nothin box of wood with metal bits on. I seen some like it in a shop called The Pier in town. Got lots of stuff, all come from near me in Jakarta. One wood box at home, maybe about fifteen pee. Here, seventy pound. Crazy. I can get you better one when I go home. Bigger. The box have all little plastic bags with flour in. Miss Cat forgot it there. Maybe long time. So Tia chuck away the flour and can sell box on eBay, waitin to see who buys. Maybe some nice bitch or good-lookin ballsack might see and like for present? Or for keep rings in? Or pins? Or keys? Would be nice. Very nice. I tell you when it sell good.

'Anyway, hey, some good news for you to put in ears, Katy Perry and Russell Grant split at last! Not good news for marrieds, but good for Katy because Russell Grant a dirty randy wanker my boys say, so she better goin home to the parents who is Christian good people. And David Beckham get voted number one for sexiest man on planet. Hmm. OK, but for me it would be John Nettles. Who would you have? Probably Pat Butcher I think . . . ?'

TWENTY-FIVE

Jo

Wednesday 10am

Jo is in full voice, and horrifically off-key.

'... Birthday, dear Silvia, Happy Birthday to yooooo!'

She is holding a bright pink shop-bought Miss Piggy cake with a single candle sticking straight up out of the very pink snout. There is a number crudely scrawled over Miss Piggy's forehead. '60!' Jo has very obviously added this herself with a blue icing pen.

'Make a wish darling. I know what mine would be. But it's not my birthday. Come on, Sissy, summon everything you've got. And ... blow!'

Jo forms a blowing mouth as if she is expecting Silvia to imitate her, like you do for a small child. Whilst Silvia has been captive and incapacitated, Jo has thought of her as she did when they were kids, as very definitely her younger sister. The baby sister. Something about Silvia being sick and in bed has further confirmed this historic sibling dynamic, and Jo has demonstrated her need to infantilize Silvia over and over again. Jo's needs are many. The overriding one is the desperate longing to be looked up to. Whilst Silvia is out for the count, Jo can freely fantasize about being the capable elder sister. She blows the candle out.

'There! All gone!'

Winnie and some of the other nurses on duty are watching this charade through the internal window. Winnie sucks her teeth in ongoing disbelief at Jo's loud and inappropriate choices.

But worse is to come, as Jo takes a deep cigarette-husky breath and launches into a rousing chorus of, 'For she's a jolly good fellow,' for far too long, ending with an eardrum-wrecking final line of, 'And sooo say aaall of uuss . . .'

The noise is beyond horrible. Jo has never been, and will never be, able to sing. She was the kid who was asked to mime at the school speech-day church service. Not only does she lack any tuning as such, she also has no idea about volume control, so all her glaring mistakes are delivered at full throttle. There is no danger of missing them.

The nurses can hear it all through the thick walls of Suite 5, unfortunately for them, and when it is over, they are tangibly relieved and glad to busy themselves with anything other than Silvia for a moment.

Although Jo didn't organize it this way, it works perfectly

for her that they are all so distracted, for Jo has a plan. Today, on her sister's sixtieth birthday, Jo is going to present her pièce de résistance, her biggest shot yet at waking her poorly sister up. Jo has brought Sgt Craig Lawrence to the hospital.

Craig is sitting next to the nurses' station, on a plastic chair, in a row of four empty chairs where many many anxious people have perched on the edge, waiting for news of beloveds. Plastic chairs infused with raw dread. Craig is twenty-six and his new uniform is chafing him somewhat. Although he knows he must appear composed, he is anything but. All of this is new to him, in fact, and he is desperate to impress. He is of average height and quite stocky, a man who pays attention to his personal grooming, a metrosexual man, no stranger to a five-blade razor and an expensive moisturizer. His face is tight with squeaky-cleanliness and his dark blond with subtle high-lights hair is combed neatly and gelled. His sergeant's hat is nestled in the crook of his arm. He has been told on many occasions that he is handsome, and he can't resist believing it. He has pleasing symmetrical features and large blue eyes, a tribute to both his Scottish and Scandinavian parents.

This is his first visit to a hospital as part of his job and he is sweating profusely. He repeatedly wipes his brow and upper lip. He hopes it is discreet. Policemen aren't supposed to appear nervous. Policemen are in charge. Apparently.

The trolley lady stops on her way past him, and offers him a cup of tea. She doesn't do this typically, and he is acutely aware of that. It's the uniform. It elicits respect and a strange form of gratitude. Perhaps a passing policeman has helped the trolley lady in the past, or delivered her drunken grandson home in the back of his police car from a city-centre brawl, or winked at her when she broke ranks and crossed the street during the May Day carnival? Perhaps. Or maybe she simply remembers the old days when she was young and the mere sight of a bobby patrolling the street made you feel safe.

Whatever it is, she has stopped and given him a cuppa with a shop-brand rich tea biscuit on the side to boot, and as a result he feels a tiny bit important. He likes feeling important. It doesn't happen often. Actually, it doesn't happen ever . . .

Craig has heard the caterwauling from Jo inside Suite 5 and knows that in a moment she will pop out to collect him. He swallows his tepid tea in one gulp and tugs his jacket down to prepare.

Jo is busy scoffing a slice of the Miss Piggy cake and licking her fingers. She is using one of the thick grey paper bowls that are stacked on the shelf above Silvia's monitor, as a plate. Why they are there, she doesn't know. Is it to do with weeing or puking? she wonders. In which case, they are superfluous since Silvia can do neither unassisted. She describes the cake taste so that Silvia might derive a vicarious pleasure from it.

'So, first of all, the icing appears brittle but is in fact soft, more like a sugary wrapping really. The cake itself is like a Madeira cake or, no, more like pound cake. Very yellow, very plain, quite moist. Absolutely no attempt at a cheeky layer of jam or confectioner's custard or cream or anything, which is a tad disappointing, but hey, look at how cheerful the whole Miss Piggy pink face is. DIVINE. One thing I would say though is that, weirdly, when you pop a piece of Miss Piggy cake in your mouth, although you know it's undeniably cake, you can't help it darling, you expect to taste bacon. I'm not sure if I'm glad or disappointed not to. Odd.

'Anyway Sis, it's lovely and I know you would love it. Fancy a bite? Fancy it enough to open your eyes and sit up? Eh? No? OK. Well listen. Big news, exciting news. I have someone here for you to meet and I don't mind telling you darling, this guy is going to change your life. He is a policeman hon, but don't panic, you've done nothing wrong. He has something import-ant to tell you, and I think you might want to wake up to hear it, frankly. Hang on.'

Jo goes to the door and pops her head out to beckon Craig in.

He stands up, picks up his black tote bag, and walks into Suite 5. As he enters, Craig has to catch his breath. He has never seen anyone in a coma before. It's disturbing. Craig fal-ters for a second and stops in his tracks.

Jo has become inured to the shock of it, even after such a short time.

'Come in. Don't worry, it's alright. Think of her as asleep. Now I'm going to stand here ...' Jo positions herself at the internal window, blocking any view into the room from the nurses' station '. . . you just carry on, as you normally would . . . but quietly . . . please . . . yes?'

'Of course . . . just put this down.'

Craig quickly looks around, and goes to the corner of the room where there is a plug point. He puts his bag down, unzips the top and takes out a large ghetto blaster, which he plugs in. He turns the volume way down low, takes a deep breath, puts his hat on, and presses 'play'. The unmistakable if muted first few bass-slapping bars of Tom Jones's 'You Can Leave Your Hat On' start to sound. Craig swaggers to the side of Silvia's bed.

''Ello 'ello 'ello, I believe there's been an incident around these parts, and a laydee has been injured. Well love, my name is Sgt Sirloins, and I need to take down a few particulars . . . right now . . .'

With that, he turns round, bends over and, in the same alarming movement, he whips off his uniform trousers which are Velcroed at the side. It would have been deft if the Velcro wasn't so stubborn at the ankles, where the trousers firmly remain joined. He is wearing a black thong and so, were Silvia to wake up at this moment, which thankfully, of course, she doesn't, her first sight after eight days of unconsciousness, would be of a hairy pimply pale bent-over bum.

Craig quickly straightens up in time to dance to the first lyrics of the song as they start. He gyrates and mimes along.

Baby, take off your coat, real slow.
Baby, take off your shoes, I'll help
You take off your shoes.
Baby, take off your dress, yes yes yes . . .

Craig is following the instructions of the song as best he can. He manages to get the jacket off in time and is pleased with that, so he does extra-sexy pursing of his lips, and plenty of hip thrusts. He prefers the music to be louder, as it covers the huffing and puffing he only now realizes he does whilst getting undressed. He's never noticed that before. Yes, this is definitely slicker and sexier when the music is throbbingly loud.

And when the recipient isn't in a coma, frankly.

He can't bring himself to look at her because he fears the pitiful sight of her might cause his penis to get even smaller than it presently is, which is spectacularly small. If he is performing in a club, he can 'arrange' his manhood just before he goes on stage so that he presents himself at his optimum state. He hasn't been able to do that here. Nothing about the hospital atmosphere has helped him in this respect. Even the deferential cup of tea from the trolley lady has failed to make him feel big enough. He has been unable to tap into his necessary fantasy high self-esteem in this bright neon lighting and antiseptic smell. He has no command over his willy whatsoever.

Which is a shame, since his routine now demands that he

proffer his front to Silvia to show the full force of his jam-packed black thong with the giant cobra's head emblazoned on it. It looks best when it's nice and stretched, but presently the cobra is looking a bit wrinkled and empty. Decidedly unthreatening. You wouldn't be scared if you met that cobra in a desert. In fact, you might take pity on it and either pet it or club it on the head to mercifully put an end to its misery. Craig prays that Jo doesn't clock it too much, in case she decides to deduct anything off his wages for his glaring inadequacy.

> *You can leave your hat on,*
> *You can leave your hat on,*
> *You can leave your hat on . . .*

Unfortunately, as Craig is attempting to leave his hat on but get his shirt and tie off (which he really wants to do soon, because his torso is fairly impressive and may mitigate the effect of his less than perfect penis), he is hampered by the still-attached-to-his-heels trousers. As he has swung round to face Silvia, the pesky trousers are strangling his ankles and pre-venting him from throwing some of his more impressive moves. He tries to kick out wildly with his feet, but fails, and the overall impression is of someone having a fit, which isn't sexy. And sexy is what it's all about.

Frankly, Jo isn't finding the display particularly sexy, but she is definitely unable to look away as more and more of Craig's streaky spray-tanned body is revealed. Jo hasn't been in close quarters with an increasingly naked man like this for some time, and is transfixed. Even the smell of him is fascinating, a sort of zesty lemony sweaty niff, which is presently permeating the room like a determined creeping citrus mist. Maybe the power of that overwhelmingly heady odour alone will jolt Silvia into wakefulness?

Jo, like Craig, longs to turn the music up. This whole exercise seems wrong without loud thudding music. She hasn't seen anything like this before, but she knows that's how it should go. She feels ever so slightly disappointed that he has chosen this very obvious music. *The Full Monty* music. Such a cliché. Silvia wouldn't approve of this choice. Almost anything else would have been preferable. Jo's eyes flick frantically between the curious sight of the now naked Craig – naked, that is, save for the thong, the socks and shoes with trousers attached and, of course, the hat – and Silvia, who is fully clothed for bed, and a hundred per cent staunchly disinterested. Not a jot of any reaction on her face. Nothing. Jo realizes that without the aid of loud music, this endeavour is going to go for nothing, and will have been a total waste of time.

Craig is just getting to his dénouement and if anything is going to rouse Silvia, it would be this moment, but not if Silvia can't hear it. She needs to know her cue to open her eyes if she is going to. It's fast approaching, and Jo can't help herself, she lunges towards the ghetto blaster and whacks the volume up to full fat, just as Craig releases the catch on the side of his underwhelming thong to play his ace, and reveal all. As Jo turns back from her crouched position at the controls of the ghetto blaster, Craig is also mid-turn and mid-reveal.

A thrillingly awful moment occurs when Craig's flaccid penis and Jo's flushed cheek come into brief contact.

'Sorry.'

'Sorry.'

They both shout above the music, awkwardly.

'*You can leave your hat on . . .*' bellows Tom.

Craig loudly joins in with the last sentiment of the song.

The kerfuffle is tangibly chaotic and Winnie is aware of it, even though she is with a different patient in Suite 8. Once again, she speeds down the ward with a low, stealthy grace. Winnie is an NHS Exocet. Especially when Jo is in the building. Winnie is on high alert. She flings open the door of Suite 5 to see a sight she will forever wish she could forget. A naked man, the colour of an old tangerine, scrambling around under Silvia's hospital bed, trying to find his hat.

'Oh dear Lord! Wha'appn 'ere? Jo, what you tinkin? Get dis dyam h'idiot outta here right now. You tink Silvia want dis ya foolishness? Me don't h'even know de awake Silvia, but me know she don't. Nobody do! Look 'pon dis stupid ragamuffin, 'im so orange, 'im a fruit! Wa di blouse 'n' skirt! You in a whole-heapa trouble wid me, Jo. Get 'im gaan!'

Craig frantically tries to gather up his clothes and leave, but the bloody trousers still tugging and lolloping around his ankles torment him and in no time at all, he falls over, like a felled orang-utan, so Tango-ed and lumbering is he.

'Sorry nurse, I just need to . . . sorry . . .'

He flounders about, trying to get up and pack up and get out. Jo has her head in her hands.

'Winnie, I'm so sorry. This isn't what it looks like.'

'Me no know what it look like, me only know what it is. Disrespectful. Das what. Aks yerself why you bring dis bodderation here? Look 'pon dis chaos!'

To Craig's further shame, Winnie picks up the cobra thong which has pinged off and is now dangling on the side guard of Silvia's bed.

'Bwoy! A wa dis?!'

Craig reaches out tentatively to retrieve the offending article.

'It's . . . um . . . my thong . . .'

'I know is what, ya wutless nasty fool. Pick it up an' move yu backside before I box yu face. Ya hear mi now?! I'm serious. Gwaan!'

Craig snatches up the thong, and his other clothes. Jo helps to rip off the obstinate ankle-grabbing Velcro trousers, and assists him to scurry off, which he does, bumbling out of the door, holding the pile of clothes in front of his groin to protect his modesty. The nurses at the desk stifle their giggles. As he runs down the corridor frantically searching for the toilet where he can get dressed, he speeds past the trolley lady who looks on aghast, and has many treasured and long-held values about policemen shattered in a nanosecond.

Back in the room, Jo feverishly yanks the plug of the ghetto blaster out of the wall and, thankfully, the wretched music stops. That is, however, the single positive thing that's happening presently. Winnie is the only person Jo has any real respect for in the hospital, so it is doubly awful that it's the lovely, honourable, hard-working Winnie who is standing at the door with her hard-working hands on her hips glowering angrily at Jo right now. Jo is immediately catapulted back to her childhood when so often she would be the one on the receiving end of the reprimands from her mother, even if both she and her sister were equally culpable. Silvia was always the favourite, seemingly blameless one.

'Right, sidung 'pon dat chair, sista. Yu better start talkin. Gimme some reasons for dis craziness. C'mon.'

Jo sits on the visitor's chair.

Winnie pulls up the other visitor's chair and sits next to her. She is furious with Jo for this ridiculous disruption, but she knows that she won't get any sense out of Jo unless she is gentle, and anyway, Winnie firmly believes that true strength is found in gentleness. So long as she can keep her tongue under control, that is the preferred route, always, for Winnie. It isn't what Winnie has witnessed or experienced herself, inside her own family, apart from her mother, but it is what she knows to be right. Winnie's Christian engine drives her to try and look for the best in other people. She prays that, conversely, this is how others might interact with her, but she fears that life doesn't always work that way. This all helps Winnie to sit with Jo, in the middle of a hectic shift, and hear her reasons without judging her too harshly.

The two women sit side by side at the foot of Silvia's bed and their needs dovetail nicely. Winnie's need to protect Silvia and therefore understand and guide Jo. Jo's need to succeed in waking up her sister, and to face her more real and profound fears. Stuff she doesn't like to think about, or talk about. Stuff that makes Jo recognize the awful truth of feeling so much the lesser for so long. Certainly less than Silvia, and for most of the time, less than almost everyone.

Winnie knows in her relatively few and recent dealings with Jo that this is Jo's truth. All of Jo's behaviour around Silvia points Winnie towards Jo's massive want. Winnie reaches over and covers Jo's hand with hers.

They sit quietly like this for a few moments, snatching a chance to just be. The chaos of the last ten minutes is still ringing in the air of the room, but it gradually quietens into a distant noise, replaced by the more familiar sound of Silvia's assisted breathing. The room is full of the now. Of the critically ill Silvia. The reality of it is tangible and unavoidable.

Jo is the first to speak, and her voice cuts through the sadness of the room like a knife through jelly.

'I am sorry, Winnie. I really am. I thought . . . I don't know . . .

I thought it was kind of a wild thing to do, bit crazy y'know . . . saucy, for her. She would've laughed about it if she was . . . y'know . . . the old Silvia. Would've found it sort of revolting and amusing and, well, it certainly would've got her attention.'

'H'indeed. Yes. Yes. Hmm . . .'

'But obviously it . . . hasn't worked. Nothing works, does it? Nothing I do. Never has, to be honest. All I'm trying to do is to think differently. Come up with something to give her a reason to want to come back . . . y'know.'

'So, sorry, yu tink she purposely unconscious?'

'No, well yes. Well, no, not exactly. All I know is that Sissy is a phenomenally strong person and if anyone could push through and wake up, it would be her. Except that . . . she's very different, these last few years. Very . . . changed. Personally, I blame that awful woman Cat. You've seen her in here, haven't you Winnie? I mean, honestly, what do you think . . .?'

'Not fe mi to say . . . but . . .'

Jo isn't listening really. She is revelling in the fact that someone, anyone, is listening to <u>her</u>. Being the listener herself isn't her bag . . .

'Because I think Sis has made some weird decisions. Well out of character. I mean, she's always been a bit selfish, but to not see the kids, not answer their calls, not even acknowledge Willow, honestly, it's not OK, is it? D'you think?'

'Well, you haffi remember she . . .'

'Personally, I think it's cuntish. Sorry to use that sort of language Winnie, I know you're churchy, but really, it's the only word that'll do. I mean, even if you have hooked up with someone who's obviously very strong-natured, very bossy, and frankly, very weird, _even_ if that's who has a massive strange, bloody inexplicable hold over you, don't you buck against that when it comes to your bloody kids? Don't you?'

'Mi not sure she . . .'

'I mean, come on! She wasn't even speaking to _me_ in the end. Not that it's the end, sorry Sissy, if you can hear me. It definitely isn't the end, that much I bloody know. It can't just be . . . this. It can't.'

'Well, Silvia not so . . .'

'You don't understand. That is my baby sister. I am older than her and it's my job to bloody look after her. Except, of course, she won't bloody let me! As usual. Has to do it her own way. Has to be the bloody winner. Well, well bloody done, Silvia, you are doing it all your own way, bravo! But you know what, in the end, you're not the winner, are you? Because I'm here and you're . . . there!'

Jo stands up.

Winnie keeps hold of her hand to placate her.

'Now den Jo, yu haffi stay calm . . .'

'So _I_ am the winner. Yes, _I_ am the one . . . who's in front . . . for once. _I_ am the one who is . . . alive . . . oh God.'

'Shhh now, come on . . .'

'I don't mean alive. Of course she's alive, you know what I mean. I am the ... longer-lasting one ... everyone always thinks she's the valuable one, she is the one who matters. My name has bloody always been "Silvia'ssisterJo". That's it. All one word. Attached to her. That's why I'm here. To be a connection to her. Well, sorry if I'm not special enough on my own, everyone! Sorry if Jo isn't sufficient! Sorry, dead Mum! Sorry, bloody old stupid Dad! Too drunk to even notice there is an alive daughter. Got a dead wife and a half-dead favourite daughter, sorry Sis, but you are, both favourite and half dead. Yes. So, sorry Dad, if you've got an alive daughter who would quite like a chance to dance on your feet please, or be arms-linked in the street, or share a tawny port with, or be given a big illustrated copy of *Beauty and the Beast* when I have <u>my</u> measles jab. Sorry I'm not enough! You twat!'

'OK. OK ...'

Jo crumples back on to the chair. She cannot staunch her tears. These are tears Jo has refused to allow for a very long time, and so the build-up is quite a considerable reservoir. Jo's whole body shudders as she lets it flow out. This is the kind of crying that really hurts.

Winnie knows it matters, she can see that this isn't part of Jo's typical histrionics, this is real pain. Jo means everything she has said.

And Winnie is right, Jo hasn't filtered any of it through her usual screen of jollity and eccentricity, she has connected, at last, with some long-held feelings of bafflement and outrage about how she was, and maybe still is, perceived inside the family. The difficult memories of her mother's early death, and of how she was left feeling like the reserve-bench mother to the family at age nine. She was slammed into that role far too early. To watch her beloved mother decline so quickly and be eaten up by what she and her sister were told was 'the muscle monster' was agonizing. Even Mummy herself didn't really explain it, and chose to use baby language around the subject of motor neurone disease.

Why? To make light of it? To puncture its power? Well, that didn't work because 'the muscle monster' ate Mummy.

Limb by limb.

Then it took her speech.

Then it took her.

Jo tried to stop it, she rubbed Aqua Manda cream on Mummy and gave her everything from the medicine cupboard she could find. Mummy obligingly took all the cough medicine and laxatives and Germolene in a sort of game where Jo was the nurse. Except it wasn't a game for Jo. It was the difference between life and death. Daddy was getting very drunk and Silvia was busy playing, but Jo was consumed with crippling worry, and stayed indoors, near Mummy at all times, watching her closely and administering all her own solutions.

Of course there were real doctors too, but Mummy was often too tired to remember what they'd said, and Daddy was always elsewhere. Jo once caught him in his study, crying. It was so strange and frightening to see. Jo decided then and there that she would have to be in charge, so that's what she did, she charged at life headlong from that precise moment onward. She might now recall those very frightening times and have to see and feel it all again.

Here she is. In a room with another beloved, who might just . . . die . . . like Mummy went and did.

Jo had to do a speedy fast-forward through her childhood when that happened, but of course, something in her remains staunchly, defiantly, nine years old, even now, demanding to be responsibility-free. Nine years old. That is the state Jo longs for.

She feels as if she didn't get enough of it then, so she lives it now, off and on. She is profoundly nine years old in a parallel, hidden life that lives simultaneously alongside her 63-year-old present life. Usually, she can juggle the two successfully, but in this moment, where her sister is gravely ill, which Jo inexplicably regards as her own fault, she has trouble differentiating between the two. Old, confused memories flood back, and all Jo knows is that she must, must try to save Silvia.

As Mummy was floating away, when she couldn't even speak properly any more, she used to repeatedly point at the then six-year-old Silvia playing in the garden, and then point at Jo to indicate she must take care of her little sister. Mummy obviously knew that Daddy wouldn't manage it very well. Jo would whisper again and again, 'Don't worry, Mummy, I will look after her. I will,' and she would watch Mummy visibly relaxing. It was so clearly a huge comfort. The promise was made, and Jo kept it as best she could after Mummy died.

For three or four years, Jo looked after Sissy while Daddy fell apart. He wanted to care properly for them but he just couldn't, and when his drunkenness and his loud grief became too much for them, they were sent to live with their paternal grandmother until Jo had eventually got a job in a small bohemian boutique, and was allowed to live in the poky flat above it. That's when she brought Silvia with her, and encouraged her through school and uni, to broaden her horizons. Jo persuaded Silvia to study, and travel and read, although Jo had very little time to do any of those things herself.

All that care. All that nurturing. And look at her now. Jo has failed. She has let Silvia down and she has let Mummy down, and she feels wretched. In the torrent of tears is a small stream that is purely those of nine-year-old Jo.

Winnie puts a loving arm around her and offers a tissue from the pack she keeps in her regulation uniform pocket for just such an occasion.

Jo blubs, 'Thanks for all your advice Winnie. You've certainly helped a lot. I won't forget what you've said. And, again, sorry. I was just, trying . . . to . . .'

'Yes, yes child. I know. It all OK. Jus' forget it now, yes?'

'Yes. Yes. Sorry. Yes.'

'And no more nonsense, yu hear mi now?!'

'No more, no. Only one thing I thought might help. Not help her wake up or anything, not wake up, I don't think I mean that, I just thought it might help if I brought Dad in. She hasn't spoken to him for about forty-five years. What d'you think?'

'Well, hmm, mi tink that would . . .'

'Yeh, I thought so. Thanks Winnie. For everything. I'll be back soon. God, you are so . . .' Jo points to her head and to her heart '. . . you really are. Amazing. See ya!'

And she is gone.

TWENTY-SIX

Ed

Wednesday noon

Ed is on the visitor's chair. He is mid-flow about his favourite subject and stroking a carved wooden circle he is clutching in his hand.

'I mean, you'd think a tree would just be there, fulfilling its usefulness and sort of y'know, doing what it's told in terms of growing, but beech is a misfit. It's like the misbehaver in the tree family. It's unpredictable and surprising. Capricious. That's a lovely word, isn't it Silv? Wonder if people in Capri are capricious? But that's exactly what beech is. Moody and idiosyncratic, because they can appear to be big and showy and ... commanding, but quite honestly, at the drop of a hat they can just give up and fall over, unlike so many other trees which are, let's face it, sort of generally seen as monuments to solidarity and longevity. Like giant wooden anchors that secure us to the past. So this big old matron just ... went crazy and uprooted herself. It's not as if the weather was really even to blame, I think she just decided to . . . collapse. Bloody drama queen.

'Anyway, it gave me a good excuse to chop up some firewood and I decided to bring you this today, on your sixtieth birthday. To be honest, Silv, I was going to carve it into a heart shape, but then I thought, no, that will give completely the wrong impression, and I know you hate mushy stuff, so I have left it a circle. Which seems more apt somehow.

'We may not be directly connected by the heart any more, so to speak, but we are still bound in the same circle, kinda, with the kids and everything. It's to represent how sort of concentric it all is, y'know life, relationships, trees. It all makes sense to me. I love all these circles.'

He looks down at the wood, scrutinizing it.

'They are connected but separate if you know what I mean. One inside the other. And. I think, looking at the trunk of this lazy ol' dame of a tree, she was about sixty. So. There. A sixty-year-old circle, for a sixty year old. Happy wooden birthday Silv.'

He lays the thick disc of wood on the bed above her stomach. It looks oddly as if Silvia has died when it lies there. Why? Too stately or something. He removes it immediately and places it under her hand gently, so that her fingertips are touching it. All he knows is that this is what he would want if it were him in that bed. And that's the best he can do.

He stands, and starts slow rhythmic pacing around the

room. He is familiar with how many steps wide, and how many steps long the room is. He can't get around it completely, because of the bedhead being up against the wall, and various free-standing machines and a cupboard prevent him from encompassing the boundary. That's what he would like to do. Yes, he would like to beat the bounds of this room. Understand the extent and the limitations of it, meanwhile marking a protective parameter he could be the custodian of.

His instinct to safeguard is key for Ed. He tried to do that in his family and he feels he failed. He most certainly does it in his wood, every day. He literally patrols the borders of his land to check for damage or intrusion before walking back into the heart of the wood to double-check all is in order. He is the keeper, and he takes it extremely seriously. He is also a creature of habit, or has become so. He finds routine comforting. He seeks out any opportunity for reassurance. On his daily round of checks, he circumnavigates his forest in ever-decreasing circles so as not to miss anything. It's an effective way of searching thoroughly, and observing detail. Lots of animals do it like that. So does Ed. He carried out his custodial duties just like that this very morning.

At the end of his patrol, every day, he finds himself at the very centre of his wood, at the queen beech where he and Silvia once pledged their love and where he tried to end himself. This is his nucleus. This is where he stops, he rests and he is positively charged, so that he can cope with everything else going on in his life without flipping into massive anxiety about his many inadequacies. It's Mother Nature's Prozac, and he has a serious habit.

This morning, when he sat under the huge flourishing queen tree looking up at her dense crown, he was taken with a sudden consuming feeling of abject loneliness. It was a familiar gut wrench for him. He didn't experience it with all the attendant horror of before but it tugged at him nevertheless. Yep. He can confirm with absolute surety, that he is most certainly a profoundly lonely man.

He stops pacing. He sits down. He dives right into the centre of his thinking, with no introduction.

'Don't take this the wrong way Silv, but I see now that I didn't know what lonely was 'til I married you. That sounds awful. It is awful. It was awful. I don't mean that I had never been alone, that's completely different. Solitude is fine, being alone is fine. Being lonely is not. I came to that marriage with you, prepared to do anything it took to make you happy. Truly. I know that sounds wanky and self-pitying now, but honestly, that is the bloody truth. I was naive, in love and ... open to anything.

'I know I can be a tosser, I worry too much and I'm a bit needy. Yes, I know that. BUT. Something I know now, that I didn't know then, is this. You are the lonely one. You came to the marriage drenched in it, and I didn't see it. I just kept trying to fix you, any way I could think of. But nothing was ever going to fix it Silv, was it, because by then, all those years after your mum died and your hopeless, selfish dad did everything to cut off from you, it wasn't just that you felt a loneliness somewhere inside, it was that you were and still are, MADE of it. Made of loneliness.

'It has shaped everything about you. Even the things I was perversely drawn to – your feistiness and your opinionated confidence. All of these things about you have loneliness as the main ingredient. Perpetual, howling loneliness. Which you were driven to share. Thanks. And y'know what Silv, the cruellest loneliness I felt was when you started to refuse to communicate with me. Doing exactly what your bloody father did to you. Stepping away from me, and never explaining it. A gradual slowing of the drip drip. A tourniquet. Drip ... nothing ... drip ... nothing ... nothing ... nothing. Slow slide into emotional poverty. Until, one day, I realized that there was no flow left. It was entirely blocked, utterly strangled from your side. I was left on my side to carry the heaviness of that particularly rampant infection of loneliness.

'Unlike you, I had no previous form with it, no process to deal with it, so it nearly finished me off. But guess what Silv, I've got beechwood in my sap, and beech flourish on thin, acid soils. They challenge the soil, the weather, the planting, all of it and they bloody prevail. Look at me, I've even got the bloody trunk of a beech now. Yep, got the bloody girth, indeed, but also got the plasticity to adapt and respond to the space I've got around me to live in. In fact, I will shape the space around me. And that's what I've done. I've put everything I love and trust around me to help me. Nourish me. The wood. The kids. Willow. They are my medicine to fight off the disease of loneliness you infected me with.

'I am doing that. I know I am. I'm winning. I just have to work out who Ed is, who the actual bloke is that I am. I have to coppice myself 'til I can grow back nice and thick. Ha. I have put myself in the centre of my wood, under the shade of that big ol' queen, but I need to see some sunshine soon myself, I really do . . .'

Instinctively, Ed stands up and walks to the window where he can still catch a few rays on his face if he stands on his tiptoes and tilts his face towards it. So little sun comes into the quad below. The light on his face is lovely.

'There is one advantage to loneliness though, Silv. It lends a very particular kind of beauty to everything. You so desperately need to see beauty to mitigate all the shitty stuff, so what happens is, the trees are greener, the sun is warmer, and bread tastes breadier than it ever did when I thought I was happy and not lonely. It's like the world is inviting me to come out to play, so it's got its best bloody jacket on. It does look amazing I must say. Not this, not this bloody awful empty yard down here where the sun doesn't get a chance, but <u>my</u> world out there. It's phenomenal really.

'I've just got to find the . . . courage is it? . . . or confidence or something. Yeah. It's all waiting for me, but I'm still holding back. Why? Why am I? I still feel empty, that's why, I think. Haven't found my balance yet, not completely. I can see a chance, I can see opportunities but I haven't quite got the balls yet. I am stabilized, my roots are down. I just need to . . . . decide that I am capable of . . . triumph. Deserving of it . . . and I'm not there yet. I am faking it to make it at the moment, which is OK, but . . . I dunno . . . I have huge plunges into solid bloody doubt. And. It really pisses me off . . . because I want to be . . . better . . . Yep . . . I want to be a better, much better man . . . than this . . . damn.'

Ed feels a sting of tears behind his eyes. He doesn't want it. He knows that if he gives in to it, he will be uprooted for days. He takes ages to recover when he gives in to these difficult truths. He prefers to live in an emotional limbo where he circles his difficult stuff. The landing on it all is very bumpy for him.

At this very crucial moment, he decides to leave Suite 5, and get back into fresh air, get back to work in the wood. He sweeps up his coat.

'So anyway, I'm off now Silv. Sorry to rant on. No actually, I'm not sorry. Some things just have to be said in the end, I think. And it helps me to work it all out. So. That's me done for today. Bye love.'

He feels a powerful interior wobble as he opens the door to leave, but one he can cope with, rather than one that renders him jelly. One thing he knows for sure is that he is a lighter man than the one who came into the room today. Only a tiny bit lighter, but . . .

As he steps outside, he nods to the nurses' station where Winnie is sitting and she smiles back at him.

If Silvia could sit up in her bed and look out of the internal window she would witness something very small but very significant. This is what she would see. She would see Ed nodding at Winnie, but still moving. He doesn't want to stop for fear of exposing his current emotional crumbliness. Winnie smiles and watches him move by, but her eagle eye has clocked his wobble, and she rises up instantly to catch him up. She walks by his side for a few steps, 'til he slows down to a stop and turns to talk to her.

It looks from here like he is speaking quietly and honestly to her. She is nodding because she really is understanding. For the second time in as many hours, Winnie is listening, and because she hears him, Ed can talk. He can tell her some of what he has just had the courage to tell Silvia, and by saying it again, his load is massively lessened and his truth is affirmed. Winnie is a safe port. She places her hand on his arm. He places his hand on her hand and continues to get lighter and even lighter.

That's what Silvia would see.

TWENTY-SEVEN

Cat

Wednesday 2pm

Cat is placing Silvia's birthday card on the shelf next to the ugly grey paper bowls and beneath the poster of Connemara. On the front of the card, there are two enormously fat old ladies sitting on a bench side by side, watching a bowls match, with the sentiment underneath, 'Edna and Wendy rave on'.

It's not funny or silly enough to be good. It's a cheap copy of those picture cards that actually can be quite funny, which Cat hurriedly picked up in the hospital shop. She stood by the till in the shop and scrawled 'Happy 60th Birthday Silly, from your partner . . . in crime . . . xx' inside, licked the envelope and stuck it down, brought it upstairs and immediately opened it when she arrived in Suite 5, with the gum still wet on the back.

'Ooh, who's this one from?' she pretended badly as she opened it. 'Ha ha ha, it's hilarious. Two fat old ladies on a bench.

"Edna and Wendy rave on". That'll be us one day Sil, so it will. If you ever bloody wake up. And one day, Silly, I will sign a card to you on your birthday which will say on the front "To My Wife" or "To The One I Love", and you will happily let me do that because you will happily be with me. Wouldn't that be just great? Yes it would . . . It surely would . . .'

Cat is gabbling and fractious. She has been increasingly unable to disguise her panic in the last week. She is a woman with a knapsack full of secrets and hidden stuff, and that knapsack is very very heavy right now. She can't afford for the straps to break, and she is having to fake walking straight ahead without any of the heaviness weighing her down. At the same time, she is juggling the genuine heartache and immense frustration she is feeling about Silvia being so incapacitated.

Cat is not good at ordering her mental chaos. She never was. Then life became very messy indeed, and she had to force herself to stay calm and cover up. She only just managed this with Silvia's help, but now she feels cut adrift from her anchor and she is experiencing a terrifying whirlpool.

'That's right. Yes. That's right. Lovely funny card. On your birthday. Sixtieth birthday. Wooh! Sixty! You don't look it hon . . .'

She does. Silvia looks dreadful. Cat takes swift sidelong glances at her, almost too afraid to dwell and notice too much. The grey roots of her dyed hair are longer, more pronounced. She is very pale indeed. She has no eyebrows now. No one has bothered to paint them on. She has no lipstick on her dry thin lips. She looks older and sicker and more helpless and therefore hideous to Cat. It's more than a woman with such a pronounced clinical absence of empathy can bear.

Cat is falling apart. She has missed work at the surgery this morning. She called in to the practice and faked a pathetic sore-throat voice to the receptionist to explain that she wouldn't be in.

'Hello Kay,' she rasped, 'don't know if you can tell, but I've landed myself a shockin' dose of pharyngitis. M'throat feels like someone's had a scourer to it. I'd best not come in while I'm infectious. Can you make sure I'm covered? Thanks.'

Cough. Cough. Fake cough.

When she was mid-lie, she suddenly had a flashback to her young, teen self doing exactly the same thing, to skive off lessons, except now of course, she's much better at it. Even back then, at school, she felt justified about the lying, because she didn't need to be there, she could pass exams easily without attending much.

She is brighter than most people. Academically brighter, that is, that stuff is easy-peasy. Emotionally, spiritually, intrapersonally? In these areas, Cat is utterly stunted. Ask any of her patients and they will know an extremely effective medical machine of a person, efficient and diligent. They feel safe around her, trust her totally.

Ask Silvia, and she will know a doubting, childlike, volatile, incendiary person, who often breaks into displays of roaring aggression. Someone who, when detonated, could explode the universe they inhabit along with everyone who happens to be unlucky enough to be in the vicinity. Cat is a woman with little to no hold on her temper, and hell, does she have one. Her temper is the portal to profound furies she has, as yet, only ever plumbed twice.

The night she murdered Philip.

And the evening she fought with, and then shoved Silvia off the balcony.

But then, once you have killed someone, in cold blood, a scuffle on a balcony is as nothing. Not that she intended for Silvia to fall, she didn't. She needs and 'loves' Silvia very much. But she, yet again, lost contact with her inner core of reason-ableness for a few minutes, and a mammoth violent fury was unleashed. In these rare moments, a red mist descends upon Cat's brain and anger is all. There is absolutely nothing else. Just rage. What was it even all about? Cat doesn't want to recall, but begrudgingly, she does.

Silvia was out on the balcony, smoking. Right there was the first irritation for Cat. Cat is a GP. She doesn't smoke because she has witnessed the gruesome consequences time and time again amongst her patients. Hundreds of diminished, cough-ing grey people made entirely of smoke and cancer come through her surgery doors. She has a nose for it now. She diagnoses in seconds. It's a curse of sorts. 'Hello Mr Wilkins,' she says aloud. Inside, she clicks into her internal scanner, 'Hello Mr Wilkins, advanced adenocarcinoma, non-small cell lung, sternum and lymph, about eight weeks top.'

It's like a wine taster. They eventually know which vine, which side of the valley, which vineyard. Sometimes, which picker. Cat instinctively knows stuff she wished she didn't, so consequently smoking is a habit she abhors. She knows how it claims its victims and she doesn't wish to witness that with Silvia. Silvia, however, is stubborn and ferociously independent, has always smoked since she was fourteen, and is not prepared to pack it in. Not now, of all times. Silvia has enough stress to deal with. Smoking helps. Besides which, Silvia has sacrificed so much else for Cat, the smoking is a step too far. She holds on tight to that. She has relinquished the big stuff. The small stuff, she guards.

Cat reprimanded her in no uncertain terms.

'Silly, I just can't witness you slowly killin' yerself right in front of me very eyes like this every day. It disgusts me so it does . . .'

Whilst being treated like a naughty child, Silvia retreated into pure petulance for her sulky response.

'Well, don't look then.'

'How extremely adult of you.'

Cat's sarcasm further fuelled the argument rocket.

'Put the fag out now, and come inside, its feckin' freezing out here.'

'No! I bloody won't! Go away Cat, and shut up. I can't bloody bear the sight of you!'

And with that, Silvia sealed her fate.

Silvia had been drinking sea breezes and, as always, she had become extremely maudlin, rehashing all kinds of difficult matters in her head. The alcohol induced a mixture of courage and insensible stupidity in Silvia. She wanted to talk about so many sensitive issues, but she always knew there could be a cost for provoking Cat.

Who else could she talk to? With time and stealth, Cat has isolated Silvia from virtually everyone who cares about her. It wasn't so much that Cat insisted on the separations, it was more that Silvia knew they would be in everyone's best interests, so she submitted to their extraordinarily secluded life together. Silvia could sometimes barely believe she had surrendered so entirely, but in actual fact, like most of the ugly awkward stuff of life, it had happened in spurts of drama interspersed with great swathes of ordinary, harmful, flowing time which incrementally caused the great unjoinings, until now, when Silvia realized just how unconnected she is.

Silvia could not tell about what happened with Philip. That would be the end of everything. It would be the biggest betrayal of Cat. It would all be . . . over.

Besides which, Silvia hadn't been there when it happened.

Cat came to Silvia one evening, five years ago, when Silvia was still with Ed, and sat at their kitchen table, drinking Chablis and chatting for all the world as if nothing were even slightly amiss. She was good at lying, good at covering up. She was already in giant love with Silvia and Silvia could feel her closing in. Despite her cool, controlled exterior, Cat is an obsessive possessive creature and wasn't going to stop at anything in her pursuit of Silvia. Back then, Silvia couldn't imagine for a moment how dangerous Cat's intentions might turn out to be. She always felt so sorry for Cat living with such a cold, rude man. The more Silvia knew of him, the warmer she felt towards Cat. So, Silvia, the otherwise emotionally rather awkward woman, discovered she could nurture. But nothing she did was ever going to be enough. Cat wanted EVERYTHING Silvia could offer, then much more.

Cat saw Silvia and her obsession with her as a vital chance to get away from Philip. She did indeed try the simplest route, by telling him she loved Silvia and wanted to go, but that was when Philip turned even uglier and threatened to fabricate all sorts of lies, and have her sectioned. Make sure everyone would know of her dangerous mental illness. Silvia was outraged when Cat told her about these threats back then. Cat told her in hushed quiet private moments, away from Ed.

If Silvia was conscious, now, perhaps she might take a moment to reflect on what Philip always accused Cat of. Philip was unquestionably a controlling bully of a man. A total arse and a snob. But. Perhaps Philip knew something more of what is at the core of Cat, and being a total bastard doesn't necessarily mean you are wrong about everything. Does it? Perhaps Philip knew Cat walked the thin line between sanity and crazy oftentimes.

Silvia gradually came to know it the closer she drew to the predatory and unhinged Cat. Slowly, throughout their time together, Silvia would witness more and more of Cat's complicated relationship with her own mind. Far from being measured and sensible, Cat flirted with outer extremes of thinking. Perversely, Silvia found it quite exciting to begin with. She was flattered by the attention, and she found the secrecy thrilling. Not just the clandestine nature of the relationship, but the hidden elements of the actual woman. Cat was not what she seemed. Ed was. Ed was exactly what it said on the tin. Reliable and steady, and ... yes ... dull. Even Silvia's kids were a bit predictable. They were exactly what kids were supposed to be, endearing and funny and sweet and naughty.

Silvia found herself confessing to Cat back then, when she was just a patient.

'Ed and the kids, they're great and everything, but they're just so ... cripplingly ... normal. I can't help it Cat, I find the day-to-day stuff of family life completely suffocating. I live in a coffin of it, I die a bit each day in it. I know it sounds awful, I should be grateful really, but it's all so supremely predictable.

Where's the excitement? I just can't fake being interested in Pokémon or Postman Pat any more . . . Oh God.'

So, when Cat came along and started to pay lots of attention to the flattery-starved Silvia, she caved in easily.

She also liked the fact that in her situation with Cat, she held the power because she was the loved one. Or so she thought. That power would bounce wildly around inside the relationship like a cricket ball that's been tampered with. It depended entirely on Cat's needs, and Cat's moods. And. Over and above all of the extreme outer edges of Cat's behaviour was the other key, deadly element. Cat was, and still is, in the grip of a demanding menace. Unfortunately, Cat O'Brien is the humble servant of a greedy mistress. Cocaine. And there couldn't be a less suitable person for the post.

Cat has spent the morning turning Silvia's flat upside down, looking for the box she keeps under the bed with her supply in. She is fuming that it is missing, and because it is missing, Cat is unravelling, experiencing a shaky sniffy flu. She is presently in the throes of a paranoia so pronounced, she could believe that the comatose Silvia has somehow purposely hidden her stash, as indeed she has promised to many times before. Cat's tenuous link to any inner calm is under severe pressure.

She doesn't like to admit to the scale of this dependency. She can't; she is a successful GP, a respected upright member of society, it would be unthinkable for her to allow herself to know just how much she wants that drug. As far as she is concerned, it's a bit of fun at the weekends, a buzz, a lark. It doesn't interfere with her work in any way whatsoever. She is in charge of it, she is the boss, and it's all harmless. In fact, it's a bit exotic if anything. A little bit cool. Like she believes other people's lives might be, that aren't hers.

Her life is muddled and complicated. She has to spend a lot of time suppressing thoughts of what happened with Philip. How she sedated him with diazepam crushed up in his porridge, so easy to mask the taste with maple syrup and hot milk. How she watched him gradually get drowsy and limp. How she injected him with an alarming amount of diamorphine hydrochloride. Heroin. One whole gram. A drug she was easily able to obtain, since she is the one at the surgery in charge of returning unused drugs, and this was the pain relief quota for a patient with terminal bowel cancer who had died a month ago. His family handed her the surplus drugs, for her to dispose of safely. Cat would order in, and Cat would do the returns, so in effect she could control how much diamorphine she could cream off.

She'd never done such a thing before, and she didn't intend to ever again, but at the particular moment she took it, she had no conscience whatsoever. In fact, quite the opposite. She was choosing a method of death for Philip which was relatively painless. Ever the conscientious medic, she didn't elect to torture him with a slow, sentient death. That would be morally corrupt. She gave him, instead, a woozy slide into unconsciousness and a quick tip off the edge of life. Merciful, clean and neat. Somewhere in Cat's perverse field of logic, that was the noble and correct thing to do. Despite his unkind treatment of her and all his horrific threats.

The only, tiny moment of hesitation she experienced was when she was drawing up the syringe. Her natural medical instinct to get doses correct kicked in for a nanosecond until she remembered with a jolt that, on this occasion, she wasn't looking to save life or relieve pain. She was killing. It was a matter of switching into her cold, robotic other self to do it.

Once done, she sat back and watched him. He jerked and spasmed a couple of times as his body acknowledged the murderer coursing through his veins. He looked at her occasionally with his trancey eyes, although she felt sure he wasn't seeing her clearly. She was amazed at how calm she was. It wasn't hard to watch him die. She felt detached from it all. Quite numb. If Cat had to analyse her own pathology at this crucial moment, she would certainly tag it as psychotic. But Cat didn't allow herself to investigate it. She is supremely skilled at sidestepping anything that will force her to confront her terrifying, malevolent self. She doesn't visit that voluntarily.

When, eventually, Philip was dead, Cat sat for another whole hour looking at him. She wanted to be absolutely sure he was gone, and there was something about sitting quietly like this, together, that felt oddly respectful, as if she was acknowledging his passing with a reverent grace. The way you should when someone dies. Cat saw no reason to disrespect him in this very personal moment.

Perhaps it also helped to make her feel polite. After all, it would be difficult to equate 'polite' with 'cold-blooded killer', wouldn't it? Murderers are evil bad people who belong in prison so that the rest of us can feel safe. Cat isn't that. She is an upstanding contributing member of society, valued and respected by her community. And polite. Very polite. She's not a murderer. Like murderers are. Most certainly not. She detaches herself from that label. Gives it no power whatsoever.

So, on that dreadful difficult day, the non-murderer rolled her warm dead husband into a big old tent bag, zipped it up, fastened the clips on the sides and lugged it into the back of her estate car parked in their garage, and drove over to Silvia's house where she sat at the family kitchen table and drank Chablis with Silvia and Ed.

Eventually, when Ed went off to bed and left the two women alone, Cat took a deep breath and told Silvia what she had done. Silvia was already a little bit drunk, and to begin with, she just couldn't believe it. She even laughed.

'You're joking Cat. Stop it. I know you're joking. Please say it's a big fat joke. Darling. Come on. Seriously. Please. Cat. Please.'

Cat watched Silvia sober up very quickly until they were both speaking in rushed hushed tones the way you do when something is horribly true, and shockingly urgent. The way you do when a murder has just happened . . .

Silvia was confronted with a fait accompli.

It was done. Cat had killed Philip. Philip's body was in the boot of Cat's car.

Silvia felt sick. Sick that it had happened, that Cat had made it happen, that Cat had made it happen in such a pre-meditated way, and that Cat's eyes were so ablaze with it all as she was recounting it to Silvia. Whilst Silvia listened to the telling, which was chillingly calm, except for that small give-away fire in Cat's eyes, Silvia's stomach lurched. Then her head became uncomfortably tight on her skull, then she started to taste acid in her throat. It was the clunking realization that she was about to make a colossal life-changing decision.

If she kept Cat's awful secret at this point, she would be leaping into the dangerous darkness where Cat lives, along with her. There would be no return from there. She would be inextricably part of it. Actually, she already was. Five minutes before, Silvia had been utterly innocent, she had no know-ledge of this horror, and now, five minutes later, she is in it with Cat. She is colluding by even hearing it all. It's all so very weird and menacing and dreadful and yet she is drawn. She wants to be, longs to be complicit.

Silvia can feel the sinister change in light on her soul as she moves further into the shadow of death. In an unbelievable

222

moment from which she would never recover, she has a life-altering lapse of judgement.

She doesn't waver.

She doesn't hesitate.

Silvia says, 'Shh now. Listen. This is what we do . . .'

We. They are 'we'.

And that's it.

In a careless trice, Silvia betrays everyone else but Cat. She makes the most foolish decision of her lifetime, and consequently, she loses her family. In that tipping second, the splitting starts, because that's when Silvia jumps into a deep murky pool where she knows her children can NEVER be permitted to swim. She makes the decision, without fully knowing it then, that she must separate from them. To save them. Never ever must her family be embroiled in this filthy fucked-up mess.

On top of Cat's unhinged, volatile state of mind which has resulted in this deadly mire, there is also the glaring nightmare of her addiction. Glaring because that's what Silvia also saw in her eyes that night. The whole sorry mess had happened whilst Cat was buzzing, high as a kite and as confident as a queen.

Silvia doesn't like anything about the drug. She was shocked when she first saw Cat sniff a couple of lines. She felt as if she was watching a cheap Hollywood film. This didn't happen in her life. She had eaten some cannabis cake in Amsterdam with Ed once, managed to get run over by a cyclist, followed by a huge dose of explosive diarrhoea the next morning, so pretty much decided not to repeat the experience. That's how racy Silvia's life had been, drug-wise. Of course, Cat didn't display her relationship with cocaine for some time. She kept it furtive, where it belonged. In toilets, in cars, in carefully locked rooms, and she managed to keep the full knowledge of her ever-increasing love affair with it from even herself.

In the same way that Cat could disconnect from any difficult or awkward experiences in her life, she was and is alarmingly able to unplug from reality when she chooses. This trait leaves Cat unfixed very often. Adrift. Available to danger. And Silvia didn't want THAT available to her kids.

She and Cat have argued many times about it. Silvia has pleaded with Cat to give it up. Cat has even promised to, in more emotional moments. She claims, when she is high, that she can kick it. When she is the inevitable depressed opposite a day later, she is gripped by her need and can't envisage her life without it to bolster her. The toxic mix of shame, guilt and desire is Cat's familiar luggage. Nothing Silvia feels or says will change it. Cat even loves how slim she gets to stay as long as coke is her chum, forever suppressing her appetite and quickening her heartbeat. Always boosting her confidence and giving her a lovely, reliable, immediate burst of euphoria.

Cat is ultimately only ever going to be interested in Cat, first and foremost, and so her faithful Colombian compadre is the perfect complement to her bruised ego. Her arse-licking chum. Sniff. Charlie. Blow. White. Coke. She chooses to call it 'Mr Charlie', it enables her to minimize her habit, and regard it as harmless and colloquial. Not at all dirty or bad. Cat wouldn't want to be regarded as a hypocrite. Cocaine isn't a bad habit in the same way that smoking is. Smoking is what Silvia does, and it's awful. Cocaine is what Cat does, and it's fun.

So, on the night of Philip's death, when Silvia said, 'This is what we do,' Cat listened. She listened for two reasons. Firstly, Silvia would indeed know what to do, and secondly, Silvia said 'we' and Cat knew then that they would be inextricably linked from then on, and that is what she has always wanted.

Silvia knew where they could drive to, very close by, they took spades and they dug and dug. It was back-breaking. It took ages. Not a shallow grave, but a fairly deep one. The hole wasn't quite long enough when the sun started to come up, so they doubled Philip's body over and pushed it in. He was buried as he was born, in the foetal position. The two women worked like navvies and filled it in, covered it over and stood panting and sweating on top of him, treading in the soil among this dense thicket of trees as the dawn chorus started up.

Cat drove Silvia home. They sat in silence in Silvia's street, side by side, thinking about the strange night. They clasped each other and hurriedly kissed before Silvia scuttled into her home, stripped off her clothes which she stuffed into a black bin liner, showered and slipped into bed alongside the deeply deeply asleep trusty old Ed. Silvia lay still, hearing his snuffles and knowing that this marriage was now over. Ed and the kids must not be anywhere near the ugly chaos. Lying there in the dark, frantically thinking, thinking, she was struck by the lightning realization that she would, at this moment, give anything to turn back time and re-establish herself in the bosom of her boring, predictable family. Her wonderfully normal husband and kids.

What on earth had she done? She could physically feel the dread spreading in her body like poison.

When they all woke up, it would be new and different. She would have to protect them.

By rejecting them.

It was going to be appalling.

In Suite 5, Cat is fraught and fidgeting. Her comedown is dismal. She is extra irritated by the fact that, because she is a GP, she travels some distance to buy her drug, to be sure she isn't recognized. She had already spent a great deal of money, and travelled a long way, all for nothing because she can't find the bloody box. Which she clearly remembers leaving under the bloody bed. Bloody hell.

'For God's sake, Sil. I mean, it's not that I can't cope without Mr Charlie, a'course I can, just not at the moment with every-

226

one asking me all this useless bloody stuff. Endless questions. About Philip. About you. It helps me to think straight. Feck's sake – do they really think I wanted you like this? I didn't. I so definitely didn't. You ... just ... pissed me off, Sil. You know you did. Sometimes you do that. Especially when you're drunk. Why do you do that? I've told you not to. I've told you not to smoke, and you still do. I've told you not to constantly rehash old unimportant stuff. You know it's not good ... for me ... to do that. And you persisted. You knew what you were doin'. You know I hate it if you are upset. I hate cryin'. It's so ... bloody hideous. You knew you were pushin' me, so you did ...'

Cat is sweating now, and thumping her left fist into the palm of her right hand as her irritability moves up a notch. The beginnings of the red mist are starting to descend.

'If they all knew what you're like, honestly, they would see ... you know how to wind me up, sure you do. You're so ... bloody ... disappointin', Silvia.'

This said with hissing on both the words 'disappointin'' and 'Silvia'. Cat is allowing the venomous serpent in her to emerge.

'And that was it for me, when you called me a "Hoodoo". How dare you? You are the one who's brought me the bad luck, woman, not the other way round. Everythin' was ... under control 'til you came along. Who do you think you are? I have lost everythin' because of you. All for you. You. You. You. You selfish ...'

Cat tails off, trying to keep her voice down, and desperately

227

attempting to steer a steady course in very choppy seas. She is listing badly. She is taking on water at an alarming rate and she has no ballast whatsoever. Silvia is the ballast. And she is just lying there, being pointless. Fit for nothing. A broken bilge pump.

'You've got the backbone of a banana, you useless eejit. Well listen, the fact is, if any of it comes out, have no doubt hon, I will be blaming you. What're you gonna do about it, eh? Everyone knows what a bossy control freak you are. I have been under your influence for years. That's what I'll say. Hear me? Christ ...'

Cat scrabbles around in her handbag, checking again if there might be any possible remnant of old Mr Charlie lying about in the bottom somewhere, amongst the Polos and hair-brush and coins and tissues. She licks her finger and dabs around in the detritus in the hope of picking up any residue. She rubs what she finds on her teeth and gums. She waits to see if there's any effect.

Nothing. Just dirt. It's all just dirt.

'Yes, look at you. You feel so strongly about me, doncha? So much that you want to die to get away from me. Well guess what? I trump you, because the fact is, Silly I am the one who needs to get away from you. You are bad for me. Time wears on, and we all wear out eventually. So. I am leavin'. This room. And you, the bloody undead. Now. Watch me ...'

Cat O'Brien picks up her handbag and her coat. She

approaches the bed and in one final defiant and disgusting flourish, she spits at Silvia.

The saliva hits Silvia's cheek, and starts to dribble down.

Cat has finally revealed herself entirely as a snake. She hoped to feel victorious when she did that, but she doesn't. She feels immediately diminished. Worthless. Cheap. Because that's what she is. She slams the door as she leaves and a whoosh of her own indignant guilt blows her up the corridor and out.

Silvia is alone in the room again. But now, the atmosphere in Suite 5 is changed. It's completely different. The danger left with Cat.

Silvia might be dying but, at last, she is safe.

TWENTY-EIGHT

Cassie

Wednesday 4pm

Cassie is sitting at the head of Silvia's bed, close to her mother's face. Cassie's mobile phone lies on the pillow by Silvia's ear, and it is on loudspeaker, so that Willow can be heard joining in with the familiar poem Cassie is reciting to her mother by heart.

'With a ring at the end of his nose, his nose, with a ring at the end of his nose . . .'

Willow jumps in quickly, she wants to be the owl for this next part, she knows and loves it, and puts on a four year old's version of a posh, deep, owly voice.

'Dear Pig, are you willing to shell for one silling your ring?'

Cassie picks it up.

'Said the Piggy . . .'

Willow tries to oink the words.

'"I will." Oink oink.'

They both laugh and laugh.

Willow says, 'Shhh Mummy, that is the Piggy and it makes my nose go sore.'

'I know darling. It sounds good though, just like a proper pig. Come on, let's carry on. Can you remember the next bit?'

Willow certainly can, she has no doubt whatsoever, and she launches into it at full throttle.

'They took it away, marry next day, by a turkey on a hill, a hill, a hill, a hill.'

'That's right sweetheart, and what happened next?'

'They eat all the mince and slices of mince.'

'Yes, which they ate with a . . .?'

'A munchable spoon.'

'Yes. And hand in hand . . .'

Willow eagerly joins in, and mutters the words she doesn't quite know.

'On the ya ya ya sand. They danced by the la la la moon the moon, the moon. They danced by the la la la moon.'

'Yes! Well done sweetheart! Lovely!'

Cassie claps loudly and whoops her approval for the tiny person on the other end of the phone to hear loud and clear. Lots and lots of unconditional praise. Not that Cassie would consciously think of it like that. She instinctively dishes out lashings of love. Buckets of it. She relishes nothing more. Piles it on in massive generous dollops. Of course she does. She loves her daughter. That's what you do as a mum. Encourage and support. Willingly. With joy.

'Alright darling. Go and have your tea now. What're you having?'

'Daddy's done nuggets. But not chips. Corn.'

'Oh, that sounds delicious. Yum Yum.'

'Yum Yum. Stop it Daddy, shh! Mummy, Daddy says corn comes out all new in poo, like it went in. Tell him to shh. Shh Daddy. Mummy says shhh, you're rude.'

'Alright honey. Go and eat your tea, and I will be home soon. The lady loved your poem, by the way.'

'Say night night to the lady. Say Happy Birthday.'

'I will, darling, I will. Bye.'

Cassie presses the red button on the phone, and Willow is gone. She looks closely at her still and unresponsive mother, and wonders if she heard any of that delightful jabber? And if she did, did it lift her heart? She wonders what, if anything, her comatose mother would want to hear that would make her want to come up and out of her giant sleep? What would it take? Cassie knows that if it were her, the voice of her darling little daughter would surely do it. Would it for Silvia? And for her, would that key voice be her own estranged daughter, or might it be her stranger of a granddaughter? Well, Silvia has heard that voice now. The unheard before voice of little Willow.

For a second, Cassie considers a life without hearing Willow's voice. Unthinkable. It's too sad a prospect for her to ponder too long.

If only Silvia could plug into Cassie's fathomless love for her daughter, feel even two per cent of it, she is sure it would jolt her back into life as if she had jump leads attached straight to her heart. The direct descendant line from Silvia to Willow goes slap bang through the middle of Cassie, and although it's a line that has recently overgrown at one end, Cassie's fervent hope that the love still travels along it, is strong. Potent enough to rouse her? Cassie doesn't know. Nobody knows, but it's certainly worth this try.

She suddenly remembers something, and riffles around in her handbag for a few seconds to find it.

'. . . put it in here somewhere . . . know I did . . . stupid . . . so much crap . . . ah! Here it is . . .'

Cassie has, in her hand, a brass curtain ring. She holds it up in front of Silvia.

'The ring, Mum, the ring at the end of his nose, his nose. D'you remember? I so believed it was the real one. Couldn't get over how amazingly lucky you were to have it. I've guarded it very carefully, you'll be pleased to hear. It lives in my jewellery box. Which you also gave me. It's tan leather with a popper on the front, and red velvet inside, remember? I think it's for travelling or something. Didn't your mum give it to you? Think I remember you saying something like that. Anyway, I love it.

233

And this piggywig's ring has been kept safely in there for, ooo, for . . . fifteen years or more. God. It's a curtain ring, isn't it? Ha ha. Yeh. Still, the piggywig didn't know that, sure he was delighted with it . . .'

Whilst Cassie was rummaging around in her handbag, her fingers brushed against the letter that's there. She knows she has to read it out to Silvia. She really doesn't want to, but she has made a promise to her brother and she will keep it. She has delayed long enough, distracting herself with the poem and Willow and the ring and . . . anything but that letter.

The time has come.

Cassie reaches back into her bag and brings it out. It almost burns her fingers, it's so incendiary.

'There is a letter here, from Jamie. It's come all the way from Afghanistan, and he's asked me to read it out to you so . . . that's . . . what I'll do.'

Unfolding the blue airmail paper, she is trembling as she starts. She has already seen the letter and she doesn't relish the fact that the slicing words on the paper will soon be words in the air. In the open air, which will convey them into Silvia's ears. And then possibly into her heart. But a promise is a promise and Jamie used up his valuable and limited phone-home time to call her expressly to ask her to do this. So she must.

'Here goes . . .'

Dear Silvia.

I can't call you Mum. I don't want to. You haven't been one to me for the last five years or so. Just want to make that clear, right? OK.

Well, I'm sitting here in a hot stinking tent in Lash Vegas (which is what we call Lashkah Gar), writing this bluey to you from the patrol base. Dad and Cass have told me what happened to you, although, frankly, I'm not sure anyone really knows what happened. I don't get how a woman like you can just fall off a balcony? Unless you were pissed. Or pushed. Or both. Anyway, it's happened now, and I know the docs have told everyone to talk to you in case you can hear. Personally, I don't care what you can or can't hear, but Dad was so bloody insistent on me contacting you, especially on your birthday, so here it is. Cassie will do the honours.

So, what can I tell you? I could go off on a big one about what a bitch you've been, and how you fucked up everything in this family, I specially can't get over just how bloody mean you've been to Cassie and Willow . . .

At this, Cassie falters slightly. Although she read the letter last night, therefore nothing in it is a surprise, she is caught out by just how important it feels to have her hurts acknowledged openly. Last night, she was slightly looking forward to this somewhat revengeful moment where Silvia might hear how her brother felt in this respect, but now that the moment has arrived, she feels the actual pain of it more than the anticipated satisfaction of having it possibly land on Silvia.

She looks intently at Silvia's face for signs of any reaction. As always. Nothing.

She ploughs on.

. . . but there's no point harping on about it, the damage is done and know what? She has survived it. We all have.

Maybe I should tell you why I'm in a tent, which is in fact a makeshift medic centre, before I'm moved back to Camp Bastion soon. Couple of weeks ago, our unit were deployed temporarily to the Garmsir District Centre, as part of an operation I'm not allowed to name in this letter. Except to say we were heading into difficult territory. Pongos had gone ahead supported by Afghan troops, to distract and bait Taliban we knew were there. Our orders were to duck in a day behind, and take command of a cell headquarters identified inside a particular cluster of mud-baked compounds. When the day came, I was given a terp to marhsall, who was pretty green. This was his first op out of interpreter training, and he was shaking. Called Ajani. Twenty-two years old. Bit younger than me. Looks like a proper jinglie, and don't get all arsy and leftie about us calling the locals that. It refers to their vehicles which are more often than not adorned with shiny jingly-jangly stuff, and make loads of noise, so wind yer leftie liberal neck in!

Anyway, Ajani is a small bloke, his uniform is far too big for him and he stood there holding his field kit and his rifle and looked like someone's eleven-year-old brother. His kit is bigger than he is, and so is his bottle. I could see he was having trouble controlling his jitters, but I could also see that he wanted to, so massive respect goes out to the little fella for his big courage.

It's tough for the interpreters out here, some of their friends and neighbours begrudge that they work for the British forces. It's too much of a head-fuck for a lot of them, and they regard the terp as a traitor or something else dodgy. They even receive death threats sometimes. Crazy. I mean, this guy speaks Pashtu and Italian as well as English, he's really bright. We had plenty of gags about how he was the only one in the corps who could order a curry or a pizza or fish and chips in the local lingo, and get away with it.

Anyway, fact is Ajani – dead bright, but dead green. I took to him. We shared our fags, and yes Silvia, I am smoking again, but frankly, I don't think you can hold that against me. Ajani and I had a good swapping

237

system set up. Three of his local fags for each one of my B&H's. You have to have good lungs to cope with the Afghan tabs, they taste like the bloody camel shit they are but hey, a smoke's a smoke in hell.

Eventually, it was time to board the cab (helicopter to you), which was already fully loaded with various provisions and ammunition freight. So much so that we were all jammed in tight, and I found myself crammed in on the starboard side, able to see out through the freight-hook hole. The Chinook shakes you about a fair bit on the flight, but I was aware my right leg was going hell for leather, and when I checked it out, I realized it was Ajani's left leg, shoved up tight next to mine in the scrum, that was shaking like a leaf. Poor sod. I pushed my leg harder against his to steady him and he looked at me. The fear on his little brown mug and the bewilderment in his wide eyes is something I won't forget.

Although I have actually forgotten a lot else about that day and following night. It's all hazy memories for me, some are flooding back at odd times, but a lot is gone. I'll probably never remember now.

Through the hole in the cab deck, I could see the Afghani terrain below, in the late afternoon sun. Whole place was drenched in pink. Female colours everywhere. Looks like a girl's country. But it so isn't. In fact, any time you see women, you wouldn't know that's what they are, they're so covered up. Can only see flashes of dark eyes through the letter box in the headgear on the odd occasion they pass us on a street patrol, or perhaps if we see them scurrying off when we enter a compound.

So anyway, the flight was pretty uneventful, no one bothers to speak as the racket in the cab is too loud. I just kept looking out through the freight-hook hole and I could sometimes see the silhouette of a 'helo whooshing along the ground when the sun was out from the clouds behind us, throwing the shadow down. Looked like a giant dragonfly in the distance. But it was us. Heading into trouble.

As we descended, the cab filled with dust and sand whipped up by the rotor. The dust is like pink talcum powder. Gets in your eyes and mouth. As the stern ramp opened, we all grabbed our kit and piled out. Could hardly see anything for the amount of dust in my eyes, so knelt down, face averted, 'til the roar of the rotors diminished. Once the noise abated, we could see again, and what we saw was a vast expanse of bollocking nothing under a baking hot sun.

We had been dropped a good 8km from the target and had a long hot walk ahead into the night, then set up a makeshift harbour position, to rest for a few hours before a dawn assault. Thank God the ground was fairly

flat, but it was still muggy and we were all carrying
plenty of weight, Osprey, cot vest, 360 rounds of
5.56mm, 9mm pistol, SA80 A2 rifle, 6 x 9mm mags,
grenades, extra batteries for the GPS gear, bayonet,
dagger and daysack with six litres of water. Easily
eighty pounds of weight. My own oppos, including
Geordie Jim, the medic, a bloody giant of a brick shit-
house, were having trouble keeping up straight, never
mind spindly Ajani with his trembling matchstick legs.
He could have buckled at any time, and he was carrying
half the gear, but he kept going.

The sudden quiet was palpable. Weird. Heavy. Only
the sound of boots and movement and heavy breathing.
We walked for hours into the darkness, eight of us,
excluding the medic and Ajani. As junior Capt, it is
ultimately my job to use the maps and decide where to
stop, which was a rocky outcrop about 3km from the
target, known as Red 1.

Kit off, settle down. Was cold. Got v. cold soon as the
sun set. No fires, too risky, but cigs allowed, under
cupped hands and only local tobacco. Vague shapes
huddling together, back to back, facing out in a 360°
circle, ARD. Hushed chat and continual smokes.
Every other word is an expletive. From everyone. No
one speaks without swearing. At all. Eyes adapt slowly,
and starlight becomes v. bright gradually as vision

learns the night. We ate dry rations, and drank water. No brew due to no fire. Got a few restless hours of kip, during a 50/50 watch, but circumstances kept us mostly alert.

About two hours before dawn, lit up for the last time before moving out, and we convened for the final briefing. I give Ajani one of my cigs, for later. He gives me 3 of his. I drew out the plan in the sand with a stick. We'd already had the detailed briefing back at base, but just as a rudimentary reminder. One headtorch only to illuminate it. Keep the light low to the ground. Definite feeling of heaviness. The numbers aren't good. Recce reports reckoned about fifty Taliban with AKs, probably. Eleven of us. With the addition of Irish 1 as backup. We're pretty much fucked. But shit, we are professional Marines and it's in precisely these circs that we prevail. Come on, you wankers, let's see your steel.

I know how important it is that I don't waver. I'm in fucking charge. Fuck. Think. We need to secure that compound with as little damage to civilians as poss, but there will be innocents there. That's how Taliban work. Using local jinglies as cover. You rarely get sight of them, they are like fucking ghosts, but they are a ferocious and fearless enemy, and tactically astute in theatre. All I have to know, and all I have to let my men know, is that we are more so. We are more than them, in *every respect. And that, luckily, is what I do genuinely believe.*

So, it's kit up and move out, stealthily. It's still pretty much sub-zero temperature, so the walk is welcome if only to stay warm. I see that Ajani, like me, is sporting a new beard. He looks puffy and tired. I can't see me, but I bet I do too. Funny how fear translates into fatigue. And how quickly the adrenaline converts it back into energy. As we push on, I remember with every step, just how important it is to be fit. In mind and body.

I look around and see the faces of these men, each one of whom I would, at that moment, die for. I would. I would take a bullet for any one of them. We are a team. These people are my family. At that precise moment, I felt that I belonged in that family more than I've ever felt that I belonged anywhere. We were together in every way, comrades hardwired to our most basic instincts, which on that morning were mainly about survival, guile and . . . well, fuck it, yes, I'll say it . . . love. These were my brothers, and I loved them as such. Still do.

You wouldn't get it. No one gets it unless they've been here. Grandad might, I suppose he was a pongo. This place makes you feel stuff you wish you never had to, but which you know for sure you'll never feel as strongly ever again. I have never known as surely before that I am so completely heard and supported. My home

242

is here. Not sure that's right, but am sure it's true. We
all knew it. Unsaid. Wholly felt.

Eventually, after an hour and a half or so, and still in
darkness, we were nearing Red 1. I knew for a couple of
reasons. Firstly, we were all communicating through
personal headsets, and the recce tp were guiding us in,
plus we had our maps and GPS ace, Lance Corporal
Cunty Kevin Hodge. Sorry to use that word, know what
you think of it, but I'm afraid that is his official name for
the simple reason that he is one. I can't tell you why he
is but if you knew, you would agree. For a man with
highly questionable morals, he is a brilliant navigator,
trained with the Brigade Recce, and it's in moments like
these he comes into his own, and all prior bestial indis-
cretions are forgiven . . .

The other clue to our approaching the target was
that we started to notice small huddled groups of
villagers leaving, scurrying past us in the darkness,
going the opposite way. Fleeing, in effect. This is always
a significant combat indicator. The initial fear of their
approach is a bum-tightener. Are they friend? Are they
foe? We make out that there are children amongst
them, which makes us feel slightly easier, but the fact is,
out here, a thirteen year old will as soon lob a grenade
at you as anyone, so you never totally relax. The stress
is prolonged and incessant, even sleeping is a taught

experience. It's hard to explain. So I won't. Ajani spoke to the locals quietly but firmly, ushering them past and telling them to keep moving. Which was exactly what I was saying to my unit. Urging them towards what was in effect, inevitable attack.

Not only was there immediate danger from Talibs, there is always danger all around from IEDs. Booby traps can be absolutely anywhere, so with every step you are on the lookout for telltale signs which are obviously not easy to observe at night. Hard to see tripwires or disturbed ground where pressure pads might be. You just have to wrestle the fear into submission and keep walking. Every step a new courage.

I was already feeling knackered, both from the physical exertion and from maintaining that amount of alertness continually. A weird thing happens where your senses become so attuned that instincts you didn't know you had start to kick in, and I had learned by then to pay attention to my instincts, even if I didn't understand them. It's hard to admit that I was putting the safety of my call sign at the mercy of my new-found and hard-to-explain instincts. But, that's all I could do, so I did, and we pushed on, in the hope that my senses were going to serve us all well.

Just as the first streaks of daylight started to threaten, we trudged alongside a three-metre-wide *irrigation canal and on the other side of it, I could smell there was a field of poppies. Couldn't see them, but I knew they were there. White poppies, tall. The heads of the poppies are scored for cultivation and you can smell the opium. It's a sweet slightly sickly smell, especially at night. Unmistakable. As that wafted past us, we came to the brow of a small hill with the irrigation culvert on our right, from which we had our first sighting of Red 1.*

The outline in the half-light depicted two definite compounds, gated and surrounded by fifteen-foot-high walls. It would be a challenge to gain entry, but we'd made our plans and were ready. We had backup from the Irish regiment and the ANA who had gone ahead for the recce a couple of days before. They were sitting tight, waiting for us to kick off. We had no time to lose, because of the light.

What happened next was so quick that I only have a jumble in my head about it. All I remember now is that I led off down the other side of the hill towards Red 1, and I was making good headway. Ajani was right behind me, and I was flanked by Bodger McLean and Thumbs Burke. In the buzz of it all, I couldn't believe that my brain was hovering around the thought that this assault was being fronted by an Englishman, an Irishman and a Scotsman! Crazy, isn't it, that I could consider that alongside everything else, but I did.

We had hoped the Talibs weren't aware we might be approaching, but when we saw the civvies leaving, it was obvious we weren't going to be the shock we'd hoped for. What none of us were prepared for was their utter readiness. As we advanced from over the hill, we were only a few paces towards them when we took fire. I told the lads to get down, and sent a TIC (Troops in Contact) report over the net, yelling 'Contact! Contact!' and 'Go! Go!' We moved forward fast, running across open, killing ground. Everything had gone from quiet and stealthy to loud and shouting, whilst under such heavy attack. We had to avoid being pinned down.

I remember realizing how close we suddenly were to Red 1 when I saw that the Talib tracer rounds were passing over our heads, and lighting up way past where we were. I could see all the green specks flashing in the dark sky behind us as the bases of the bullets exploded and lit up. It could have been a really good Bonfire Night display if it wasn't lethal. Meanwhile the hail of fire we were running into was full on. There is an unforgettable crack-thump sound when bullets fly by. Lead wasps, Cunty Kevin calls them, and that's right. There is a popping sound and the air warps and sucks as they whizz past. You hope.

All I know is that I was suddenly on the ground, clutching my leg and Ajani was somehow in front of me.

I saw his face because at the exact moment that a touch of first light hit it and lit him up, an enemy round hit him in the head and as his skull shattered, sending shards of bone and brain and blood and hair exploding out every which way like a dandelion head, he slumped forwards on to me, smothering me with his pumping dark blood and his ruptured flesh. Clumps of hard soil and rocks were thwacking me from either side as the earth around me was being pounded by their 762 rounds, slamming into the ground. My mouth, ears and eyes were full of dust and thick glinting blood. Tasted like steel, like nothing I'd ever tasted before, like metal and bacon together. I couldn't tell what was my blood and what was his. Bastard. All I knew was the pain.

I try to shove him off the top of me; he's heavy for a small bloke. Ajani – who was dead bright and dead green, and is now just dead. I can hear muffled sounds and I can hear pounding as boots stomp on ground around me. Are these my lads? Or ragheads? Are the fucking Taliban right on us and about to finish me off? I can't see. I reach down to my right thigh to draw my 9mm but I am getting weaker with every second and I can't do it.

Is this what dying feels like? Am I going to kick it here, in this dirty shithole, leaving my call sign with no leadership? I hear reassuring sounds of Geordie Jim telling me to keep still, and he's doing something tight to my leg, he's injecting me. I hear the sounds of a helicopter – and that was it, I lost all consciousness.

Turns out the rest of my unit got the backup they needed from 1 Royal Irish, the ANA, and two Apaches and pushed on to take Red 1 with only Ajani as a fatality. Besides a couple of the Talibs who copped it. Rest taken prisoner . . . Some injuries, like me, but not too shabby, considering.

So now, here I am, patched up, drugged up, and waiting to be casevaced to Bastion. Then there'll be some decisions made about what needs to happen next – I expect I'll be taken to Birmingham or somewhere like that to recover. Need to know exactly how serious it is before plan is made. Looks like a shattered knee to me. But what the cock do I know?

Well, what I do know for sure is that life is precious, and I'm going to savour every living moment of it. And I'm going to do that in the name of courageous Ajani Sahar, and courageous Dad and courageous Cassie. Not you. You wouldn't have the first clue about courage, or what matters, Silvia. You proved that. When I was in and out of consciousness in the Chinook, with my legs splinted together, and my own blood spilling down the deck plates to my face, I thought about my family and how they would cope if this was it for me.

I knew then, very clearly, that it wouldn't matter to you because you haven't known me for so long now. Would you even find out? And if you did, would it just be like someone snuffing out a candle in the next room? Can't see it, doesn't really matter, doesn't affect you? Like that? Well, here's the thing I knew in that moment Silvia. I don't care what you think any more. My anger about you and your shit has eaten me up, you pushed me away and that push got me all the way here, but no longer am I going to let you be in charge of what I think about me.

I am going to survive this. I am going to survive you. Even if it meant coming to this hellhole to learn it. I now know it. I do not need you. I do not love you. I no longer look for your love back. Keep it, and shove it up your arse.

There's dust everywhere here. It's the teller of everything. Weather, war, everything. I've had it everywhere, eyes ears nose mouth . . . It's even inside my shit and my fucking socks at the end of the day. But as I lie here now. Finally. I think it's settling. Settling. Settled.

So. Happy Birthday, and that's it.

Bye then. J.

Cassie folds the pages and replaces them in the envelope. She sits and thinks, with Jamie's words still in the air, and the sound of her mother's breathing.

Never altering.

TWENTY-NINE

Winnie

Thursday 10am

Winnie is about to carry out her regular checks on Silvia, making sure all the machines are functioning properly and she is as comfortable as she can be. Winnie twice washes her hands with the alcohol-based sanitizing gel from the dispenser on the wall, and as she gets a wake-up whiff from the nostril-singeing menthol assault of it, she has a passing shudder of horror at the certain knowledge that most of the visitors in this and every other ward won't bother.

Winnie remembers the training film they were shown about MRSA, and the terrifying statistics she learned, like the fact that 53% of healthcare workers have traces of MRSA on their hands at any one time. A hospital is the ideal environment for the bacteria to flourish and for the transmission of infections because so many people are in direct contact, living and dying, side by side so closely. She discovered that there are 17 strains of MRSA, and many can kill you if your immunity is compromised and you are weak. Add the virulent and ugly C. Diff to the equation, and it pretty much transforms a hospital into a kind of luxury bug hotel.

The superbugs have checked in and they are getting stronger with every antibiotic encounter they have. They are partying in every room of the hotel, especially the communal areas. They are getting drunk at the bar, and having parties and weddings and weekend breaks, and conferences, and basically taking the piss. They don't stay quiet in their rooms any more, they are out and bold and loud, and hitching a ride to anywhere on any dirty hand they can find.

Winnie is determined that she, at least, will not be a carrier. Not knowingly, at any rate. She knows how vulnerable her very poorly patients are, and she would do nothing to exacerbate their often tragic situations. Winnie is a person who, in a quite old-fashioned way, takes the most enormous pride in her work. She will always do the absolute best she can, and if washing your hands regularly to minimize the risk of infection is part of that best, then of course she will comply. It's simple and easy. Why don't others see it the same way?

Likewise, she would never enter a room without greeting her patient with a cheerful hello. It's only right and decent to her. It's good manners, and Winnie was brought up right. On top of which, she has plenty to tell Silvia today. Plenty. Because a miracle has happened since yesterday afternoon.

'Marnin' Silvia. It's mi, Winnie, comin in to check you darlin. Jus so you know, it a blustery nasty day, an' Deyvid Cyameroon still de prime minister. Lord help us all. He is hatin on the poor ol' NHS. So. Ya nah miss nuttin, sista, in fact, ya might even be better off fas' asleep! He he he. Now let's have a lickle look at dis bag.'

Winnie deftly lifts the sheets where Silvia's urine bag hangs, attached to the catheter. Even when her patient is unconscious like this, Winnie likes to be sensitive and subtle about it, so she folds the sheets back in such a way as to reveal as little as possible of Silvia. Discretion and dignity at all times are Winnie's modus operandi.

'Dere, let's give you new bag. Shame de bag cyaan match your shoes, eh?! He he. Now den, dat should feel better.'

Winnie carefully replaces the old full yellow bulging plastic sack with a new empty fresh one, and she cleans all the connections to be sure. She then raises the top of Silvia's bed a little bit higher, about 20°, so as to allow for good drainage of venous blood, and she makes a note that it's time Silvia was turned to lie on her side for a while. She knows that if a coma patient is in one position too long, the lowest portions of the lungs become passively congested with blood, and the respiratory functions of the alveoli are then impaired. This then becomes frighteningly fertile ground for the development of numerous infections, but especially of bronchopneumonia.

Winnie can't turn Silvia alone, so she will summon help in

a minute, but meanwhile, she wants to tell Silvia what happened without anyone else in the room, so she proceeds with her regular checks of blood pressure and temperature, plus respiratory levels, while she relates her tale excitedly.

'So, now, when mi see Mr Shute, sorry, "h'Edward", leavin here in such a rush yesterday, mi notice 'im stress 'n' vex. I arks 'im if he wan' go getta caffee. 'Im say yes, so we go to de h'appalling café dungstairs and 'im get two cup overprice liberty-teykin muddy water call' caffee. Serious, Silvia, dat caffee is made by a sadist, it so horrible. We both sippin it so polite, den I get it in mi throat where it burn up so, an' mi start fi cough real bad. Den we both laffin at jus' how rank it is. Laffin an' coughin. So much dat mi snortin like a pig! It so funny, and h'Edward face light up so when 'im smile, don't it? 'Im a lovely man, Silvia, in't it? An' 'im speak so high of you. 'Im say 'im sad de marriage broke up, but 'im h'understan you needin to move on, have new life. Dats good. For both. Yes? Mi can see 'im sad dat you sufferin now Silvia. 'Im have a good heart. An' 'im pay de eighty thousand pongs it cost for di h'atrocious caffee, so mi know 'im generass.

'H'anyway. We talkin an' talking 'til mi jaw ache, mainly 'bout you an' Cassie an' Jamie, but h'eventually, mi tell 'im all about what bin goin on wid mi son Luke. It so pyainful for dat bwoy. Mi heart bleed, truly . . .'

All the time, Winnie is observing and checking Silvia. Checking her airways are clear and clean. Checking for skin

253

integrity and muscle deterioration, checking for ulcers, check-ing her mouth for saliva. Gently, in rotation, she moves all Silvia's joints to avoid stiffness, and all the time, she is noting the lack of response and she is documenting everything effi-ciently on the charts. She doesn't want to miss a single trick or clue, and she is super diligent, even though she is talking all the time. Winnie is a supreme multitasker.

'Him get beat up by dis group of mean gyals at school, long time now, but 'im only tell mi Tuesday eveling when 'im come home wid him head bruk open, and plenty scratches dung 'im beautiful lickle sad face. Mi could see where he bin bawlin. Lines o'tears. Valleys dung 'im cheeks. Poor lickle mite. Scared 'im 'til he shiverin like a leaf. Dey mash 'im up really bad. Tek 'im book bag an' 'im dinna money an' 'im iPod 'im save up for wid 'im birtday money. Dem give 'im big bodderation fe nut-tin! All becaa why? Becaa 'im so lickle an genkle? And black? And becaa dey can.

'Mi tinkin it might be my fault, becaa mi teach 'im not to use 'im fist, to try an' negotiate if dere is problems. But dese gyals is proper bullies dey don't want talk, an' of course, 'im feel worse becaa dem is gyal. He supposed to be de big man and bash dem up if dey treaten 'im, but 'im only nine years h'old and dey in senior school, an' dey massive! Bully gyals. Wyait at de syame bustop, so dey got plenty chance to give 'im liks. Fe what?!

'I seen dose gyals. Tree of dem. One is pyale an lang an maaga, one is slabba-slabba, fat as a wyale, an de las' one is white trash wishin she a black sista wid corn row too tight an big ol' ugly bangles an' gold bling ev'ywhere. De parents should be h'ashame. Mebbe dem no know, but mebbe dem de syame. Whatever, mi cyaan have mi bwoy mess up like dis, look 'pon 'im all mash up. Dat fat one bash 'im in 'im teet an' now the front one come loose. Dat sight mek mi vex an' mi all ready fi go dung where she live. I know dat flat, an dat gyal, she dead! She mess wid my pickney, I mess wid her face, beccaa she need to know 'bout di truut when it come to bullying. You always gonna meet a bigga bully dan you one day, missy, an' see me ya! Me a go box up your face so bad, you will ny'am ya own teet, truss mi. Mi a dweet! Serious. Mi a tersty fe her blood, mi dat vex. Mi could kill.

'I was tinkin an dreamin of all de isms an schisms I would lay on dem nasty gyals when mi hear a lickle whimperin quiet noise. It Luke crying h'again, but dis time, it beccaa of me. Mi frightenin 'im wid all de cursin an' shoutin, an' stampin about. We no do dat in my family. I teach 'im not to. An' now I am doin it bad. 'Im beg me not to go rung to dey flats. 'Im say it a go mek it worse an' 'im have enough crosses. 'Im lickle tears reach into mi heart an' I soften up an' calm down. Mi cyaan bear it when 'im cry. Mi never could. Mi haffi comfort 'im, an' 'im mek mi promise not to go dere, not to say anyting, an' so dats what I do. H'eventually, h'after mi fix up his face wid TCP, 'im fall asleep on de sofa in front of de Simpsons, an' mi let 'im stay home wid mi mudda yesterday.

'So you see, Silvia, mi full of sufferation when mi see h'Edward here, an' mi see dat similar sufferation in 'im face when he left, so dats why we have the caffee an' dats why mi tell 'im all about Luke. An' mi cyaan believe how much 'im lissen. Proper lissen. An' alla de time mi see 'im tinkin and tinkin an' arksin questions. H'Edward truly h'interested in what mi tell 'im an' 'im a hatch a plan inna 'im brain to help. Mi cyaan believe 'im takin time to tink it troo. H'after all, dis nuttin to do wid 'im. It not 'im problem. Mi tell 'im so, but 'im h'insist 'im help. H'Edward say 'im know all about bullyin an' how it leave you feelin bad 'bout plenty tings.

'Mi not sure if 'im bullied at school or where, but 'im seem to feel de pain when 'im talk it over, 'im eyes look sad, so best not to intrude 'pon 'im personal ting an' tings. Mebbe one day, dat might be possible, but not jus' now. H'anyway, 'im say it all "outrageous" an' fe to have "zero tolerance". 'Im arks if de school do anyting to help? Well, mi say, some other tings happen in the pass wid Luke, not so bad as dis time, but de school not really respond, an' Luke beg mi not to get h'involved fe fear it mek it worse, so really, we stuck wid it.

'Bwoy! H'Edward get all heat up 'bout dis an' 'im talk about "institutional racism" bein de "downfall of dis country" and "stealth evil" an' how de police got de same, and so schools copy, an' let dis level of crime creep up 'til it so normal an' big an' bad, we letting racist thugs kill h'innocent black boys jus' walkin on the street, an' dose wicked boys run free an' laff bout it fe years. Boastin 'bout how good it feel to get rid of dat "pointless nigger" an' how dey wish dey could do it one at a time 'til we all dead. Dis is what happen if no one stop dem. 'Im tink what happen to Luke "a race hate crime" an' "intolerable". You should see 'im face Silvia, 'im full o' fury!

'So, h'anyway, 'im say "Leave it to me", and 'im tek mi phone number. When 'im leave, mi finish mi shift an' go home, but allatime since mi talk an' reason wid h'Edward, mi honestly feelin more . . . safe . . . jus to have 'im support feel good. Becaa 'im properly lissen. Lissen an' care.'

Winnie opens the tub of cream on the shelf and, with skilful manoeuvring, starts to apply it to Silvia's lips, and back and heels and, eventually, bottom. All the time, she is gauging the warmth and dryness of Silvia's unresponsive body. It has, on rare occasions, been in an intimate moment like this, where she has a good deal of physical interaction with a patient, when virtually imperceptible but nevertheless present signs of response can occur.

A groan, a flickering eye, the wiggle of a finger.

Winnie has never failed to be excited when this happens even though she is well aware that it may ultimately signal very little. But then again . . . it may well be the tiny start of something seismic, and the thought of missing that is too awful.

Although Winnie is talking and what she is telling Silvia is urgent, she never for a second loses sight of her purpose in this room, and she is vigilant at all times. It's with her innate

257

and natural instinct and her eagle eye that Winnie notices the clamminess around Silvia's neck and at the top of her back. She notes it and makes sure she washes and dries these areas with extra care.

'So, mi at home cookin up dinna an' checkin Luke getting 'im spellins done when h'Edward text mi an' arks where mi live becaa 'im wan' to show mi something h'important. Well, is no time at all before 'im knock 'pon mi door an' 'im come in, jus' in time to share mi Saturday soup. Usually mi mek it onna Saturday, but it Lukie's all-time favourite, so mi mek it fi 'im yesterday to help soothe mi lickle man from his tribulations. H'Edward like it. 'Im nyam it quick an' clean de bowl out, like 'im wan' eat dat too!

'So, den 'im give mi a letter to read, an' 'im tell mi 'im compose it fe mi to write out in mi h'own handwritin', sign an' give to de school today. Mi have de h'original here in mi pocket. You wan' mi to read it? OK . . .'

Winnie unfolds the sheet of A4, and reads it out.

Dear Headmaster,

I write to bring to your attention an alarming incident concerning my son, Luke Dixon, who attends the primary school. He was waiting innocently at the bus stop on Tuesday morning when three young women from your senior school harassed and then attacked him, causing him considerable bodily harm and emotional distress. I have had to keep him at home since then, due to his profound anguish after this appalling persecution. The behaviour of all three girls, representatives of your establishment, is not only sickening in its malevolence, but worryingly indicative of a serious disrespect for the bullying charter you surely must implement at your school. A charter which, incidentally, I would like to have the opportunity to view and share with other equally concerned parents, at your earliest convenience.

I am sure, in your capacity as supreme legislator at your school, you are aware of the law concerning hate crime. The law is indeed especially muscular concerning environments such as schools, where appreciating diversity is key. Should one's establishment be deemed 'institutionally racist' for instance, I feel sure it would be appropriate to instigate an investigation involving all school personnel, and should the school be found guilty of, say, neglecting to counteract any bullying/racism/ homophobia, that might well be interpreted as aggra-vating the offence – the sentence for which, I believe, if tried on indictment, could be 5–7 years. A sobering thought, and one I hope you might dwell upon, albeit briefly, before you dismiss any chance of your school being identified as such a repugnant bed of worms.

Might I remind you that a hate crime is any criminal offence motivated by hostility or prejudice based on

the victim's race, colour, religion, size, sexual orienta-
tion etc. Really, it is any incident that is perceived to
be prejudiced by the <u>victim</u> or <u>any other person</u>. In
this case, my small son is most definitely the victim,
and I would be proud to step forward as 'any other
person'.

I am sure the elimination of harassment and hate
crime is a priority under your jurisdiction and therefore
you would be bound to extinguish any trace of a hostile
environment. I hope I can count on your support, and I
am more than willing to come and meet with you along
with my representatives to those ends.

I intend to furnish the Office for Civil Rights, the
Department of Education, and the National Union of
Teachers with all above information, including the
names and addresses of all three culprits, and of two
further witnesses should they require.

I am convinced you will appreciate the sensitivity of
such an issue for my dear son, and I trust whatever
course of serious action you choose to implement, you
would not in any way embarrass or compromise him.
Such an outcome would only compound his troubles,
and further victimize him.

I look forward to hearing your plan in the very near
future, and I urge you to do the right thing, and declare
war on hate crime in your institution. A man of your

experience, stature and position should surely need very
little persuasion in this particularly crucial endeavour.

With the greatest of respect and in full anticipation of
a positive outcome.

Yours sincerely . . .

'An' den dere is de place fe mi to sign. Phew! What you tink bout dat letter?!! Eh?! H'Edward is very very clever. 'Im put dat headmasta inna h'impossible to get out of position. 'Im gotta dweet, int it? 'Im definitely gotta punish dem evil gyals. An' jus' in time, mi tink, becaa dey jus' the type to keep on bullyin 'til one day somemoddy get kill. So mi tink dat H'Edward could be savin a life or two wid dis letter.

'I write it out h'immediately an' sign it. H'Edward is laffin alla de time, tellin mi 'im not really sure 'bout de law on hate crime, but 'im try to sound convincing so de headmasta sit up an lissen. He he he! We laffin togedda but mi see a lickle spar-kle in 'im eye, an' mi tink dis letter very h'important fe dat man to write. 'Im workin something out. Mi no know who might have bullied 'im in de pass, but something like dat gone on, an' 'im putting it to res' writin dat letter.

'So, I tek it right up to the headmasta secretary an' place it bang on 'er desk an' mi look 'er in de eye an' say calmly "Dis matters". She nod, an' mi gone. So Silvia, we wyait an' we see, yes? We let time an' nature tek it course. An' we let God do 'im work. An' wid h'any luck at all, dem tree h'ugly bitches drop dead in h'unbearable h'agony . . . wid dem h'eyeballs sting an' dem hair on fire!! Ha ha! Now mi not so Christian, eh?! Ha ha!

'No, but serious, mi grateful to you Silvia, becaa if you not in here, me nevva meet h'Edward and 'im nevva help to protec' mi boy. It was a good sight to see dem sittin dere togedda las' night talkin about dose nasty gyals. Luke able to speak 'bout 'im feelins more wid another man. An' 'im see it not weak to feel terrible, an' 'im see dat true strength is in de gentleness of a man, not de fists an' fury. Yes. Yes Lord. Dat is truut.

'So. OK. Now. Mi wan' to get anudda nurse to help turn you a lickle bit, an mi can see you feelin a bit hot again Silvia, an' ya temperature bit high fe me, so lissen darlin, mi gonna get de doctor in to have a lickle check on you. Don't worry, Silvia, it probably nuttin. But we gotta be sure. Better safe than sorry. Yes. Better safe. You hold on dere darlin. Mi sort it . . .'

And so exits the room probably the only person in Silvia's present who has no axe to grind, no anger or hate or questions. Winnie wishes only good things for Silvia. Winnie hasn't even stopped to consider what it might be like to wish good things for herself.

Good things like, perhaps, Ed.

THIRTY

Jo

Thursday noon

The quiet fug of the room is shattered by the clatter and clank associated with getting a 92-year-old man into a hospital isolation room like this. Jo has used one of the pound-a-time wheelchairs stored at the front door of the hospital, and they are notoriously unwieldy. She felt misguidedly confident that it would all go smoothly. She picked him up from the Poppy Park care home where he lives and, as requested, the carers there had made sure he was up, fed, washed, shaved and dressed ready to go.

Jo has several times in the past attempted these tasks herself, but she finds it disturbing when her father occasionally slips into a temporary bubble of his dementia and is inappropriately rude or lewd. The carers at his home are used to it and shrug it off, but Jo spends a good deal of the short time she shares with her father dreading the next awkward moment.

She so wishes she didn't, she wishes she was truly the kind of Earth Mother who can deal with anything that comes her way. She didn't have kids, so she missed out on the cute, palatable sick and shit and snot that motherhood brings. Instead, she seems to have skipped directly to the entirely intolerable sick and shit and snot of old age that daughterhood brings, and she is immeasurably grateful to the angels at Poppy Park for doing so much of the difficult stuff.

Even better than their patient understanding and handling of crotchety old men, is their patient understanding of crotchety old ex-army men. These are a particular breed of chaps whose needs can be difficult to understand. Men whose lives, in some cases, since the age of sixteen have been ordered and regimented. Men who are used to being ranked and barked at. Men who are more comfortable in male company. Men who speak the same coded language. Men who signed the Official Secrets Act. Men who fought for their countries and their lives side by side. Men who loved each other but weren't permitted to acknowledge it. Men whose shared broad humour masked a thousand fears and inadequacies. Military men. Men like Stanley.

Most military men are never 'ex-military', it's a lifelong commitment. The army is not a job, it's a life, and so therefore whilst you are still living, you are army. You are 'Pongo' and much as they rarely admit it, absolutely EVERYTHING else comes second, including wives and certainly children.

For Stanley, army life was charging on as it should, the family moving from posting to posting, camp to camp, following his work, until the terrible day he discovered his wife had motor neurone disease. He loved his wife very much indeed, obviously not as much as he loved the army but still, very much. More than any other woman. He hadn't wanted anyone other than her and was utterly faithful to her, even though some of his more exotic unaccompanied earlier postings presented plenty of racy temptations that various of his oppos couldn't resist. Not Stanley. He was always fiercely loyal to Moira and his darling daughters, Jo and Silvia.

As the ferocity of Moira's illness became apparent, Stanley had a shocking epiphany. Once, when she was going through a particularly distressing episode of muscle twitching and painful cramps, he put his arms around her and with all his brute force, he clamped her very close to him until her poor body stopped spasming. She was calm for a moment, and so he released his grip. And as if powered by giant batteries, she started to jerk and twitch once more. Again, he hugged her tight, again she relaxed. Again he released, again she started up. Although it was tragic, the undeniably comic rhythm of it simultaneously struck them both as hilarious and they started to giggle and then laugh uproariously. The juddering and the laughing intermingled and it became a strangely beautiful union that moved him deeply. In that instant he realized that a momentous shift had happened, and for the first time, an astoundingly ironic time, he knew he loved this wonderful vibrant woman more than he loved the army.

And now, <u>now</u>, she was leaving him, in the most achingly traumatic way.

He had to witness the rapid and savage attack of the brutal disease on Moira's poor body, without being able to protect or defend her in any way. He felt useless, emasculated. As the steady death of neurons in the motor cortex of her brain, her brain stem and her spinal cord kicked in, virtually all voluntary movement ceased, and she became a woeful sight, an exhausted tortured wretch. She could hardly swallow, and her breathing became increasingly difficult. It was at this desperate phase of the violently merciless illness that Moira experienced the particularly cruel symptom referred to as the 'pseudo bulbar effect', an emotional incontinence which meant she had sudden and inexplicable episodes of exaggerated, uncontrollable laughter or crying or smiling, usually at complete odds with her mood.

Stanley could see these extremes were very difficult for the girls to deal with, very confusing and upsetting, but there was nothing anyone could do. Least of all him, the husband and father, a man unable to help or save his wife. A useless man. A failed man. All of his dreadful helpless feelings troubled Stanley increasingly until Moira's harrowing end, and they increased beyond. The sight of his two little motherless daughters was more than he could stomach. His sad situation reconfirmed for him the army mantra that the army comes first. If he had truly lived by that, then surely this wracking agony of loss would be considerably less. He would've lost only his second love, not his first. That surely would've been more bearable. Anything would be more bearable than this, because this was seven kinds of hell.

He had no idea whatsoever how to cope with it. So he didn't. He threw himself into army life, into his matey male friendships, and into a large bottle of whisky. There, at least, he could erase for a while the enduring images of Moira in her last, pitiful days, which plagued him in every waking moment. It was during these turbulent times that Stanley's own mother stepped in and insisted the girls should come to her since he was so clearly not coping. His drunkenness was just about tolerated at work, where his colleagues felt so desperately badly for him that they were prepared to muddle through and cover up when they could. He had a few warnings and was eventually sidelined to a desk job where his deterioration wouldn't be so public or obvious, and that's how he limped on until his retirement.

From the day she went to live with her grandmother, Silvia chose not to speak to her father. He had already frightened her with his boozy bluster and bellowing, but through all of that, the truth was, she still wanted him to be her dad. After all, he was the only parent she had left, and she was bursting to be somebody's daughter. Stanley was, sadly, too drunk to notice and too crushed to care. Silvia couldn't forgive his rejection.

So, now, Jo eventually manoeuvres Stanley into a corner of

Suite 5, with all the concomitant crashes and bangs that go with the likes of Jo in charge of an errant and frankly disobedient wheelchair.

Winnie holds the door open and witnesses it all, wishing she could take over and navigate the chair herself. She has learned the trick, after all these years, of pulling the patient backwards in it, rather than attempting to push it forwards, forcing the badly designed small front wheels to lock. Instead, she has looks on as Jo eventually settles her ancient father into the room.

Winnie sees the strain on Jo's face.

'You wan' cup o' water? Fe you an' daddy?'

'Oh yes, please Winnie, thank you so much.'

Jo takes her coat off and sits herself down in the visitor's chair, close to her dad. She reaches over and takes his coat which is folded neatly on his lap, and she tidies his collar back under his blazer.

'There. Better. Very handsome, Dad, very smart. I'm sure Sissy would be very impressed if . . . she . . . could . . .'

Jo looks at her father. She hasn't properly looked at him today because everything has been such a rush, and she was determined to get him here come hell or . . . high . . . hell.

'Let me know if you need the toilet, Dad. We're in the right place, Winnie or one of the other nurses can help, but you need to give me a bit of warning, OK? It's up the corridor, the Gents is further than the Ladies. Anyway. Here we are . . .'

268

She looks again.

The old man is staring at Silvia. He says nothing. He hasn't said much at all on this journey today. Jo thinks that perhaps he is a bit apprehensive, but she can't be entirely sure that he knows where he is, or what is going on. He has periods of intense lucidity but, mostly, he is living the winter of his life in a blur of misty confusion. He seemed willing to come at least, so that's good, but now he is finally here, he is very quiet.

He does indeed look extremely dapper, if a little shrunken, in his grey flannels, crisp white shirt, regimental stripey tie and dark blazer with the beautiful embroidered badge of the 2nd Battalion Essex Regiment emblazoned on the pocket in all its purple and gold glory. For the very first time, Jo looks closely at it, and notices there is a sideways sphinx perched on a block reading 'EGYPT' at the top of the image which seems, mainly, to be a castle with a key dangling from it. A sphinx. That's odd. Perhaps it was a particularly important battle, or something, she has never thought to look closely or ask.

He has had a careful shave, probably one of the carers did it for him, but they have followed very carefully the line of his natty whiskers in the formation he has shaved them for maybe seventy years. He has a good-sized moustache, a bit like Errol Flynn, which, at its sides, joins on to the bottom of his thick sideburns. He still has plenty of hair although it has, of course, receded and is now entirely snow white. He looks very distinguished and irrefutably army.

Today, he has chosen to wear his medals. For display? For armour? Who knows? They are all lined up on a bar, brightly striped ribbons with silver discs hanging beneath, and bronze stars and pewter crosses. Jo doesn't know what they signify exactly, but they are extraordinarily impressive. War medals, the Burma Star, the Africa Star, his Distinguished Service Cross, his Military Cross and more. A row of shiny honours, hard won.

His face is craggy and his expression is haunted but he is still a handsome man. His heavy-rimmed brown tortoiseshell spectacles sit perched on his nose, the lenses tingingly clean. He looks through those sparkling glasses, right at Silvia, with his milky grey eyes. His gaze doesn't falter. He is intent on her. His hand is wrapped around the top of the extendable aluminium cane he uses to aid his wobbly walking, and Jo notices his worn and scratched rose-gold wedding ring, which stands proud from his shrinking old fingers. It is tapping against the metal cane as his hand continually shakes.

Tap tap tap.

'Don't be afraid to speak to her, Dad, somewhere in there, she can probably hear you. You just have to ... sort of ... tune into the right channel sort of thing.'

He continues to stare.

Jo realizes that, actually, she does the same thing with him, tries to tune in and find a level at which they can successfully communicate. He too is in a similar limbo to Sissy, somewhere between life and death. Jo is uncertain where either of them reside. They are not yet dead but neither are they fully alive. In a way, she is the last one left from the tight little foursome they once were. She feels a wave of sadness about that. She didn't expect to be without parents <u>and</u> a sibling, it seems too unfair. She shakes off the thought. Dad and Silvia aren't dead . . . yet.

In place of the sadness comes an overwhelming sense of responsibility and, for a brief moment, Jo allows herself to experience being something akin to a mother, or a wife. Something she has never been able to be. Both of these people need her right now, to be their advocate and protector, and Jo guiltily enjoys the position she finds herself in.

It's good to be necessary, especially after a lifetime of feeling entirely the opposite. It's a shame the circumstances have to be these, but when you are Jo, you will take all the fulfilment you can get, anywhere you can find it. She settles for a paltry little amount of love, every time. The bar is low, and in this room right now is about as much as she can ever expect, so why wouldn't she allow herself a tremor of pleasure about it? It's a bit unfortunate that both participants are captive, and in questionable health, but she can overlook that in order to have her needs met.

Just as Jo is revelling in her importance, Stanley seems to emerge from his daze, and starts to speak.

He is distressed.

'Has she fallen over?'

'Well, I suppose in a way, yes, she has Dad. She fell from a balcony, that's why her injuries are so severe.'

'What?!'

Jo speaks louder, as if volume will resolve his confusion.

'SHE FELL OFF A BALCONY! HURT HER HEAD!'

'This is what happened last week, isn't it? The first symptoms show in the arms and legs, she has been dragging her foot . . .'

'No Dad, she fell off a balcony, she didn't just fall over.'

'Yes. That's right. The twitching starts soon.'

'No Dad, she fell off a . . .'

Jo begins to realize that Stanley is imagining Silvia to be Moira. She tries to clarify it for him.

'Dad. This is Silvia in this bed. Your daughter Silvia . . .?'

'Tell Mummy it's over soon, not long. Not long . . . darling . . . settle down . . . there there . . .'

His voice peters out as his head slowly falls forward and Jo sees that he is crying silent tears which fall directly down from his stooped head into the glass in his spectacles, which fill up like tiny sad swimming pools.

'Oh Dad. Come on now . . .'

Jo goes over to gather her father into a reassuring hug, and as she leans down to him, he raises his stick and starts to strike her. It is sudden and shockingly forceful.

'No Dad, stop it! Please! That hurts!'

272

'Get off me! Get away!'

Jo reaches for the stick to defend herself from the blows, and she wrenches it out of his hand. In the ugly demented chaos of the moment, Jo locks eyes with her father.

Amongst the frenetic confusion, he clearly says, 'Give us a kiss then.'

'Stop it Dad!'

Stanley attempts to stand up and reaches out towards her just as Winnie enters the room, carrying the two glasses of water.

'Wha's all dis?! Come on grandpa, sit back dung in de chair. You OK Jo?'

'Yes, yes. He just has ... these moments. It's nothing. He's confused ...'

'Of course he is, it all a bit much, yes?'

'Yes. That's right. Yes.'

Jo doesn't want to play mum or wife any more. It's too real and complicated, and she doesn't have the patience.

Stanley groans a bit, sits back in his wheelchair and gradually calms down. He accepts the water from Winnie and seems placated. He looks at Jo, and although she is nervous to look him directly in the eye again, for fear of him kicking off, she does, and there she sees her familiar kindly old dad looking back at her and smiling.

He says, 'Shall I treat you to ice cream? You like that, don't you? Come on then, nipper ... you want a flake?'

He slips back into his old skin and she knows there is nothing to fear. For now. How she hates these demented ghostly glimpses of a man she longs to be loved by. He was her closest ally in the young family back along.

She and Daddy.

Sis and Mummy.

That's how it was . . .

'I think I'd best get him back, Winnie. It's his lunchtime. He's better off in familiar surroundings.'

'Yes, yes, h'okay Jo. Yu wan' some help to put 'im in de car? De porter can do dat.'

'Yes. Yes please,' says Jo.

'Yes please. Ps and Qs, please. And thank you,' says Stanley, copying her. 'We should leave Mummy to sleep while she can.'

His voice is croaky and weak.

'Yes Dad, that's right,' says Jo, as she gathers up both of their coats.

Winnie thankfully takes charge of the wheelchair, and deftly turns it round so she can get Stanley out of the room backwards, with as little fuss as possible.

As he rolls past Silvia backwards, the last sight he sees of her is her head, the head of his darling Moira, with all the tubes and fuss of the ventilation support attached just as she actually had at the end.

'Bye honey pie. Sleep tight . . .' are his last words to her.

And he is out the door and into the slipstream of the busy corridor.

When Jo eventually gets him safely ensconced back into his room at Poppy Park, one of the senior nurses takes her aside and asks to speak with her on a delicate matter.

It would seem that this month's cheque has not turned up?

Jo was under the impression that her father's army pension paid for his care here, so what did she mean?

Oh no, the nurse explains, it all changed five years ago, when Stanley was moved into a different level of care due to his dementia. In order for him to be 'bumped up to top flight', a cheque has been arriving each month for the not inconsiderable difference. Stanley said the signee was his daughter, so the nurse has assumed this was Jo.

It isn't.

It's Silvia, who won't be signing any cheques in the near future.

Silvia.

Who sold her family home for no obvious reason.

Silvia.

THIRTY-ONE

Cassie

Thursday 2pm

With the beeping of the ECG machine and the regular gasping of the ventilator as her metronomes, and the visitor's chair as her dais, Willow is in full voice, performing for 'The Lady'.

She sings, or rather, shouts.

'Have you ever had a penguin come to tea? Penguins, attention!'

She salutes, maintaining the demeanour of a penguin at all times.

'Penguins, salute!'

As she starts the next verse, she vigorously waggles her arm, and continues like this throughout. She starts with one, then increases to waggling both arms on the following verse, then both arms and a leg, then both legs, then both legs and a head and so on, until in the final verse, she is jumping about and jiggling her whole body wildly like kite tails in the wind.

The whole display is hilarious, and Willow is lapping up the encouragement and laughter of her mum and Winnie.

'And so don't ever have a penguin come to tea. Penguins, attention! Penguins, goodnight!'

Cassie and Winnie whoop and clap.

'Well done darling, well done!'

'Yes! Very good lickle cutie! You so clevva!'

Cassie gathers Willow up in her arms, and hugs her tight. She is aware that Willow's eyes are darting over towards the bed and its curious occupant. Cassie agonized over whether to bring Willow into this strange environment, she wondered if it would disturb her, but in the end she reckoned that the possibility, however slight, that Willow's presence might help Silvia to surface was just too significant to ignore.

Cassie also decided that she would break the cycle of rejection, and lead by example. She would be the bigger person and do the right thing, rather than let the toxic infection of hurt spread any further. Willow might have uncomfortable memories of this experience, but at least she would have been here. She wouldn't, in the future, be able to level any blame at Cassie for denying her the chance to at least see her grandmother, or 'The Lady', as she knows her.

Cassie finds it hard to explain the peculiar relationship to Willow, it's so unlike her close bond with her other grandmother, Ben's mum. Willow wouldn't really understand that this log of a person is a grandmother, she has had nothing to do with her, so didn't know her before she became a log. Maybe, ironically, that is a plus in a way. At least Willow doesn't have to feel a massive sense of loss or anxiety, which she would surely feel if the two of them had a proper connection.

If she knew Silvia. Properly knew her.

'Come on puddin', why don't you use your colours and make The Lady a lovely picture for her wall?'

'Dat would be so cool Willow, mi haffi get back to work now, but I be in later an' see what you done, yes?'

Winnie winks at Cassie, this is special treatment because children aren't usually allowed on this ward, but Winnie has told Cassie she will make an exception in her case, and allow Willow in when she is on duty today. Winnie feels strongly that the hospital rules regarding children in the ITU are archaic and cruel, and that this is the most crucial time when visitors should be allowed free access to their critically ill loved ones. They may never have another chance. Sometimes, medicine and all the tightly controlled rules surrounding it should take second place to people.

Today is one of those days. Winnie wants the people to take precedence over bureaucracy and regulation. Besides which, she owes Ed and his family massively, so she is happy to bend the rules. Winnie leaves Cassie and Willow alone with Silvia. The three generations in one room.

It's personal and it's important.

Cassie puts Willow down and goes about making a little art corner for her with all the paraphernalia she insists on bringing in her 'art bag'. She has crayons and felt-tip pens and paper and colouring-in books and table mats stolen from T.G.I. Friday's with puzzles and patterns to colour. Cassie lowers her mother's over-the-bed swing table right down to Willow's height, and sets it all out for her.

Willow is curious.

'Why is The Lady making that noise?'

'Well, at the moment The Lady can't quite do her own breathing because she is very poorly, so that machine there is doing her breathing for her, and that's the noise you can hear. That's all.'

'I do breathing on my own, don't I?'

'Yes honey, you do. And very well. You are an excellent breather, I think.'

'Yes. I am. And I'm not poorly.'

'No, you are very healthy.'

'Yes, because of fruit. And oranges.'

'That's right.'

'Did The Lady forgot to eat her oranges?'

'No, she fell down and hurt her head.'

'Oh. And now she's having a little sleep.'

'That's right.'

'Will she wake up soon?'

'I don't know. I hope so.'

'Does The Lady like cheeses?'

'Um, I think so, yes. Why, darling?'

'Cheeses will help her . . .'

Willow starts to draw intently in her pad of paper.

'Right. How will cheeses help The Lady, Willow?'

'Cheese always helps people, maybe gets her better, so she wakes up?'

'Hmm. I've never heard of that, but maybe . . .'

Willow laughs at her mother.

'Yes Mummy, you have heard of it. You're just being silly . . . cheeses makes everyone better if he likes because he's made of God.'

'Oh I see. Yes, I am silly, because I usually call him Jesus . . .'

'You're funny Mummy. Look, I am drawing my family . . . there's Grandma, and Daddy and Granddad Eddie and you. Now I'm drawing me . . .'

'Oh, I love that picture, and I'm sure The Lady will too.'

Cassie goes closer to her mother and looks at her face. It seems changed, oddly clammy and not quite Silvia's normal ruddy colour, in fact she could swear she sees a subtle hint of a blue hue about Silvia's skin. Then she looks closer and thinks she can't. The machines seem to be making all the usual noises, the breathing is exactly as it has been these last few days, and she looks comfortable on her side. Cassie takes a deep breath, and walks to the window. She looks up at the sky and notes that big rain clouds are rolling in.

'Ooo, I think there might be some rain later, Woo Woo. We won't have to water your tomato today. It will get plenty to drink from the sky.'

Cassie gazes at everything outside: the quad, the sunshine-starved grass, the wooden bench where a gaunt man in a threadbare dressing gown sits puffing away furiously at a thin cigarette, the precise reason he's in here. He is the very epitome of a sad sight and Cassie's heart hurts just to look at him.

That's the trouble with hospitals. They are full of desperate sick people. It's hard enough to safeguard your reserves of courage to deal with your own particular infirm, never mind dealing with the sights, sounds and smells of other people's. Cassie is an exceptionally sympathetic person to boot, and it's a challenge not to empathize too much when you are surrounded by misery and fear, like you are always in a hospital like this. She could sob right now at the woeful sight of that thin man and his thin cigarette, imbuing him with all her pained imaginings, his poor timid wife who only ventures out when supported by this formerly strapping capable man. Admittedly, they mainly went out only to get fags but nevertheless she will no doubt be rendered housebound by this dreadful circumstance.

And what about their son in Dubai who will have to make the difficult decision about whether his father is sick enough for him to take time off his important lucrative job to come and see him one last painful time before he dies?

And then there will be the harridan of an unkind greedy daughter who will boss the frail mother into selling the house and giving her everything. The sickly dad has always been a buffer between his daughter and the vulnerable mother. He has protected her until now, when he himself is too pitifully weak . . .

All the time Cassie has been engrossed in speculation, busily living and suffering other people's lives for them, little Willow has been singing quietly, a random made-up song about rain and tomatoes and God, who made both, whilst she toils away at her important picture.

'It's finished, Mummy!'

This jolts Cassie out of her fertile imagination where she could happily remain all day, in a limbo of no responsibility. However, back in the real present, she relishes the responsibility of motherhood, it's so easy for her to want to be there for Willow, look at her now, holding up the fruits of her toil. Cassie walks to her and takes the picture to have a good look.

She has drawn the outline of a house, and inside is a row of people. Cassie recognizes them all immediately: Ben with his customary beanie hat on, his mother, Willow's gran, Granddad Eddie with a wheelbarrow, then Cassie herself with a mass of red hair in felt tip, holding hands with Willow who is always a mini version of Cassie with the same hair but wearing her red duffel coat and green frog wellies. Outside the house, to the side, is a massive tree, most probably a beech.

'It's to show The Lady who my family is, and the trees and the cat.'

'What cat, darling? We don't have a cat, do we?'

'Yes, we do. Jess. That's my cat.'

'Jess? Do you mean Postman Pat's cat? The black and white one?'

'Yes, that's my cat too.'

'I see. So, where is Jess on the picture?'

'Not on the picture. Over there ...'

With which, Willow points at Silvia.

Cassie looks. Willow has drawn extensively on Silvia's face with black permanent marker. Since Winnie turned Silvia on her side, her face is now dangerously, irresistibly accessible to a creative four year old. As Cassie comes closer, the full extent of Willow's ingenuity is revealed. She has drawn big black whiskers on Silvia's cheeks, made her nose entirely black, dotted between her nose and upper lip, and in a very un-catlike way she has inexplicably made two big round red rosy circles on her cheeks.

Cassie raises her hands to her face in shock, and gasps. How could this have happened without her noticing? Cassie is transfixed by the sight, her eyes are wide open and she is silent, slowly drinking it in.

'The Lady be's Jess the cat, then she can come in our family with my mummy and daddy and Granddad Eddie and Grandma. The cat will do sleeping all the time, like The Lady, see?'

'Yes darling, I see. Yes. Mmmm.'

'I think The Lady likes to be a cat because she didn't say not to ... did she, Mummy?'

'No Willow, that's true.'

Cassie can contain her shock no longer. It has tipped from the initial gut lurch into incredulity, swiftly followed by uncontrollable giggles. She is helpless to do anything about it, the hilarity of the moment consumes her. Everything about the situation is so wrong in lots of ways, yet seeing her mother painted like this is somehow so right. It's right because she deserves it, and it's right because a little innocent grandchild should be able to paint the face of their grandmother without it being any kind of problem whatsoever.

Maybe not with permanent marker, but still ...

'Oh, Willow. I do love you ...'

Cassie is almost convulsing with laughing so much and Willow is happy to join in. It could be that she had done something wrong but Mummy is so happy that it must be OK so she feels free to chortle along with Mummy.

The two of them hoot away.

'Oh my blimmin God, Willow, it's ... genius. Ha Ha!'

Willow starts to jump up and down with glee at just how

284

happy Mummy is. She claps her hands excitedly, and grins as wide as a Cheshire cat.

This is the very moment that Winnie comes in, along with the young doctor who has something she needs to tell Cassie.

Cassie absolutely knows she shouldn't be laughing at this key moment, but the running tap of her giggles is jammed full on, and however hard she tries, she doesn't seem able to stem it. The absurdity of it all, Willow shrieking, the sight of her cat-faced mother and the gravity of the moment all conspire to collapse her into a doubled-up fit of the tittering shakes. Cassie attempts to at least alter the volume but all efforts are pointless. The seriousness of the doctor and Winnie's palpable shock at the daubs on Silvia's face add to it. The pressure to keep a straight face is enormous. She can't. Her eyes water with the effort of it, and she coughs to try and regain some composure. Her body is so tightly held in, so tense against the giggles as she attempts to get her breath, the humour in her is brimful and ready to explode.

So much so, that just as she gets a handle on the guffawing and starts to quieten down, a tiny but undeniably audible little high-pitched fart escapes from her.

Willow hears it.

Everyone hears it.

'MUMMY! You done a poppity!'

'Oh God, sorry. Ha! Ha! Ha!'

And now Cassie is off again, snorting and slapping her leg to try and control the gales of laughter.

Amid all this bluster, Winnie gently coaxes Willow to follow her out to the nurses' station, claiming that she wants to show her picture to the other nurses. Willow skips along beside her, holding her hand, happily prepared to exhibit her work publicly. Winnie quietly shuts the door.

The doctor and Cassie are left alone in Suite 5, and to the accompanying backing track of Cassie's struggle to stop laughing, the doctor quietly explains that, as a next of kin, she must inform Cassie that Silvia has contracted a nasty infection.

Cassie can hardly take it in.

'Blah blah opportunistic pathogens, blah blah blah weak immune system, blah blah nosocomial pneumonia, blah blah test blood and urine, blah blah . . .'

Cassie notes that the young doctor is not much older than her, maybe five years or so, no more. She notices the small anchor on a gold chain around her neck and wonders what it signifies, or who gave it to her? She is fascinated by a mole on the cheek of the doctor and how it moves when she speaks. She is distracted by anything other than what the doctor is saying. She doesn't want to hear that at all . . .

'. . . blah blah being treated with antibiotics, Ceftazidime, blah blah give increased oxygen, blah blah not great, blah tell family, blah blah . . .'

Cassie is aware of the doctor's hand on her arm.

'You OK with all this?'

'Yeah,' says Cassie. 'Fine. Yes. Fine.'

As Cassie speaks, a female visitor of another patient passes the window and glances in. Cassie wonders what the woman thinks of what she is seeing. Is she filling in all the details just as Cassie would if she peeped at this scene?

Is she thinking 'Oh look. There's a poor daughter being told the devastating news that her loving mum is about to die'?

Is that what she's thinking?

Is that what's happening?

THIRTY-TWO

Ed

Friday 8am

E d is on his phone.

'Well, yes, OK, I see. Hmmn. Yes. I'm afraid I can't be there just yet, I'm at the hospital, my ex-wife is . . . very ill,' he whispers. 'Very ill, if you get me, I have to be here. Well, I suppose I might be able to get up there around lunchtime all being well. OK. Of course. Just . . . can you . . . just please be careful around the roots of any saplings, any of the younger trees . . . yes . . . of course. Yes. OK. Thank you. Sorry, what's your name again? . . . Right. Thank you. Bye.'

He clicks the red button on his phone to cut off the caller. He remains looking at the phone in his hand for some minutes whilst he processes the information. It's a bit weird, he's not experienced a phone call like that before, especially not under these circumstances. When Cassie called him yesterday afternoon to tell him what the doctor said about just how sick

288

Silvia suddenly had become, he might have been forgiven for thinking that was the most crucial piece of information he would be given in this twenty-four hours.

He was wrong.

Ed decided not to rush immediately to the hospital. He was due to see Winnie in the evening, and he very much wanted to do that. He definitely wanted to see Winnie more than Silvia. He felt a pang of guilt about it, but Cassie had explained that nothing was likely to happen immediately, besides which he believed Winnie would be able to shed some light on the situation for him.

He came to the hospital at midnight instead, and slept in the sadistically uncomfortable chair by Silvia's bed, lulled by the wheezing of the ventilator. He could hear her breathing become increasingly gurgly as the long night wore on. Various night-duty nurse spectres wafted in quietly at measured intervals to top up her intravenous line with antibiotics and sedatives and diuretic drugs. They whispered to him as they did it, as if not to wake her. If only they could wake her, he thought. Perhaps they were whispering in order not to wake him, but he was only drifting in and out of shallow sleep. A mere waft of air would have woken him. How he would have welcomed a waft of fresh air. Why is the room kept so sealed and hot? This air is now so over-used, there is precious little oxygen in it.

To distract himself from how stagnant and unnatural this

environment is, Ed has held on to Silvia's solid disc of wood he gave her on her birthday just a couple of days ago, it anchors him to all he cherishes. To the natural, normal world outside here. He is acutely aware that he may not be returning to that world for a little while, and that, maybe, when he does, it will be after Silvia is dead, because Silvia is . . . bloody hell . . . it's true . . . Silvia is actually dying.

He looks at her pallid face. He knows it's true. No doubt.

But actually, he remembers he has just promised the police he will try to get back up to the wood when he can, so maybe this won't quite be his last visit. He suddenly realizes that he hopes not. Against all the odds, he finds he wouldn't mind visiting her in here forever, if it means she is still alive.

He feels compelled to keep talking to her, telling her all his stuff, so he does.

'Bloody hell, Silv, that was a copper on the phone, sorry to take that call in front of you in here, I know you'd find that unfeasibly rude. Anyway, turns out they want to dig up a patch at Foy Wood. Some bloke's dog has sniffed something up near the big old queen beech. It's probably a dead dog or something, or a placenta. Some of those dreadlock girls from the campsite love all that, their offering to The Green Man or somesuch loony stuff.

'It's apparently in the oldest part of the wood – you know it well Silv – but ironically that's close to where I have planted a whole new set of saplings in the hope that the big old nurses will shelter them a bit, so I hope they don't go and dig too close to them, they've only been in there for a year or so, they're still taking hold. Still, not much I can do. I'll bob up there later to see what's happening. Hope they don't cause too much chaos . . .'

Silvia lies there. Being breathed for.

'Sorry love, not your problem. So. Here's another day Silv, another morning. I wonder if there's any time happening in your world? Well, just in case it is, let me bring you up to speed, I didn't want to blether on in your ear through the night. In case you were sleeping . . .

'I want to be straight up with you Silv. I don't think there's any point in fannying about. Cassie called me to explain what the doctor said, that you have a pretty serious infection. I was about to kick off to be honest, I thought you might have caught it in here, well, of course you caught it in here, but I thought perhaps the hospital is at fault or something . . . y'know, dirty. Winnie told me that yes, you have, of course, contracted it in here, but it's not so much to do with cleanliness as with your immune system being so weakened. I'm afraid you were probably going to catch anything that's been floating about here. Let's face it, hospitals are full of bloody infections, it's the worst place to recover in many ways.

'So. Hmmmmm . . . It's not good Silv. But listen, they're giving you heaps of antibiotics . . . and you are a strong person, we all know that. You've got to want it though Silv. You've got to want to live . . . and I'm not sure that you do, I wish I knew. I really wish I knew everything you want. We are all guessing, and for all we know, we could be getting it totally wrong, but look Silv, everyone is doing their best for you and trying to go about it in the way we think you would want. That's all we can do.'

He picks up the disc of wood again, unconsciously comforting himself. He pulls the chair over and sits close to her head. He looks at her face. It is hard to do because she looks so undeniably like a dying person now, so . . . collapsed.

How can she have gone from alive and vibrant to this living dead in less than two weeks?

It's astounding, terrifying, how speedy it's all been.

Her face still has the marked remnants of Willow's face painting. Although the nurses have attempted to get it off with various different methods, it won't quite shift, so she still has traces of cat whiskers and nose. Funny how quickly you can get used to it, thinks Ed. It even sort of suits her, in a silly way.

Throughout the night, sitting next to his ex-wife, Ed has found himself several times being drawn towards in-sync breathing with her machine. It's as though his breathing and hers have magnets. Eventually, they pull towards each other. It's happening again now, while he sits quietly here with her in the morning light. He wonders if his natural unmetered breathing is too fast, since he has to slow it down considerably to breathe at her pace. At the machine's pace. He doesn't like the fizz he can hear in her lungs, it's definitely becoming more noisy. He feels powerless to resist the rhythm and it's pointless to try.

Why not breathe along with her?

Maybe that is some sort of company, the union of the two bodies. The synthesis of simply coexisting simultaneously.

'Sometimes Silv,' he whispers, 'there is absolutely nothing you can do about suffering, except just suffer it. But I feel for you. I really do. However asleep you might be, this can't be nice. And I want you to know I'm here, OK?'

With that, he covers her hand with his and gives it a little squeeze. He doesn't really know who she is any more, but he wouldn't want her to be standing at the gateway between life and death on her own. He thinks that we surely all would need a chum at a time like this, and Silvia has precious few.

He has no idea what has happened to Cat. She hasn't been seen at the hospital since Wednesday, and no one can get hold of her. Much against their better instincts, but for the sake of Silvia, both he and Jo have been trying to contact her, all in vain. She appears to have disappeared. Ed is surprised by this. They seemed inextricably linked. To the exclusion of all else. Much as he doesn't like how exclusive their friendship is, he utterly expected Cat to be in attendance at a moment like this. Still, the old faithfuls like himself and Jo are not giving up.

In fact, Jo is due to come in soon, and Ed wants to tell Silvia something before she turns up. Just something he wants her to know.

'So, here we are. Two old twats. Been through a lot together Silv. Yes. Got loads of amazing memories. I was looking through the old photo albums with Cassie on Sunday – she was amazed I had so many . . .'

He doesn't elaborate on this thorny subject. He could never quite believe that Silvia gave them all to him, appearing to reject her entire history with their family. He's never explained this to the kids, believing it to be too painful a fact.

' . . . and we did have some great times, didn't we? Holidays in Cornwall with the kids, that time we had to be rescued by the coastguard just outside Mevagissey, on the inflatable, remember? Oh God. My fault. Mr Nautical bollocks. And the magic coin pasty competition? Jamie lost a tooth to that. My fault again. And the "giantest mermaid in all the universe"? Your head poking out of the sand. Cassie spent all day on that. Proper art. Heartbroken when the tide came in. Had to dig you out quick.

'And what about Christmas? All the Christmases? I bloody love Christmas. I know you hated all the naff stuff, the fifty white teddy bears in festive tartan up the stairs? The old strings of lanterns my mum and dad used to have, the knitted nativity? Ha ha, God, I loved that. So did the kids. So did you I think, eh? We all cracked up when you replaced Joseph with the peeing boy. Ha. His pants up and down all through

Christmas, pissing into the crib. Dirty bugger. "Mummy, Joseph's weeing on Jesus again!" Ha ha ha. Loved it.

'Hmmmn. Yep. We did have some good times all together. Mustn't forget that, Silv. Mustn't forget. All goes into the pot. And helps.'

But all this isn't what he wants Silvia to know.

This is.

'So. Anyway. Winnie, from here, and I met up last night. Mainly to talk about a problem she's been having with her son. I drafted a letter for her . . . But anyway. I decided to show her the wood. I gave her an old pair of Cassie's walking boots and we drove up there. I didn't know if she'd like it, didn't know if she'd be into nature and stuff but honestly Silv, it was like watching a kid at Disneyland. She says she doesn't get much time to be outdoors and she'd forgotten how much she loves it.

'I didn't want to bore her with all my tree stuff, but I thought she might be interested in a few facts and thoughts, y'know. So we walked and talked about how trees of course have no brains, yet miraculously, they can adjust and create and sort of learn. About how this wood was here when we came into being and how it will certainly still be here way way after we've gone and how bloody awesome that is. Immemorial Equilibrium. Yes. Indeed. I told her about how the pattern of the branches on the great old beeches imitates the pattern of the leaves and she started to cry. I thought I might have upset her but she said she was crying with . . . wonder. Pure wonder and joy.

'She said it was just like us, and our kids, the branches and the leaves, imitating each other, and she said how thankful she was that Luke finally had a man in his life . . . who . . .'

Ed finds it difficult to carry on. He is choked. He is struck by how much it all matters. To him, to Winnie, to Luke, to Cassie, to Jamie, to them all.

'. . . who might be the kind of example he could follow, who is . . . kind, she said, and true. Who is a good dad, she said. She said that Silv. That I am a good dad. And a good man. And a good granddad. She said she knew that because of the way Willow drew me in the picture. Oh, there's the picture . . .'

He walks to the wall to check it closely.

'Ha, yes, I see. There's me with the wheelbarrow! Bless her. She loves riding in that. She really does. Look at her frog boots. She's done those ever so well. Ah. Yep. Good.'

He turns back to Silvia,

'So. That's what she said anyway, and honestly Silv, it meant the world. And I couldn't help myself, I just had to . . . y'know . . . kiss her. God. I did. I kissed her, and we were standing there in the whirl of the wind in the trees, and it was bloody amazing. Exchanging breath with her and with the trees all at once. All the oxygen blending together. Fresh, and bloody amazing.'

He can't stop saying 'amazing'. He is clasping the wooden disc to his heart without even knowing it.

'And then. THEN. She sang! Just lifted up her head and sang out loud. And we walked and she sang. Bloody wonderful. Her voice is amazing. Amazing. She is amazing. Unafraid and real and amazing.'

Ed is remembering the astounding moment Winnie sang out a beautiful gospel hymn he didn't really know.

> *I come to the garden alone*
> *While the dew is still on the roses*
> *And the voice I hear falling on my ear*
> *The Son of God discloses.*
>
> *And he walks with me, and he talks with me,*
> *And he tells me I am his own;*
> *And the joy we share as we tarry there,*
> *None other has ever known.*

Her voice is phenomenal. It's pure, strong and exultant. He took her hand and walked through the trees he loves so much, with this shining woman. He's not a religious man, but he felt blessed in that splendid moment.

Still today, he feels lucky and grateful. And excited to see her. She is due on duty again this morning. He is desperate to lay eyes on her, to reassure himself it's all true. He knows it is. But he wants to see her. He wants to see her forever. And look out for her, and her son. He longs to protect them, to come alive again as a man. Willow has helped to balance him. Cassie and

Jamie have always appreciated him, yes, but now this woman and her dear son are going to complete him.

He knows it. He can't wait. He's got so much for them all.

'So, the thing is Silv. I sort of understand something now, I've been thinking about it all night sitting here next to you. I realize that, in our marriage, we were both in different marriages really, I think. We were a bit like bacon and eggs, where y'know, the chicken is involved, but the pig is really committed? I totally gave myself to it just as we promised, "for better or worse", and you didn't see it like that. So consequently, you were able to give up on it, and I haven't. Even 'til now. I just couldn't let bloody go.

'But now I see I absolutely fuckin' must. I must. And not just for me, but for you. Unless I break away properly, finally, you can't either, and now is the time you must. Because, Silv, my darling Silv . . .'

He goes to her and touches her arm.

'I think you need to die, don't you?'

Suddenly, Jo storms through the door.

'I'm here darling, it's alright now!'

THIRTY-THREE

Tia

Friday 9am

Tia passes the day room next to the nurses' station and sees Jo being comforted by Ed and Winnie. She is sobbing and shuddering like a small child. Tia knows why. Cassie has called to sensitively explain it might not be long now, and that if Tia wants to see Silvia for the last time, she ought to visit soon.

Tia respectfully walks past, and comes into Suite 5.

'Hello Mrs Shit! Tia here. Miss Cassie call me an' tell me you doing the dying soon, so I can say goodbye today. She say you have the hospital infection bug. They is dirty turds in here, who gave you the nerve to get killed here? They should let Tia do the cleaning. I don't kill you. I do good cleaning like you know for years. No bugs gettin past Tia. No way. They can all muff off. Tia cloth clean with TSB anticeptical every day. All bugs dead. Not allowed to kill Mrs Shit. I should bring in Tia's

299

cloth and mop. Get it fresh. Stop them killing all the other sick cockheads in here.'

Tia bustles around the room, tidying things that are already tidy, eventually settling down in the visitor's chair.

'I not stay long. You got to die soon, an' family comin. Tia not family, but know Mrs Shit long time, isn't it? So Tia make this for you.'

She furtles about in her bag, and then, very carefully, she brings out a Tupperware container.

'Cos before when I bring Mrs Shit best favourite curry in here, the nurse check my bag each time now, an' they ask Tia to leave all values outside. But today they all busy with cryin so they don't see, so Tia can bring for you . . .'

She opens the container and brings out a small, home-made offering. It is a bowl made from interwoven palm leaves, containing lots of little things Tia thinks are significant for Silvia, trinkets and gifts to help her on her final journey. There are a few grains of rice for nourishment, likewise a satsuma and a star fruit, there is some salt for purification, a small plastic heart, a pound coin, a cigarette, a pebble and a shell. All of these are covered over with colourful, fragrant, brightly coloured petals from jasmine and roses, and honeysuckle and daisy. In the middle is a small tea-light candle which Tia lights.

She sets it down safely on the floor, under Silvia's bed.

'This to say thank you for the life of Mrs Shit, and send her back home to heaven, so she can get born again, but this time a new different thing. Maybe a fish? Or a tree? Or a cat?

'Ooo, that's to tell you about Miss Cat. Tia is cleaning at Mrs Shit house yesterday, an' see Miss Cat drive her car up, comin in. Tia thinks no way hosepipe, so quick to double-lock door inside and sit down quiet, keep still so Miss Cat not get in. She tryin key, no good, swearin an' bad words. She kick door, angry shoutin then long time, she go. Tia not let her in. Miss Cat not good in there. Not good. Not good for Mrs Shit. Mrs Shit get all sad pussy face since Miss Cat come. So Tia go back in and finish clean.

'This time Tia see in drawer by Miss Cat side she sleep. It a heavy drawer, but only hankie in, so why heavy? Tia feel right to back an' it push back wood away. Got tape holdin up a bag in. It's got a man watch and big ring for weddin, inside says "Philip + Catherine 2.3.1991" and smaller woman ring with same. Gold rings. So Tia thinks Miss Cat never comin back, so good to sell rings and watch. They on eBay now. Lots bids.

'Tia goin to get more talkin medicine for husband with that money. He likes the talkin an' he start to do smilin, little bit. The talk doctor say it good to bring in my boys to join in next time. And Tia. All together for talkin. Doctor think he get well, take time. Tia make sure two sons dress up nice for talkin. They big boys since Mrs Shit see. Get new shirts. They both have 16–17 necks! Big!'

Tia sees Jo looking in and waving from the nurses' station, and she knows she should leave, and let the inner, superior circle take over. It's time. She reaches back into her bag and brings out a folded bolt of brightly coloured cloth. She lays it on Silvia.

'This for Mrs Shit. It the sarong Tia wears to marry husband. Now Mrs Shit get wrapped up to keep spirit safe in, when she travel to world of dead. And so Tia and husband can say thank you to Mrs Shit for helping to get him better, and for get boys to school. You remember what stars say in magazine Mrs Shit? They say Friday the day should "dress to impress". Now Mrs Shit dress nice. Very impress.'

She unfolds the beautiful cloth and wraps it around Silvia. The more she unfolds it, the more the beauty of it is revealed. It has come all the way from Indonesia. The pattern is a rich swirl of red and blue and green and yellow, glinting with gold thread and lots of tiny mirrored sequins sewn in delicately. The drab room is suddenly transformed into a blaze of vibrant colour, and Silvia is enfolded in a prism of vivid emerald and ruby and sapphire, of sun, sky, grass, fire, moss and sea.

Of the splendour of everything brilliant. Of life. In its loud colourful glory.

'There. Mrs Shit should let go. There is so many other lifetimes to have. Time to start them now. Not to be scared. Just to go.'

The tiny mirrors in the sarong reflect hundreds of tiny bright lights around the room.

Tia leans in and tenderly strokes Silvia's still cat-whiskered face.

'It like when my boys say to Tia, and mean nicely, "Now, fuck off!"'

THIRTY-FOUR

Jo

Friday 9.45am

Tia and Jo are hugging each other in silent solidarity outside the door of Suite 5. Each secretly believes the other to be quite mad, but they are glad of the comfort this physical exchange provides. Silvia offers them a common sorrow to share, and both of these women rarely have a chance these days to touch another human being in such an intimate, consoling way. They hold on to each other for quite a long time with no embarrassment whatsoever.

Both have a chronic want.

When Jo burst into the room earlier, all of a flutter, she broke down pitifully the moment she saw Silvia. However obvious Silvia's illness has been thus far, never has the dreadful raw reality of it hit home as much as now. The certainty of what's happening is palpable. No one is speaking in a careful, sensitive way any more. The finality is beyond doubt, and Jo finds the truth very difficult, although she is now forced to accept it at least. She had to leave the room and let it all out. Thankfully, Ed was there to help and so was the wonderful Winnie who has oftentimes been strict with Jo. They calmed her so that she can now come back into the room better equipped.

Jo enters the room with a certain amount of trepidation, and sure enough, the second she glances at Silvia, she loses it again, just like before. She is a hopeless mess, but Ed has had to go back up to his wood for some reason so she knows she has to face this. After all, nothing is really that different in here except Silvia's colour has changed, she looks paler, and bluer. She has the faint remains of a cat painted on her face. There is an extra drip up, connected to a syringe driver in a locked Perspex case.

Nothing else has changed, and yet everything has.

Hope is lost, and that is the massive overriding difference. Jo tried to maintain as much hope as possible previously in this room. She believed it might be catching, and that some-how, in her faraway place, Silvia might hear the call of that hope loud and clear, and if she could, she might swim towards it through the darkness and out into the light, where Jo would be waiting. Now though, that former hope in Jo has faded and is replaced by a giant grief-in-waiting. Jo knows she must keep a lid on this. The time hasn't come yet, but her dread of it threatens to tip her up.

Jo bursts into more tears.

'Oh God, sorry Sis, I just ... y'know ... sorry. God. What a baby I am ... pathetic. It's just all so bloody ... hard.'

She sniffles, and blows her nose and starts to gather herself emotionally.

'I can't believe it's come to this. A bloody infection! I had so many other ideas for stuff to stimulate you ... like tickling therapy, a live band, fish nibbling your extremities, lots of great stuff like that. I really believe one of them will work eventually, but an infection trumps all of it, frankly. I bet you're bloody furious in there somewhere darling. I wanted to carry on with everything, still keep going, but they're all saying what I have to do now is accept. Christ. How? If that's it then, I have to accept that I have completely let you down, haven't I? Yes, I bloody well have. Oh God. Sorry Sis.'

She snuffles into her tissue and shrugs her submission with gasps and groans.

'But y'know what? Here's the thing. I can't control the universe. I wish I could, but I can't, and you are a very bright star Sissy. Very bright. Mummy knew that and that's why she asked me to guard you, but I'm sorry, I just couldn't and actually, y'know what? I can't go on being part of the Silvia constellation. We have all paid homage to you, circled you, making sure you come first and making sure everything is alright for you, but I don't think you are even aware of it, it's gone on for so long. We've all willingly been the satellites in the Silvia cosmos, so much so that I would have taken all ... this ...' she indicates the machines, the bed, the tubes, everything'... from you if I could have. I would rather it was me. That's how I've always thought of you. You are the main planet, the brightest one, and I am simply in your orbit.

'But honestly babe, I've got to stop all that because everything in the universe needs a counterpoise. Balance. Equality. It's no good if I keep giving you centre stage to fill. It's too much, for both of us, it's too much. I have always thought that sisters can't occupy the same space, so I've given in to you. But ... why? I think I've always avoided explicit competition in case you bloody win! But that's no good honey. Sometimes you will win and sometimes I will, but either way we should wish each other well.

'I just can't keep on feeling guilty this has happened to you, it's bloody exhausting! And as Ed says, it's quite simply not my fault. It's not!'

Jo sounds like a petulant child as she blurts this out. No wonder. That's pretty much where her emotional development has been arrested. Almost exactly when her mum died. When she was nine years old.

Jo reaches into her pocket and brings out a photo she spent most of last night looking for, after Cassie called. She knew it was in a box somewhere, but did she have it or did Silvia? She riffled through everything she could find to no avail. She climbed into her trusty VW and drove over to Silvia's. Jo had a key, and let herself in. She rummaged through every obvious box. Nothing. The bureau, the top of the wardrobe, under the bed. Nothing. Then, suddenly, she heard an old-fashioned ring-tone. It was Silvia's phone ringing, but where? She followed the sound, all the way to Silvia's handbag on the table in the hallway. She took the phone out and the lit screen announced that Cat was calling. Bloody Cat! Just a day before, Jo might've made the effort to speak to her, to encourage her to come to the hospital, to explain how critical the situation is, but for some reason that night – some properly accurate, sisterly, instinctively protective reason – Jo has no hesitation pressing the 'IGNORE' button, cutting Cat off.

Why was she calling Silvia's phone anyway?

As if Silvia could answer.

She must be drunk or something. Even more reason not to speak to her.

As Jo replaced the phone in Silvia's bag, she sees her sister's open purse, and there, in beside her credit and loyalty cards is the photo. The very photo. Sissy has been carrying it around with her all this time, seeing it every day. It is a photo of the two little girls, Jo and Silvia. They are about eight and five years old, standing in their new raincoats. The photo is black and white but Jo clearly remembers hers was blue, Sissy's was red with matching Start-rite shoes. They are outside Madame Tussauds and they are each holding a monkey. Their faces are full of barely contained delight. They are happy. Of course they are happy, they are safe and loved and they have a mum and a dad and they have no reason to doubt life will always be like this.

This is the photo Jo has in her hand now at Silvia's deathbed.

'I've brought this, Sissy. It's us with the monkeys, remember? It's the real us. Two sisters who will always love each other, whatever happens. No one else is us. No one else has had what we've had, good or bad. I have loved being your sister y'know. I have learned so much, and honestly, I didn't know it 'til now. That's the truth. You and me. Big and small. Together. Forever. You will always have me and I'll always have you, whether you're here or not. Fact, darling, fact.

'Now, listen to me, you go well, whenever you're ready. Just so you know – I'm ready. At last.

'I'm Jo. I'm strong. And I'm ready.'

Jo sits down. She sits next to her dying sister, to be company for her.

THIRTY-FIVE

Cassie

Friday 11am

With respect for Silvia's sombre situation, the nurses have drawn down the blinds both of the small window in the door, and also the bigger window which looks out on to the nurses' station and the corridor. The window out to the quad is still clear, although the light is grim.

Cassie is standing just inside the door. She has her phone in her hand, and she is checking that all is well at home before she feels able to turn it off. She wants to clear her mind of anything else, so that she can be fully present in this room. She might not have this time again.

Cassie has felt a surge of responsibility since the doctor chose to tell her first about Silvia's gloomy prognosis. She has been identified as the next of kin and therefore the ideal person to inform. The oddly spurious hierarchy has propelled Cassie into the prime position she has been longing for. Yes.

She is family with Silvia. Close family. The doctors aren't to know the reality of the family dynamic. They assume a daughter is a beloved. Cassie can't deny that despite the horror of the situation, she is relishing the assumed role somewhat. It fell to her to make the important calls, firstly to her dad, then her Aunty Jo, then Tia and so on.

She can't get through to Jamie, there's no answer on his phone, but he's told her that quite often he's not allowed to use it, so she decided to text him and leave it at that. Cassie knows that he has stepped back purposely from the situation, so she reassures herself that he won't mind being out of the loop. He might even want that. It might make his life easier, perhaps?

Cassie is very close to her brother and has missed him very much since he joined the Marines. He was her solid ally. Dad is always a reliable support, but he has had his own sadness to contend with, besides which, she doesn't feel that it's particularly fair to dump on him about Silvia, the one person he is super raw about. He has his own mending to do concerning her. Anyway, Dad has been fantastic with Willow, who adores him, and that's all Cassie desires from him. Why punish the one parent that has stuck by her?

So, Cassie has managed the difficult situation since it ramped up a gear. She has been efficient and organized, even to this very moment. She is spinning all the plates. Dad has had to go back up to his wood to sort something out with the police. Tia has visited and gone, and Aunty Jo, who can't stop blubbing, is presently availing herself of a giant dripping bacon butty and a cup of execrable coffee downstairs in the dreadful café. An interesting breakfast choice for a confirmed vegetarian.

Aunty Jo seemed a bit better when Cassie swapped shifts with her. She is still crying a lot, but she seems calmer, thank goodness. Cassie wasn't looking forward to dealing with Aunty Jo's histrionics. She always makes a drama. Maybe now that there is an actual drama, Jo has finally understood how much the family need her to maintain some level of control. Cassie wants for there to be nothing fizzy right now, nothing to distract from Silvia.

Just before Cassie came in, Winnie and another nurse were in here, making Silvia comfortable and turning her on to her other side. It's always much better after Winnie has been into the room. Silvia gets the best attention and somehow the room feels fresh, and the situation is the best it can possibly be.

Cassie notices that Winnie has moved into a slightly different modus operandi. She is moving around quietly and keeping all unnecessary nursing away, so that there is little fuss and noise around Silvia. Suite 5 is hushed and feels something like a sanctuary for the first time. The lights are low. Winnie has even allowed Tia's offering candle to continue to burn. She has raised it up on to a shelf and the lovely smells of the flowers permeate the room. Silvia still has the beautiful fabric wrapped around her.

Cassie takes it all in.

This is now a dying room.

She steps out of her ballet-pump flats and crosses to the bed. She puts her bag down and takes from it the white bendy bear, 'Namma', that Silvia sent over for Willow when she was born. The one and only present.

Cassie has asked Willow if The Lady can borrow it while she's feeling so poorly?

Of course Willow has agreed, although it's not easy for her to let him go, even temporarily. But Willow is a benevolent little soul, and would always do the kind and right thing, to her own cost. Like Cassie.

Cassie picks up the corner of the sarong and the sheet, to where she can see her mother's body. Silvia is facing the other way now, so Cassie slowly climbs into the bed and puts her back up against her mother's. She puts her head on the white bear, pulls the beautiful fabric around her and lies still. With each laboured breath, Cassie tries to relax and chime in with the same rhythm, until eventually she succeeds and she is inhaling and exhaling simultaneously.

Cassie likes it more than she could ever have imagined. The intimacy is bliss. Her body gradually starts to imbibe the heat of her mother, and she begins to unwind. They lie spine to spine, breathing steadily. Cassie closes her eyes, and in so doing, she can, just for this short time, imagine she is loved by her mum.

It's all she wants, and it's the best.

She is being transported back in time by everything sensory in her, and she is remembering fragments of her very young childhood when she was held close, when she felt safe, when the love was guaranteed and endless. The delight is intense, but the time is short and precious, so Cassie instinctively knows what she must do. She turns over, and when she is curled up, spooning her mother's back, she slips her arm around to place the bear next to Silvia and to pull her close. Cassie is wrapped around Silvia pulling her in as tight as she can, rocking her gently. She wants to stay there together like that for always. She buries her face in her mother's red red hair. Cassie's red hair is indistinguishable from Silvia's.

Cassie reaches her mouth up to her mother's ear and she whispers quietly.

'Here it is Mum, here's the love. Have it all.'

THIRTY-SIX

Winnie

Friday noon

Winnie takes the opportunity to nip into Suite 5 for a few minutes alone with Silvia while she checks and washes her. She has told the other nurse she can do it alone. Cassie and Jo are in the day room with the doctor. They had lots of questions, so Winnie ushered them all into the small day room with the two sofas and a fish tank, to talk in private, and away from Silvia.

The fish tank is a gift from a well-meaning family who spent many difficult hours in that room when it was bare. Somewhere in that time, they must have had a conversation about what the room needed to cheer it up and they decided a fish tank was the answer. Was it unanimous? Or did one brave renegade unsuccessfully advocate a puzzle table or even a PlayStation and screen for the kiddies? The fish tank arrived on the ward two weeks after the death of their relative, and has been a nightmare ever since, causing ructions amongst the staff, none of whom want any of the responsibilities associated with it. It has to be maintained, regularly cleaned, the fish must be fed, dead ones have to be scooped out and replaced, the filters and pumps have to be checked. The ruddy thing is always leaking, and when it does, it shorts out other electrics in its vicinity, requiring engineers to be called up, who take ages to come because the tank is hardly a priority in a busy hospital. Meanwhile more fish die, and so it goes.

Winnie has come to dislike the fish tank and all its inhabitants, but, ever willing, she has taken on the responsibility with good grace, and she hopes that, as Cassie and Jo are sitting in there, no doubt hearing very difficult information, they might at least get some distraction, if nothing else, from the bloody fish tank. Winnie has recently shelled out fourteen pounds to replace all the fish after they copped it, one after another. Her stomach churned when they were down to just one ugly toady-looking fish and she introduced a new one, which it immediately attacked and ate. It transpired he was the murderer all along, of all the others. Winnie left him alone in the tank for a few days to swim about and reflect on his bloodthirsty cannibalism, and the dreadful massacre he wrought. The gory carnage.

While she was leaving him to repent in solitary confinement, she also decided to 'forget' to feed him. She felt a tiny bit guilty about it, but disgusting images of his fishy slaughter shored her up. He was an evil fish and he must go to his maker with his own conscience. Alarmingly quickly, he turned up his fins and she wasn't sad to find him floating on top of the water, utterly dead. She used the net to fish him out and took no little satisfaction in lobbing him into the big yellow bin marked 'hospital waste'.

That was a couple of weeks ago and, since then, she has populated the tank with lots of small brightly coloured happy fish who are getting on well and seem to have no desire to murder each other, mainly because they are plastic . . .

Winnie is aware that time is running out for Silvia. She wants to make sure that what little life she has left on this earth is pain-free, clean and dignified. Winnie knows that pretty soon, all of the machines will be withdrawn from Silvia if the family choose that route, which she hopes they do. She wants to make Silvia ready without interfering with any personal time the family need.

Winnie will miss Silvia in her own right. For some reason, she has talked more to Silvia than any other patient she has had. She always makes sure she addresses every patient, but Silvia is different . . . Winnie has properly confided in her. Winnie's life has been through considerable change in these last ten days, and Silvia has witnessed it all.

If indeed she has.

Whichever way, Winnie regards Suite 5 as a safe telling place.

'Mi come fe wash you, Silvia, mek you all nice fe all dose

317

visitors comin in. An' nice fe you, to feel as upful as you can. Yu have much crosses to bear at dis trouble time wid dat nasty h'infection. H'only yu know how it feel. Mi no know a wa dat. Nobuddi else, but yu. Mi mek haste, an get yu feelin fresh, yes?'

Winnie has her bowl of soapy warm water and a new, clean muslin cloth. She dunks the cloth and squeezes it out, wringing the excess water back into the bowl. It trickles down, and Winnie begins her last wash of Silvia.

This is a religious ritual for Winnie, a devotion.

The water is cleansing, purifying. It's Jordan, it's goodness, it's God.

'Mi haffi tell yu Silvia. Mi got doves in mi heart today. Dem all coo away, surprise yu cyaan hear it. H'Edward tek mi up to 'im forest last night. Bwoy! It sooo pretty pretty dere. Beautiful. 'Im tek mi so careful tro' the trees, walkin gently on de bracken an' leaves wid de giant mudda trees all arong us, so high an' wide. We go right inside, to the very miggle. High high to heaven an' wide wide to de seas. Mi nevva haffi time dese days to h'appreciate nature enough, an' it such a place of God, Silvia. He is dere, in h'every lickle ting, h'every leaf an' h'every twig, his h'omnipotence. Mi know it so clear. An' h'Edward 'im know so much about all dem tree! 'Im know everyting.

'Mi feel privilege to stan' dere wid 'im reasoning so clevva in praise of Mudda Nature an' all she finery. It speak to me, loud an' true. Mi heart fill up an' mi have no choice but to sing. Oh

318

Silvia, it full of glory. God is in dat place. No doubt. And also Silvia, mi hope you hear dis wid respec' . . . but . . . love also in dat place. And in here . . .'

She touches her heart.

'Y'know, mi meet plenty man inna dis short life so far. But not like h'Edward. None like dat good man. An 'im definitely good. 'Im made of goodness. Mi know it deep dung. It truut. When mi know facts, mi can say facts. 'Im mek mi feel ageless, light as a fedda, like a young gyal h'again. Mi tink we a go mek a life togedda, Silvia, an mi wan' yu to know becaa mi respec' yu, an' becaa yu should know, mi a go do everyting to mek it good fe h'Edward an' Cassie an' lickle Willow.

'We gonna grow eachudda good, jus yu wait an' see. Even the soldier boy I nevva met yet. Winnie goin to mek it so dere is a mudda in dat space yu leave. Mi know h'Edward goin to mek good dad for Luke, an' so it my duty an' pleasure to do de syame fe dose kids o' yours. Mi know yu would wish it so, Silvia, mi know it.'

Winnie has washed all of Silvia except her feet, which she comes to now. She takes the cloth and immerses it in the lovely water. She wrings it out, and some of the wonderful redeeming water drips back into the basin. She opens the cloth and wraps it around Silvia's left foot, encasing it in the wet warmth. She holds it tight to give Silvia any tiny morsel of comfort that simple act might provide. How lovely to have your foot held, supported, cradled. Before the cloth has a chance to go cold,

319

she massages the foot with it, separating the toes and going between, sweeping down and under the heel in a sure, confident circular motion. When she is finished with the left foot, she does the same to the right.

The ceremony of it matters to Winnie. Silvia is not religious and the family have rejected any suggestion of a vicar or last rites or anything, so this is Winnie's small symbolic way of showing her reverent respects, of giving praise and thanks for Silvia and of believing in the goodness of her soul. It is a pious and devout act. Quiet and personal. And beautiful.

When Winnie has finished washing Silvia's right foot she takes a towel and pats both feet dry. She makes sure the bedding and the colourful sarong don't encase her feet. Ed has explained that she always liked to keep them out of the sheets, in the fresh air, so Silvia tucks the bedding out of the way, and gently lays her feet on top. Her elegant long white Venus-like feet.

Winnie can hear the voices of Jo and Cassie in the corridor. Their meeting with the doctor is over. She can hear a deep voice joining on. It's Ed. He is outside now too. The family are gathering. It's time for Winnie to take her place firmly in the background. The next phase of her role begins now. She must assist with the dying, make it the best death it can be, and do her best to support the friends and family. That's all part of the nursing, and maybe now, the most important part.

She steals this moment to speak her truth to Silvia.

'Silvia? Mi feel sure yu can still hear me, yes? Yu know yu not goin to recover from dis. Yu know dat. Yu time soon come. But wait, sista, an' hear mi out, mi know fe sure dat yu a go to a better place, a great place, to paradise, Silvia, to de Lord. Go home to glory. Don't be afeard, nuttin gonna hurt yu. Dis is yu homegoing. Yu gonna be bathed in light. Yes Jesus. Yu gonna be saved. Mi jus' wan' to say, it's bin mi privilege to nurse yu. Yu a good woman. An' yu truly loved. Mi walk wid yu right to de gates, OK? So, go well Silvia, go well.'

She hurries from the room, to give the family as much time as they can have. She knows the way only a nurse knows, it really won't be long now.

THIRTY-SEVEN

Family

Friday 12.30pm

Winnie closes the door behind her, leaving Silvia alone for the first time since last evening when Ed arrived to keep the night vigil. They have all switched and shared the time with Silvia between them, like handing a baton on in a relay race against the clock. All have tried to give each other some space and somehow, as it remarkably does at crucial times like this, it has worked seamlessly. There has been a hushed respect, which has flourished inside the diminishing time. There isn't room for selfishness here, they must all give the best of themselves.

Inside Suite 5, there is only one energy.

Silvia.

Her life force is fading but right now, she is still alive, and while she lives, she is the pivot for them all. She is why they are circling around, collecting together to share however it is going to be. She has drawn them in.

She.

Her.

She.

Silvia.

Jo, Cassie and Ed are clustered together in the corridor. Ed is wide-eyed, unshaven, and stunned. Winnie brings them all into the windowless day room with the fish tank beaming its cheerfulness out brightly in the corner, she touches his arm reassuringly, and she goes to fetch tea. Something has ruffled Ed badly, but what's happening here in the hospital is more pressing, so he listens carefully whilst Jo and Cassie explain in detail the conversation they have had with the doctor.

Cassie speaks pointedly to her father.

'I think this is it, Dad. The doctor said the infection is bad . . .'

'Getting worse, gaining control, grim . . .' Jo chimes in, ensuring the story is as overdramatic and alliterative as it can be.

'Yes,' Cassie agrees generously, allowing her aunty to indulge, 'basically, they can't really do much more now. She is going to find it increasingly difficult to breathe . . .'

'Gasping, choking, wheezing, drowning . . .'

'Aunty Jo, I don't think we need to . . .'

'No, of course darling, sorry, I'm just drawing the picture for your dad . . .'

'Right, well, she said they would recommend taking her off everything, the drips, the ventilator, everything . . .'

'The catheter would, of course, remain . . .'

Jo is determined to be precise. The detail is presently keeping her focused. The bigger picture is too horrific.

'Yes. Umm . . . they're saying it's our decision entirely since there's no living will or anything . . .'

Ed rubs his stubbly face, and says, 'Actually, this isn't a hard decision, for my part I mean. I know it's tough, it's bloody awful, but the fact is, I remember having a conversation soon after we were married actually, yonks ago, about exactly this sort of scenario. We were driving somewhere. Dunno. I thought she was being a bit morbid at the time, but I clearly remember her saying she wouldn't want to be kept alive "like Frankenstein", should she not be able to live decently, sort of thing, y'know, independently.

'I remember because I violently disagreed. About her, I mean. Yep, she definitely said that. Or words to that effect. Typically contrary. Stubborn. God. I never thought . . .'

Cassie is relieved.

'Really? Right. Well I suppose it's obvious then . . .'

'Oh Christ, we're going to kill her!' Jo gasps.

Ed is forced to take control.

'Jo! Will you stop your bloody nonsense. This is hard enough without your drama. Stop it please.'

'Yes, yes. Sorry Ed. Sorry Cassie. It's just . . .'

'I know,' says Cassie as she pats Jo on her hand, 'but it's the right thing. We all know it is, and from what Dad says, Mum's already made the decision, it's out of our hands.'

'Yes. Yes,' Jo concedes.

'It's going to happen anyway Aunty Jo, we're just making sure she's comfortable.'

'Yes, that's right . . .' Jo is astounded at how mature and collected Cassie is. Cassie is so much Silvia's daughter. 'Yes, of course. Sorry.'

Winnie brings in the tea and they all pounce on it. A familiar hot wet sweet taste. Something normal amidst the strangeness. It is massively comforting, a liquid blanket over them all.

Winnie sits down next to Ed. Very close.

'Yu let mi know when yu decide, yes? No hurry. Nothing happen 'til yu say. An' I mek sure it's me who do everyting. So she safe. She safe.'

Ed pipes up.

'Well, I think we all agree? Yes?'

Jo nods her head vigorously. Over-keen now, determined to be supportive and part of this family team. Desperate, in fact, not to be left out, desperate to matter. Cassie blinks her consent, solemnly.

'So we will sign whatever you need, just please make sure she is in no pain?'

'Mi tell the palliative team fe come along and check everyting right now, and togedda we prepare her. Get rid of all dose h'ugly tubes. Bet she glad to get dem away.'

Cassie's small voice cuts through.

'How long, Winnie?'

325

'Very difficul' to say h'exactly darlin, but I h'expect not long. Inside dis hour mebbe? You h'okay wid dat?'

'Yes,' Cassie says.

'Yes,' Jo says.

'Yes,' Ed says.

The three-line whip is complete, and Winnie rises to do her duty. As she gets up, she strokes Ed's back, a daring intimacy in these circumstances, but she wants him to know what a sure and certain anchor she is.

He stands up with her and mumbles, 'Can I speak to you? Out there?'

She leaves the room, and he follows, letting Cassie and Jo fortify themselves with tea. When they get into the corridor, he realizes that it's all too busy there, too public, so he motions that they should go into Suite 5. They slip into the room. As soon as they are alone, they both simultaneously want to hold each other, but equally, they both instinctively know this is the wrong place for that. It would be unseemly, inappropriate, selfish. So they don't.

But Ed has to tell Winnie something, he speaks fast and low.

'I've been up at the wood. With the police. Bloody hell, Winnie . . .'

He clamps his hand over his mouth, he hasn't said any of this out loud yet, and it's utterly shocking. Agitated, he pulls his hands through his hair. He is trying to think of the right, careful words. He can't, so he just says it as he knows it, and it tumbles out of his mouth in an odd staccato fashion.

'They found a man. All curled up. Bent over. A dead man. An actual bloody person. Dead. Been there some years, they reckon. Inside my boundaries. In my bloody wood! Dead. Completely dead. Rotting. Under one of my big old nurse beeches. Right there. Where I walk all the time. Probably walked all over him. A lot. Never saw a thing. Dead. A bloke. A dead bloke, an actual bloke . . .'

Winnie puts her hands on his shoulders.

'OK, h'Edward. Calm now. Dat is crazy. Yu mus' be shock'd. Who dey think dat it be?'

'They don't know yet. They asked me if I knew. Of course I don't know. I asked them if I'm a bloody suspect, why are they asking me? Chrissakes!'

'An' what de say to dat?'

'They say I'm not as yet. They . . . apparently . . . ninety per cent of this sort of thing . . . they match the dental records to missing persons . . . then they often find out very quickly who they are. They usually do, they said. But they might ask me a few more questions or something, I don't know . . . I told them what's going on here and they were fine for me to come . . .'

'Of course. Yu have nuttin to worry, becaa yu h'innocent, h'Edward. Truss' mi.'

'Yes, yes. I suppose so, but it's so strange. I don't want to tell Cassie. Not right now . . . with all this . . .'

'Of course. Dats right. Don't yu worry. It all come out darlin, it all come out. It jus' a bit shockin, in't it? Mad. Come. Sit dung.'

Ed is willingly led by her to sit in the visitor's chair. His heart is beating fast. He has the images he has just seen recurring in his mind, buzzing about, horrific fragments dipping and diving in and out of his thoughts.

He found it hard to make sense of the scene that greeted him up in the wood. When he first approached, he saw the tape around the site and the tarpaulin erected over the top and for one heart-thuddingly bizarre moment, he thought he might find out that it was himself in there, cold on the ground, with a noose around his neck. He suddenly imagined that his suicide attempt back then had somehow been successful and everything else since was some kind of other-world reality. That he was actually dead. He shakes off this notion as swiftly as it had slammed into his thoughts, but it certainly shocked him, jolted him.

As he approached and they checked his identity, he realized just how awful it was when he saw disturbing glimpses inside the tent. Tufts of hair on a muddy leathery scalp, bone and flesh in shapes and colours he couldn't recognize or process, whilst still knowing, in a harrowingly real way, what it was. He was aware that he stopped breathing, then that he suddenly had to. And then, on the intake, the revolting stench filled his nostrils, which told his brain what was truly happen-

328

ing. His brain immediately informed his stomach that this was entirely, horrifically unpalatable, and he began to retch. He had to walk away from the site and vomit nearby. He was shaking, unable to control the hammer blows of revulsion smashing him in the gut.

The violence of the shock caught him unawares, and his general tiredness from a fairly sleepless night did nothing to help. He had no resilience. Who would? How many people ever witness such a thing? A murdered body, halfway dug up from its rude muddy grave. Haunting.

Still now, Ed feels the brutality of it, but he can't indulge in it. Silvia must be his focus today, it's unlikely she will have a tomorrow.

Winnie has stood quietly next to him, letting him gather his thoughts.

'Come back out now darlin, mi need to get all dis offa her, and mek she ready. Yu should go an' splash yu face, get a h'apple, be wid yu daughta . . .'

'Yes. Yes. I will, yes.'

He takes her hand as she leads him back out.

The door closes, once again leaving Silvia alone. With the white-hot secret hanging heavy in her air.

Back in the day room, Ed slurps his tea and looks at his lovely daughter's troubled face. What a complicated, difficult time this must be for her. He is struck by just how brilliantly she is handling it all. He makes a mental note that Cassie may feel much more of it all later, after . . . he will keep an eye out for that. She is a supreme coper. He is aware of that. Look how she has coped with everything so far. She is a mother, for heaven's sake, and so young.

His phone pings. It's a text. The detective involved up at the wood has sent it. He said he would communicate in this way considering Ed's circumstances. In fact, he said he wouldn't communicate whatsoever unless there was an urgent need.

It reads simply:

Would you know of a Catherine Mary Bernadette O'Brien?

Yes. He does.

At this precise moment, a figure shambles past the open door. Cassie and Jo are facing into the room, so they don't see, because they are distracted, talking about the fish tank and how it is the only colourful thing to look at in this appalling, windowless room.

Ed sees it though. He sees a shape at least, he just caught sight of it briefly before it exited from his vision. A bent shape, a hunched man, clumsily walking with . . . what was it? A stick, a crutch? Something.

This is a busy hospital, of course someone is walking with a stick. Ed knows in a blinding certain instant that what he fleetingly saw wasn't a someone. It was his someone. He senses his own, smells it. Like a returning Emperor Penguin will instantly find his own singular chick amongst a vast horde of them. He knows he is right, and he is out of his seat in an instant, and into the corridor, where the figure has his back to him.

'Son?'

Jamie turns awkwardly and sees his father coming towards him, arms outstretched.

'Bloody hell, Jamie, it is you!'

Although everything hurts, Jamie eagerly surrenders to a massive bear hug from his dad. Cassie and Jo have heard Ed's shout and join on to a boisterous joyful bundle in the corridor. They are so happy to see him, to see him alive, that, for a moment, they all forget why they are there.

Gradually, the screech and twitter of their hysteria subsides, and Ed ushers them all back into the drab day room to brief Jamie. He disappears into the room amid a hail of excited questions from his family. He is back in the fold.

He is back.

Just in time.

In Suite 5, one of the other nurses assisting Winnie is wheeling out the last of the standing machines. Winnie wants it to be as un-hospital-y as possible for them all, so she has removed everything she can. Silvia is no longer attached to anything, and there are clean dressings on each part of her body that was. She has a large dressing on her neck, and smaller ones on her arms and hands. Winnie has rolled up two small clean towels and placed them under Silvia's hands to support them. She has made a comfortable V-shape of pillows behind Silvia's shoulders and head, and she has raised the head of the bed so that Silvia is half sitting, half lying. The sarong is wrapped around her, and her feet are still out of the bedding at the foot of the bed.

The room is much quieter since all the bleeping and wheezing machines have gone, but they are replaced by the sobering sound of Silvia breathing unassisted. She is struggling on each breath and the gurgle of her throat is ominously audible, but she is heavily sedated so she isn't physically distressed at all. She is in a deep narcotic slumber, she is in a coma, so there are no signs of response. Winnie is pleased it is fairly tranquil.

She takes the brush, and tidies Silvia's hair.

'Dere. Yu look pretty. Nice an' pretty.'

Winnie leans over and, quite unprofessionally, she kisses Silvia on the forehead, and goes to gather up the family.

Silvia breathes.

Then doesn't.

For a bit too long.

Then does.

In the day room, Winnie is introduced hastily to Jamie by Ed.

'Winnie, this is my son, Jamie, and this is Winnie, my ... Mum's nurse ... her friend ... my friend ... umm.'

'Yeah, OK Dad. Hello Winnie.'

'Yu hurt bad?'

'It's OK thanks. My knee's buggered.'

'Any pyain?'

'Not presently.'

'OK. Yu tell mi if yu need anyting?'

'Yes, of course. Thank you.'

'Mi tink it's time yu should all go in . . . yes?'

They all mutter and start to move towards Suite 5, with Jamie at the front, the vanguard. He limps and winces when he forgets occasionally just how shattered his knee is. He has metal pins in it and he isn't supposed to be walking on it at all yet, his operation was only a few days ago at a hospital in Birmingham. He was recovering quietly when he received the text from Cassie about just how serious the situation with Silvia is.

He didn't want to come, it's too painful and he didn't want to ever see her again or grant her any of his time or effort. His barriers were firmly up, but then there was something achingly plaintive about Cassie's text. He could tell she was being brave and stepping up to be the organizer, the little mother. It broke his heart that she should think she has to do that. He knew that he must support her, whatever the cost to him. He won't allow the dysfunction and coldness of Silvia to filter down into their lives so much that they forget to support each other. Even though Dad is here, big brother looks after little sister. Those are the rules, and they're right. He requested compassionate leave, he's on R and R anyway, so here he is.

For Cassie.

Or so he thinks.

Just as they get to the door of Suite 5, they hear a kerfuffle and when they look back they see a dishevelled, angry wide-eyed sweaty creature bombing up the corridor towards them.

It's Cat.

'Let me in there! I need to see her!'

Without a second thought, and with all the lightning-flash reactions of his training in a war zone, Jamie uses his stick to trip her, and as she falls, he grasps her arm and twists it to her back so that as she hits the floor she isn't hurt much, but she is entirely restrained. He slumps down and kneels across her so that she can't move a muscle.

'Aaaagh! Get off me. Help! Get him off me . . .!'

'Stop wriggling and you won't get hurt. Do you understand?' Jamie speaks low and clear.

Ed indicates to Winnie that they will need to use the day room, and she nods her agreement.

Jo and Cassie are astonished, dumbfounded.

Ed speaks, 'Jamie, listen, we need to keep her here. The police are looking for her, put her in there . . .'

Cat is shrieking, 'Let me up! I want to see Sil! I need to be with . . .'

Jamie tightens his hold on her. A small group of fascinated onlookers are gathering around.

Jamie leans in and hisses in her ear, 'You will never see her again, fact, do you understand?'

334

He shakes her, a little bit too hard, until it hurts her. And it hurts him, his knee is in agony.

'Now, get away from my mother . . .!'

On that, and with Ed's help, he staggers up, and, along with Ed and Winnie and a porter who has run to help, they bundle her into the day room, close the door and lock it.

She beats on the door like a caged animal from inside.

'Let me out, you feckin' bastards! Or I'll . . . I'll smash this fish tank and all the feckin' fish will die!'

Ed looks at Winnie, who stifles a smile. Not only are the fish fake, but the tank is plastic. Let her try. Winnie places the key firmly in her pocket.

'Well done, boyso.' Ed grabs Jamie. 'Your mum needed you to do that.'

Cassie and Jo, still astonished by the whole debacle, are stuck to the wall like stunned limpets.

Ed takes charge.

'Come on, everyone in . . .'

They file into Suite 5, Jamie now supported by his dad's shoulder.

Unlike the cacophony of the corridor, it's peaceful and quiet in here. All life is suspended. They spread out and around the bed with Cassie and Jamie hugged up together.

Cassie softly says, 'Mum, Jamie's come.'

'Yes. I'm here.'

He is hushed.

He touches her foot.

There is nothing to be done except to be there. So that's what they do.

They sit on chairs and watch and wait.

Each person has their own loud internal dialogue with her, but none speak out. It isn't necessary. It doesn't feel awkward, it feels natural. It seems hallowed somehow. Like the only place to be at this serious and significant moment. They are the right people to share it, and they know that. They watch and they think.

It's so very very quiet.

Occasionally they catch one another's eye and when they do, they smile and understand. They all have permission to just be.

Gradually, her breathing becomes more and more shallow, until they are straining to hear it.

It stops.

It starts.

It stops for too long.

All of their breath stops.

It starts.

They start.

It stops.

Winnie has slipped into the room.

They all smile at her. She is the knower.

Winnie recognizes this is the Cheyne-Stokes change in

rhythm that she knows heralds Silvia's end. Winnie is aware these strange breath patterns can be alarming so she very quietly starts to hum, to help everyone along.

It works. It's wonderful.

She hums 'Amazing Grace', and they are all glad she does.

'Hmmm.'

(How sweet the sound)

Ed leans in and kisses Silvia.

'Hmmm.'

'Bye Silv.'

(I once was lost but now am found)

Winnie takes their hands, one by one, and places them on Silvia's arms and feet.

'Hmmm.'

(Was blind but now I see)

Jo whispers, 'Bye Sis. I'll never forget you.'

'Bye Mum,' says Jamie.

'Yes, bye Mum,' says Cassie. 'We love you.'

Ed reassures her, 'You can go, Silv . . . it's OK.'

'Hmmm.'

(And Grace will lead me home)

One last strained breath.

She is gone.

Silvia isn't any more.

THIRTY-EIGHT

Silvia

Friday 1.31pm

deep   dark
  sleep   shadow
    tired soul journeys on alone

drifting   ocean
  final   tide
    rolling back towards your touch

wash sing
  soft   climb
    finish here begin beyond

turning   home
  eternal   sorrow
    forgive it foolish foolish love

feel   you
  waiting me
     I am 'til I am not

slipping   always
  loving   vanish
    light kills darkness here I am

coming free
  hold   me
    mummy
       mummy
          mummy

                mum

Acknowledgements

Billie, my darlin' daughter

The fantastic Sue Hunter (thank God for you!)

The mighty B. F.

Louise Moore

Emma Kilcoyne

Sharon Henry (M. B.)

Sue Perkins

Nigel Carrivick

Kathy Burke

Alfred Bradley

Jono and Judith Taylor

Barrie Gibson

Cynthia Hylton-Jones

Maureen Vincent

Robert Kirby

Neil Reading

Fiona McMorrough

Mark Bignell (Mike and Michelle) and all at Hamoaze House

340

David Gammell (Help for Heroes)

The astounding Frank Williams (Bootneck)

Doug Beattie

Mark Townsend

Michael Coady

Eamon Grennan

Richard Mabey

Roger Deakin

Will Cohu

Anthony Silverstone and Jemma Bellerose

Jane Pritchard, and all the doctors who helped at Ealing Hospital

Dr Andrew Scurr

Grumpy Vic at Ashridge Nurseries (Me: 'I'll call you back for more info,' Vic: 'Don't bother!')

Professor Michael O'Brien

Richard Lounsbury

David Roper

Liz Smith and all who look out for me at Penguin

Keiren O'Brien

All who cared for my beloved mum, Roma, at Derriford Hospital

And for massive support on the home front, Dave, Emma, Mike and the wonderful, wonderful Debs Walker

Dolly

Permissions